TOO MUCH TO BEAR

It looked like trouble. The bear was looking around, almost shyly. He didn't seem to be hungry. He actually seemed to want to play with the bait buckets of sardines.

Didi looked away from the bear and at her friend, who was wide-eyed, entranced by her first encounter with a real live black bear.

Suddenly the bear swatted one of the buckets and sent it flying. Then he flung another one up in the air so that it rained sardines. A change was coming over the animal, and Didi could sense it.

The bear stood up to full stature on his back feet, his nose was sniffing furiously, and his eyes pointed forward. Then he fell back on all fours, wheeled, and trotted toward Didi. And while everyone crouched as low as possible, the bear charged toward the blind, swatted it with one paw, revealing the three humans. . . .

DR. NIGHTINGALE ENTERS
THE BE

Dr. Nightingale Enters the Bear Cave

A DEIRDRE QUINN
NIGHTINGALE
MYSTERY

Lydia Adamson

A SIGNET BOOK

SIGNET
Published by the Penguin Group
Penguin Books USA Inc., 375 Hudson Street,
New York, New York 10014, U.S.A.
Penguin Books Ltd, 27 Wrights Lane,
London W8 5TZ, England
Penguin Books Australia Ltd, Ringwood,
Victoria, Australia
Penguin Books Canada Ltd, 10 Alcorn Avenue,
Toronto, Ontario, Canada M4V 3B2
Penguin Books (N.Z.) Ltd, 182-190 Wairau Road,
Auckland 10, New Zealand

Penguin Books Ltd, Registered Offices:
Harmondsworth, Middlesex, England

First published by Signet, an imprint of Dutton Signet,
a division of Penguin Books USA Inc.

First Printing, February, 1996
10 9 8 7 6 5 4 3 2 1

PUBLISHER'S NOTE
This is a work of fiction. Names, characters, places, and incidents either
are the product of the author's imagination or are used fictitiously, and any
resemblance to actual persons, living or dead, events, or locales is entirely
coincidental.

Chapter 1

The red Jeep hit a big bump that nearly lifted the two passengers out of their seats. Rose Vigdor whooped. Didi slowed the vehicle down.

"Put some Patsy Cline on," said Rose, "so I can see if my head is still screwed on right."

Didi slipped a cassette into the tape deck. A country fiddle blasted out of the rear speakers at earsplitting volume. She adjusted it. Patsy's rich alto seemed to calm everything—even the last of the brittle autumn leaves swirling against the windshield.

They were driving north on Route 9 toward Route 23, which would take them west across the Hudson River and into Greene County and the northeastern tier of the Catskill Mountains Forest Preserve.

It was a vacation of a sort for Didi. She was to be

part of a team taking a census of the black bear population, studying them in the wild, with particular emphasis on their nutrition and health just prior to denning in late autumn.

The team consisted of a wildlife biologist, a botanist, a photographer, a guide, and a veterinarian—herself, Deirdre Quinn Nightingale, DVM. Didi counted herself lucky to have been selected from the many applicants. She had never seen a black bear in the wild in her entire life.

She was also lucky to have obtained a place on the "expedition" for her friend Rose . . . having accomplished this coup by "kicking back" her honorarium. Rose, of course, was not aware of this. She thought she had been signed on as Didi's technical assistant, whatever that vague term meant. Certainly it wasn't a code term for chief cook. Didi had sampled enough of Rose's organic brown rice casseroles to vouch for that.

The team would be spending ten days together. That meant they'd be sharing their Thanksgiving meal in one of the wildest and most inaccessible areas of the Catskill Forest Preserve. To give the team free and unimpeded access, a 3,100-foot peak called Mt. Dunaway and its immediate environs had been closed to both hunters and hikers by the Department of Environmental Conservation.

When the red Jeep had crossed the Hudson and Patsy Cline had finished her songs, Rose Vigdor said, "I'm going to miss my dogs a lot."

"Trent Tucker will take care of them just fine. He's not too good with people, but he's splendid with animals. They'll probably gain twenty pounds each."

Rose laughed. "You know, Didi, I must confess something. I was thinking of having an affair with him. He's kind of cute. In a country bumpkin-juvenile delinquent kind of way."

"Why didn't you?"

"Why didn't I what?"

"Have an affair with him."

"Well, I thought maybe you wouldn't approve."

"Why did you think you needed my approval?"

"Well, he *does* live in your house. He *works* for you."

Didi didn't answer. She kept her eyes on the road.

"In fact," Rose continued, pushing her straight blond hair back under her ski cap, "the whole thing is a mystery to me."

"What 'whole thing'?"

"Their relationship to you . . . . all of them . . . Trent Tucker, Charlie Gravis, that Mrs. Tunney, and the little space princess, Abigail."

"There's no mystery, Rose. My mother willed them to me—along with the land and the house and the silverware. Of course, she didn't literally give them to me, but it adds up to the same thing. I'm under a moral obligation to keep them on. I don't pay them any wages. They work, when they do work, for their room and board."

"It's very medieval."

"That's true. I'm a regular lord of the manor," Didi replied.

"And anyway, if Trent Tucker and I had an affair, all of Hillsbrook would know. And the village people would probably think me even more peculiar. You *know* what they think of me now!"

"I really don't know what they think of you."

"Yes you do. They think I'm a fourteen-karat flake."

"Actually," Didi said, "most Hillsbrook people think it's perfectly natural for a beautiful young woman to leave a high-paying job in New York City and buy a broken-down barn and live in it quite happily without electricity or running water."

Rose grinned. "You left out that I am also engaged in the longest one-woman barn restoration project in the history of Dutchess County."

They both laughed.

The red Jeep turned off Route 23 onto a feeder

road. The terrain became more wooded, but the leaves had already vanished from the tree branches and were blowing across the road.

"Are we lost?" Rose asked.

"I don't think so. My instructions were to take the feeder road off 23 for eleven miles, until I reach a dirt road fork. Then take the left fork to Camp Dunaway."

"What will it look like?"

"Well, it's just the base camp at the foot of Mt. Dunaway. A cabin, I suppose."

"Why are so many of the trees gnarled?"

"Weathering," Didi replied.

"It's getting spooky."

"These are southern hardwoods," Didi explained. "A lot of oak and hickory. When we get a little higher we hit northern hardwoods—beech, maple, birch. And at the top of Mt. Dunaway we'll find spruce and fir—what they call a northern coniferous forest. That's what makes the Catskill Mountains so unique—three kinds of forests merging on a single mountain."

Didi cut her monologue short. She was suddenly embarrassed at her lecture. Who was she to pontificate? She was born and raised only sixty miles from these mountains but had never even taken so much as a weekend hike in them.

"I want to ask a favor of you, Didi," Rose said in a somber voice.

"Go ahead."

"If I am torn apart by a black bear on this trip, I want you to promise me that you'll take my dogs in."

"You have my word, Rose. But relax. Black bears aren't grizzlies. They're shy. They're more afraid of you than you are of them."

"No!" Rose said melodramatically. "There is a very good chance that I will not survive . . . that I will be savaged by a thousand-pound black bear."

"There is no such thing as a thousand-pound black bear," Didi said. "In fact, I think the largest ever recorded was around seven hundred pounds. And that was considered almost a freak of nature, a once-in-a-century monster."

Rose did not answer. It was obvious to her that her friend Didi didn't understand the power of bad karma. She was too much the scientist—the veterinarian—even if she did yoga breathing exercises every morning.

Rose then directed the conversation to a more practical subject: "Who is paying for this adventure, anyway?"

"You!"

"Me?"

"Sure, you're a taxpayer. And the DEC is a state

agency that exists on tax dollars and user fees. They administer the state-owned land and all activities on it."

"But why black bears?"

"The DEC determines the length and frequency of the hunting season. If the population is crashing—no hunting. If booming—longer season. They fund all kinds of animal population studies."

"Do you think they'll give us plastic identification cards?"

"For what?" Didi was perplexed.

"You know; that identifies me as an employee of the New York State Department of Environmental Conservation. With a picture of me. And it'll say: Rose Vigdor, Senior Black Bear Consultant."

"Hardly."

"Too bad. I always wanted one of those."

At the fork, Didi wheeled the Jeep left and started down a stretch of packed dirt hardly worthy of the word "road."

It ended abruptly down a steep hillock that flattened into a clearing.

Didi braked. The two women stared at the sprawling log cabin that was smack against a rocky overhang.

"It's an old cabin," Rose noted.

"No, actually it isn't. What it is, is a replica of an old cabin—a trapper's cabin."

At either side of the cabin were attached store-houses that appeared to be made of aluminum. There was a small porch and accordion doors and windows.

"No one else is here," Rose said nervously. "Are you sure this is the right place?"

"Yes. This is it. The rest of the team won't get here until noon. That's when we were supposed to assemble. I just wanted to get here early."

"To get the worm?"

Didi laughed and climbed out of the Jeep. "Let's get the stuff out of the back seat and into the cabin."

They pulled the three large duffels out and lined them up on the ground.

"God! They're so heavy," Rose said.

Didi flashed a dirty look at her. If she had listened to Rose, there would be fifteen duffel bags to contend with. Once Rose had learned that they would be camping out a few nights during the project, the would-be nature girl had gone bananas. The original list she had obtained from a manual had included the following as basic equipment for a night in the woods:

daypack
backpack
tent
sleeping bag
backpacking stove and fuel
firestarter
extra waterproof matches
candles
mess kit
eating utensils
can opener
plastic water container
barometer and altimeter
compass
maps
binoculars
camera
flashlight
emergency blanket
nylon cord
sewing kit
mirror
whistle
first-aid emergency kit
Ace bandage
snakebite kit

There had been another, even longer list for clothes. Didi had to be ruthless in editing the lists. Rose had been crushed but she had acquiesced.

"We'd better take them in one at a time," Didi suggested.

They carried the first bag up to the cabin and onto the small porch, where they set it down.

"Just slide the door open, Rose. There's no lock on it."

Rose slid the door open. It was a bit stiff and she had to push with both hands to get it fully open.

Then she turned back to the duffel, picked up one end, and, with Didi on the other end, entered the gloomy cabin.

Suddenly the duffel was pushed back against Didi's stomach with such force that she had to drop it!

She started to yell at Rose for her clumsiness, but not a word came out, because Rose had turned and seized her arm in a viselike grip.

"Oh, God! I told you! I told you! There's a bear inside!"

The hysterical Rose bolted past Didi to safety.

Didi took a deep breath and stepped tentatively inside.

What bear? There was no black bear inside.

There was, however, a huge, black-bearded man.

He was hanging by his feet from the cabin ceiling, each foot tied to a beam with a thick rope.

His eyes were wide open in his dead, upside-down face.

His flannel shirt had fallen off his gargantuan stomach.

And that stomach was riddled with bullet holes.

Didi wheeled around, stepped back outside, and leaned against the door frame. Her legs were like jelly.

Chapter 2

"Why did you cut him down?" the park ranger asked. Her name was Fay Whitely and she was a tall, thin woman about fifty with a down vest and thick-soled boots.

Rose looked at Didi, then looked back at the park ranger, then stood and threw up her hands in frustration. "You took an hour to get here! What were we supposed to do? Stand here staring at a dead man like he was a wax dummy or something? Paint his toenails?"

"Calm down, miss," said the state trooper, Frank Kermit. It was obvious that Rose was on the edge of hysteria. Didi pushed her friend back into a huge, tattered easy chair. The cabin was filled with secondhand furniture, but the interior walls, the fixtures, and the bunk beds on the north end of the pseudo trapper's cabin were brand-new. It looked as if whoever had funded and built the replica had run out of money before the furnishings were purchased and had to end up at the Salvation Army with a pickup truck.

The corpse lay on the floor, covered by a thick wool blanket. Only the stubby fingers of one hand were visible.

"His name is Sylvester Glass," Fay Whitely said to Kermit.

"A local?" the state trooper asked.

"Yes. A jack-of-all-trades. A little carpentry. A little snow removal. A little woodcutting. My guess is he was working for the DEC, getting the cabin ready for the research team." Fay Whitely turned to Didi. "You're part of the team, aren't you?"

"We both are," Didi replied, nodding over at Rose.

"Can I see some identification?" Kermit asked.

The trooper took both their driver's licenses and began to copy down vital information from the documents into his notebook. The ranger walked outside to greet an emergency fire department vehicle that had just pulled out, and which often functioned as an EMS in the more outlying, rugged areas.

More vehicles arrived, more state troopers, and soon Didi and Rose, still seated in their chairs, were surrounded by technicians poking and prodding and scraping and chattering. The body was wrapped and taken out. The floor of the cabin was searched and vacuumed. The beam on which the unfortunate man had hung was dusted for prints. Splinters were taken as samples. A hundred flashbulbs seemed to be going off at the same time.

It was as if the little cabin in the wilderness had suddenly been invaded by an alien high-tech culture.

Didi stared at the large fireplace across the cabin. Someone should light a fire, she thought. It was growing colder. She ignored the tumult about her, keeping within herself. She was still trying to overcome the shock of coming upon the dangling body, and the exhaustion of cutting it down. It had taken such a long time to accomplish because she and Rose hadn't been able to unknot the ropes that fastened the dead man's legs to the beam. They had had to search the cabin until they found the small metal toolbox with the hack saw blade inside it. They used the blade to cut the ropes, but then the body was too heavy for them and it had slipped through their grasp and landed heavily on the floor, like a bag of potatoes falling off a pickup truck.

"Do you believe all this is really happening?" Rose whispered.

Didi didn't answer. Her vacation—and that really was what this expedition was about, a chance for renewal in some primeval forest, even if it was only the Catskills—had turned into a horror even before it had begun.

Suddenly Didi laughed out loud. A disconcerted Rose stared at her, as if her friend had lost control. Didi laughed again, almost demoniacally, and then, for a moment, buried her face in her hands in despair.

At last she drew her hands away from her face. "Don't worry, Rose. I'm not cracking up. I just had this awful fantasy that we were all part of a movie— an old Western I once saw—the *Oxbow Incident* . . . you know . . . about a lynching."

"But this isn't a lynching. We have no proof that Sylvester whatshisname was—"

"A lynching is a lynching," said Didi.

"The trooper said," Rose continued, "that he might have been shot to death and then hung."

"A lynching is a lynching is a lynching," Didi repeated. "Besides, I don't believe the state trooper."

Rose didn't respond for a moment . . . then she said, "When I opened the door I did believe it was a bear."

"He was an awfully big man," Didi replied.

"Why did they hang him upside down? I don't understand. Why would they do such a thing?"

"It's the way you dress a deer."

"What?"

"When a hunter kills a deer, the fastest and easiest way to remove the deer's skin is to hang it up by its hind legs. Then you incise down the center and peel the skin away from the bone."

Didi stared at the beam where the man had been hanging. She had a strange sense of déjà vu, but she couldn't understand it. It was as if she had seen such a crime before. Perhaps, she thought, it was merely the mode of hanging, not the bullets that had riddled him. Perhaps this reminded her of the slaughterhouse she had visited briefly, the one outside Philadelphia, while in vet school. Several students had gone there to observe the testing procedures used to cull unwell animals from the rest. The well animals had been slaughtered and hung on hooks on a conveyer belt.

But that man had been hanging from that beam! Not a steer but a man.

"Here!"

Didi looked up. Fay Whitely was standing in front of her, two cups in her hand and a thermos cradled in the crook of her arm. Didi took one of the proffered cups. Rose took the other. They drank. The cocoa was hot and delicious.

The state trooper, Kermit, returned their driver's licenses to them.

"Did either of you see any dogs around when you arrived?" Fay Whitely asked Didi and Rose.

"No," Didi said, and turned questioningly to her friend, who shook her head in confirmation. "Why do you ask?"

"There were tracks leading from the cabin. A man and at least one dog. They went up the slope just behind the house. There's a path there."

Kermit interrupted Fay Whitely's narrative, "We lost them about fifty yards up the slope. But it was a man and a dog. That's for sure. The man was wearing hunting boots. It could have been Sylvester Glass's footprints. Maybe made early in the morning, before he died. It *could* have been. But Sylvester Glass didn't have a dog. And he was a big man. The boot marks are not spaced enough for a large striding man. The man who made them was a much smaller guy. Maybe, in fact, a woman."

"Are you sure you saw no dogs?" Fay Whitely pressed.

"*I* am sure," Rose answered this time, not even attempting to hide her annoyance.

Fay refilled their cups from the thermos.

Suddenly a stocky, sandy-haired man shouldered his way aggressively between Fay and Kermit. He dropped an ancient, gaily beribboned backpack onto the floor, all the while holding his gaze on Didi.

Then he asked, "Dr. Nightingale, I presume?"

"That's right. Who are you?"

He looked around in disgust. "I used to think my name was Harris Renner," he began, ". . . that I was a wildlife biologist . . . that I was supposed to meet my research team in an isolated cabin at the foot of Mt. Dunaway. But now I don't know. *What in hell is going on here?*"

It was still dark, but daybreak was close. Allie Voegler shone his large flashlight along the building wall. The beam illuminated the face of Wynton Chung. He was in the full uniform of a Hillsbrook police officer.

"Get that out of my face!" Chung barked.

Allie directed the beam to the ground. They were in the back of Agway—the department store just outside the village of Hillsbrook.

"They came out this door," Chung said, "about five this morning. A half hour before the janitorial staff arrived. They must have hidden when the store closed last night. Slept in the store. Got up and robbed it blind. Then walked out."

"How many?"

"Looks like two, but it's hard to tell."

"What'd they get?"

Chung motioned for Allie to follow. Allie was amused by the way the new officer had taken charge. After all, he was Chung's superior; it was he who should be taking charge. Still, he was quite happy with Chung's enthusiasm.

The two entered the open back door through which the thieves had exited.

"Hit those lights!" Chung yelled.

Suddenly the store was lit up—by unseen hands.

"Two assistant managers are already here," he explained.

Chung led Allie to the far side of the store, into the bedding department.

"Look!"

Allie looked at the huge bins.

"See this one? They took five pillows out of it. Thirty-nine ninety-nine each. Not a big haul. Five pillows. At least that's what we think."

Chung reached down deep into the bin, pulled up a pillow, and flung it to Allie, who caught it deftly.

"Why steal pillows?"

Chung shrugged.

"Maybe they were drunk," Allie speculated. "Maybe they didn't want to steal anything. Maybe they took the pillows, found a secure place in the store, and fell asleep. Maybe when they got up early in the morning they just carried out with them anything they could carry. A pair of goofy kids. Maybe." He walked over and dropped the pillow back into the bin.

Then he followed Chung to the candy counter. Chung handed him a piece of candy. "Try it!"

"A little early for sweets."

"So what? Eat it."

Allie undid the wrapper and popped the candy into his mouth. The taste gave him a jolt. Strong ginger. He began to chew the taffy-like substance. The ginger taste grew stronger as he chewed. He swallowed, finally. "Pretty good," he admitted.

"It's Korean candy. They stole a whole bucket of it."

"Are you sure?"

Chung didn't answer. He said, "Let's go, because now it gets interesting."

They walked into the sporting goods department. They circled a counter. The lock on the wall gun rack had been broken—crudely. Several rifles were missing.

"They took the three limited edition Winchesters and a whole bunch of ammo."

Allie smiled. He remembered looking at these Winchesters only a few months back. Trent Tucker, one of Didi's elves, had been standing right next to him.

"So there it is," said Chung. "Five good pillows. A bucket of ginger taffy. And three 30-30 rifles with ammo."

"There could be more," Allie noted.

"Right. The assistant managers are checking."

"Since when does this place have managers? I thought the owners run it."

"You're out of touch, Allie," said Chung.

Allie chuckled appreciatively at Chung's remark. And before he knew it he was laughing uproariously. "Out of touch" was a particularly apt description of his situation—of all of his situations, in fact.

Chapter 3

A log was burning in the fireplace. All the chairs had been drawn in a semicircle around it. The cabin was warm but the wind was howling outside.

It was a strangely silent place now—after the troopers and rangers and technicians and their vehicles had gone. They had been like an army withdrawing after a successful campaign; they cleaned up after themselves lest anything be left for the enemy.

Harris Renner was leaning forward in his chair, cracking his knuckles.

"OK," he said. "Now that we have this place to ourselves, it's time for me to say a few words. First, welcome. Second, I'm sorry for the tumult. Third, here's what happened—

"Dr. Nightingale and her associate came up early and found a corpse. His name was Sylvester Glass;

he was fixing up the cabin for us; and he was murdered. As of yet, no one knows by whom."

He looked around and met everyone's gaze, one by one. The botanist, Marsha Greeley, looked bored. But the "expedition" photographer, Kurt Trabert, seemed to be hanging on every word. The guide, Moe Douglas, listened solemnly, attentive, but making no eye contact with Renner. Douglas had known Sylvester Glass.

Didi and Rose were too weary to be attentive. Each was trying to keep awake in her respective chair.

Renner continued, "I'm a wildlife biologist. I despise fake religion and fake grief. I didn't know Sylvester Glass, so I can only mourn him the way I would mourn for any stranger who died in a plane crash a thousand miles away. Do you all understand what I am saying?"

There was a murmur of assent.

"And now," Harris Renner said, "let's get to work. I want to give you a brief description of our task. It will be a bit different from what I stated previously in letters and phone calls with all of you. If you recall, I said we would be doing fieldwork into the denning behavior of black bears. Actually we are going to be doing something a little more specific."

Didi roused herself. What a strange thing to say, she thought. Why hide a group research objective? At any time.

She looked around, but no one else seemed to have picked up on Renner's admission that he had withheld information from the group.

"Look at this," Renner commanded.

He was holding up a small object. It seemed to Didi to be a child's whistle, made of plastic . . . except it was blunt, with something sticking out of the top.

"Do any of you know what it is?" he asked.

Moe Douglas said in a matter-of-fact tone, "Turkey call."

"Close. A predator call. It's used in hunting. Now look at this."

Renner held up another small object.

"Looks like an elk call," Moe said.

"Give that man a prize! He's exactly right," Renner said jubilantly. He took out three more such devices and displayed them.

Then he blew on one. Out came a horrible, high-pitched squall. A shiver crept down Didi's spine. Turkey, elk, or moose—that noise sounded like someone or something in dreadful pain.

Harris Renner stood and blew the thing again, this time with more lung capacity, almost gleefully.

The sound was unbearable. Didi stopped up her ears.

"Let me explain something," Harris said as he sat down again. "Several years ago elk hunters learned to their dismay that black bears out West responded to elk calls. What do the bears think? Why do they come when they hear these sounds and similar ones? They may think a cub is in distress. Or they may think a deer is down and in trouble, and hence a good meal is on the way. We don't know. But because they respond to these calls with far more regularity than other animals, many of us believe bears have a much more sophisticated repertoire of vocalizations than we thought they did. Maybe even"—he paused as if to evaluate this audience, then—"maybe even a rudimentary black bear language."

There was a nervous silence in the cabin. No one knew where this strange monologue was going.

Didi looked up and noticed she was sitting under the same long beam where poor Sylvester Glass had hung. She felt very uncomfortable.

"I just didn't want the papers to get hold of this. You can imagine their response. Crazy scientist now claims there *are* talking bears."

Everyone laughed. Except, Didi noticed, the botanist, Marsha Greeley.

Harris Renner had changed his tone of voice. It was now full of authority—almost military—as befitting the leader of an expedition.

"So here is our task, colleagues. We are going to implant small microphones into female bears prior to their denning. We are going to place very sophisticated recording devices into the dens. We are going to record all sounds within until the following spring, when the devices will be removed. We are, as you can imagine, particularly interested in the vocalizations that will occur between the mother and the newborn cubs in the den. So . . . find the dens . . . stake them out . . . sedate the bear . . . place the mike and the recorder. That's it."

He sat back, expansive. He seemed to be waiting for comments, but there were none. Then he leaned forward and pointed at the guide.

Moe seemed to know exactly what to do and say. He stood up and described the structure of the cabin. Didi listened carefully as he spoke. "Our stove was never delivered, so we'll use the fireplace all night. But I think you people better sleep with your clothes on. One of the storerooms contains a small kitchen where you'll find an electric stove and refrigerator. There's plenty of food stocked in there. The latrines are out back. They have flush toilets, lights, but no heat. The only running water is the small sink in the kitchen. Tomorrow morning we'll all go up the slope together. Figure we'll leave around six."

"Any specific bunk assignments?" asked the photographer.

"No. Take any one you want. They're all the same: one top, one bottom."

Harris Renner stood and applauded, as if he found Moe's short speech exhilarating. "I'll make the first pot of coffee," he declared and headed toward the kitchen.

"I like him," Rose whispered to Didi.

Charlie Gravis looked straight ahead while he gave Abigail, on the seat beside him, instructions.

"Just bring the cards to Dr. Lupica's nurse. She'll know what they're about."

He waited for Abigail to exit the pickup, but she didn't move.

"What's the matter?" he asked.

"Nothing."

"So why ain't you moving?" he retorted. He was addressing Abigail, but looking out at the small cinder-block building just off the highway. There was a neatly lettered sign in front of it: VETERINARY CLINIC. DR. ARTHUR A. LUPICA, DVM. Underneath the

sign was a smaller, swinging one that read: BOARD-
ING. CATS AND DOGS.

"You forgot one card, Charlie," Abigail said. "In
the glove compartment, remember?"

He gripped the wheel of Trent Tucker's vehicle
very tightly. This interference from a snip of a girl
was intolerable. Charlie was seventy-four years
old, and he was Miss Quinn's chosen assistant.
She had given him instructions, personally. They
were simple: Write down all calls on index cards
and bring them to Dr. Lupica. He was covering for
her while she was away. Lupica had years ago
given up his large animal practice in favor of dogs
and cats. But now he hungered for rounds again,
and for the heady smell of dairy barns and horse
stalls. So Didi Quinn Nightingale was giving him
his chance. And he, Charlie, was following her
instructions to the letter—except for one tiny
indiscretion, which was really none of Abigail's
business.

"Listen to me, young lady," Charlie said angrily,
and not meeting the girl's eyes. "Hey, are you listening?"

"Yes, Charlie."

He was going to give her a piece of his mind. He
was going to tell her that she damn well *better* listen
to him, but suddenly all the anger and impatience

left him. What was the use of getting so mad at poor Abigail, thought he. Everybody knew the girl's milk pail was half empty. It just wouldn't do no good to get mad and start shouting at her. She heard what she wanted to hear. And she was such a gentle creature.

He plucked the cards out of her hand, opened the driver's side door, and went into the building to deliver them himself.

When he came back to the pickup, he removed the index card from the glove compartment and placed it on top of the dashboard.

"Now we're going to see Cleo Dopple."

"Why?" Abigail asked.

"Because her old dog Red is hurting. Lumbago it is. Rheumatism in the back. And some arthritis thrown in, too."

"Mrs. Tunney told you not to mess around with any of your home remedies."

This time Charlie couldn't contain his rage. "I don't care what Mrs. Tunney said. I'm head of our household."

Then he thrust his gnarled arthritic hands in front of the young woman.

"Look at these!" he all but screamed. "Miss Quinn may be a helluva vet. Oh, yes! Didi Quinn Nightingale might be the best damn vet in

Dutchess County for all I know. But nobody—and I mean nobody—knows more about hurting than old Charlie Gravis here."

He turned the key in the ignition. The old truck's motor kicked over.

"Do you want to come with me . . . or should I drop you off at the house?"

Abigail folded her arms. The wind blew the card off the dash. Abigail retrieved it. "I'll go with you."

Didi woke suddenly. She looked at her watch. It was just past midnight. She was fully clothed except for her boots and socks. Rose was in the upper bunk, sound asleep.

Didi turned and saw Harris Renner kneeling by the fire, tending to it. The cabin was freezing.

Didi swung her legs around, put her socks and boots back on, and went over to the fire.

"Cold enough for you, Dr. Nightingale?" Renner asked.

"My name's Didi." She crouched down in front of the firelight.

"People call me Harry," Renner said.

OK, thought Didi. We've got that settled.

"It must have been horrible walking into this cabin and seeing what you saw," Renner said in a low voice.

She didn't know how to respond to his statement, so she said nothing. She stared at his profile. She couldn't tell how old he was. But whatever his age, he was in superb physical condition. He crouched by the fire effortlessly, perfectly balanced.

Renner put on more firewood and pokered it down in the hearth. A few sparks flew out. He chuckled.

"There's something I want to ask you," Didi said.

"Ask away." He turned toward her and set the poker down. "But why don't we try the chairs," he suggested.

They made themselves comfortable in the chairs. Didi was sitting beneath that beam again, and now there was a medley of dancing shadows along it.

"All right," Harris Renner said, turning to her. "What did you want to say?"

"Why did you want a veterinarian along on this project? From what you said, it would appear you need an acoustical engineer. In other words, what am I doing here, Dr.—I mean, Harry? Don't get me wrong. I wanted to be here. But I am a little confused."

"You're going to have a lot of responsibility," he replied.

"Doing what?"

"Well, I expect you to do genetic analysis of blood and tissue. Morphometric analyses of ear skulls. And starch-gel electrophoresis."

Didi's jaw dropped. "You can't be serious!"

Harris burst into merry laughter, then immediately stifled it so as not to wake the others. "No, of course I'm not serious. Let me tell you something, Didi. Bears don't die from diseases. Well—they do . . . but rarely. Mostly they get shot during hunting season by rifle or bow. Or they're hit by cars. Or they get a hold of poisoned bait because they're stealing some farmer's crops or honey. Maybe they swallow plastic bottles they get at the town dump. Things like that.

"That's why we know so little about the diseases of wild black bears. It's also why we really *don't* need vets along on expeditions. Any more than we need botanists. Because the average wildlife biologist can analyze scats for plant identification as well as sedate bears. I know I sure as hell can."

"But you still haven't answered my question, Harry," she said. Actually, it now felt quite natural to be using his nickname that way.

"Which was . . . ?"

"Why do you want me along?"

"You might just as well ask why I wanted a botanist along, too."

"All right. Consider that question asked as well."

For the first time since she met him, Didi had the feeling that whatever his chronological age, he was in many ways a child.

"The answer is simple," he stated. "Tradition."

"Tradition?"

"Yes. I don't do research projects in the field without a full complement of scientists. In fact, if I can't get the funding, the hell with it. When I bait a black bear with a powerful sedative, I want a vet around, no matter what."

"You mean, your way or no way?"

"It sounds arrogant when you put it like that. But believe me, it's not about that."

Didi closed her eyes. For the first time she felt the warmth of the fire. She wondered if she would be able to sleep in the chair. It seemed better than the bunk.

"There's coffee on the stove," he told her.

"And there's blood on the moon," she retorted.

"What the hell does that mean?"

Didi was embarrassed. She had no idea why she had blurted that out. "It's just a saying," she mumbled, "a country saying."

"What country?" Renner teased. "Transylvania?"

Didi turned her face away.

Chapter 4

They left the cabin at 6:15 in the morning for their "shakedown" hike, as Renner had called it.

They circled the rocky ledge behind the cabin and started single file up the path.

Moe Douglas went first. Then Harris Renner. Then Didi. Next was Marsha Greeley. Then Rose. And finally, Kurt Trabert.

When the sun rose, they stopped to rest. Moe Douglas made instant coffee for everyone and served it in small paper cups. The coffee was hot, creamy and sweet, made with powdered milk.

Kurt Trabert began to "shoot" seriously during the break. He used both a video camera and a small SLR. His manner was something absolutely professional and assuring. One felt no intrusion. He just seemed to glide about.

To her chagrin, Didi was exhausted after only

thirty minutes of hiking. Her legs were trembling. She sat down with her paper cup of coffee on a lightning-scarred tree stump.

Rose, who looked to be in even worse shape, stretched out on the ground.

A snow flurry whirled around the resting party and then moved off.

"I knew I brought the wrong kind of boots," Rose said.

"You brought three different pairs, Rose. One of them has got to work," Didi noted. She looked down at her own boots and her eyes caught movement on the stump. She instinctively recoiled. But it was only a wood beetle scurrying.

"Bears love them."

Didi looked up. It was the botanist, Marsha Greeley, looking at what had grown to a pulsating clump of beetles. She was smiling at it as if she had recovered an old friend.

"I thought you were a botanist, not an entomologist," Didi said.

"The thighbone is connected to the hipbone."

Marsha Greeley was what people used to call compact. She was wearing baggy clothing and boating sneakers instead of boots. She was the only one in the party who carried a walking stick. Her face was highly expressive and her mood, whatever it was, seemed to register instantly. Didi figured her to be about thirty-five years old.

"Is this your first project with Harris Renner?" Didi asked.

"Yes. Although I'd heard of him. I heard he's a fine scientist. He did a lot of good work in Canada, early on."

"Are you from Canada?"

"No. Why do you ask?"

Didi shrugged. She didn't know why she had asked the question.

"I was born in Boston," Marsha told her, "and went to school at Cornell. I teach now at the University of Vermont at Burlington."

She bent over to catch one last glimpse of the now-dispersing insects, then straightened.

"I never knew that bears ate beetles," Rose said, bringing her knees up to her chest.

Marsha smiled a little. "Bears will eat anything. They like ants better than beetles, but they eat anything and everything. They're the most omnivorous creatures on the face of the earth. And that's why scientists love them. Their spoors are wonderlands of digestive analysis."

The botanist laughed wildly then, as if to make fun of her own ridiculously high-blown phrase, a wonderland of digestive analysis.

"At least that's why I love them, anyway," she continued. "In the spring they eat herbaceous material of all kinds. In the summer they eat berries. In the fall they go for acorns. There is virtually nothing growing in the entire forest that a bear will not taste one time or another."

"What about human flesh?" Rose asked.

The botanist laughed. "Well, they will eat almost any kind of carrion. They do love fish and bird eggs. Even a dead porcupine is considered haute cuisine by a black bear."

This gastronomic conversation was interrupted by Moe Douglas, who yelled out, "We're moving!" and then came around with a plastic bag for everyone to dump the coffee cups into.

The hike resumed . . . upward . . . ever upward in a soft ascent. But while the mountain sloped nonprecipitously for the most part, Didi quickly realized that Mt. Dunaway was unlike any other mountain she had ever climbed. From a distance it seemed like one of hundreds of small, heavily wooded conical peaks in the Catskills. But the hike up the mountain revealed a very peculiar terrain.

Mt. Dunaway was broken terrain. There were crevices, rock croppings, abandoned quarries. One had to look where one was going every step of the way. Maybe that was the reason for her exhaustion.

Didi began to understand why Mt. Dunaway had been selected for the project. It was ideal for black bears. At least it seemed ideal in Didi's mind, from what she had read in her cram course on the animals after she was accepted in the project. She had learned that bears seek out territories with high-quality escape cover. And Mt. Dunaway surely had that—an uneasy black bear could get out of sight and away in seconds, through small canyons, tree falls that created tunnels, old streambeds, quarry walls, dried-up riverbanks.

And Didi had read that the most common types of dens were tree cavities, rock cavities, ground excavations, and surface dens. Surely, Mama Bear could pick any kind of den she wanted on Mt. Dunaway and find it.

They found the first sign of black bear about twenty minutes into the second leg of the journey. Harris Renner pointed out a series of tree scrapes. Then some scats. And then clear tracks. They all gathered around the tracks and stared. Moe Douglas bent down and studied them. "Old tracks," he said. "Maybe three days old." But everyone felt a tension, a growing excitement.

They hiked a half mile more and Harris uncovered the first den. He scooped leaves and broken branches away from a small hillock to reveal a large, shallow depression dug into the earth.

Each member of the party was invited to peer in briefly.

Renner said, "The success of our project depends on our ability to find dens. But not ones like these. Because you can tell that this is an abandoned den. It hasn't been used for years. We need to locate dens that were used last winter." He smiled. "If they were used last winter the odds are good they will be used again this winter."

"Male bears would more likely hole up in an old den. But it's females we're after," added Moe.

"Right," Renner agreed. He looked around at his team. "And now I want to get down to the nitty-gritty. Dr. Nightingale and I had a conversation last night about the professional responsibilities of certain members of our team. I'm afraid I was a bit flip in my response. Now I want to clear it up—for her, and for all of you."

Didi squirmed. She thought last night's conversation had been a private one. She looked at Rose, who was grinning at her like a Cheshire, as if to imply that she, Rose, knew that the private, nighttime conversation with Renner had been about something else entirely.

Renner continued, "Everyone on this project has

specific and important tasks. Tomorrow we will split into two groups and go out searching for dens. Once the dens are located, our work will then start in earnest.

"Now, I want you all to understand this. Few research projects go into the field today with such a high complement of professionals like we have. They're usually one-person operations. But it wasn't really frivolous of me to demand such a full house. Here's why—

"The minute we locate a viable den, our work really starts. Dr. Greeley—Marsha, that is—will take spoor samples from the vicinity to determine diet and nutritional content. She will also create a rough map of existing vegetation in the area—types of trees, shrubs, and the like.

"Then the fun starts. I will place sardine bait buckets in the area. They will be laced with sedatives. Then I will use the calls I showed you yesterday. When a bear arrives, takes the bait, and is sedated, Dr. Nightingale and her assistant will start their tasks. Didi will stethoscopically examine the bear to verify that she carries a live fetus—or perhaps twins, which are increasingly common. She will also examine the bear for old wounds, infestations, and infection.

"I will place a miniature microphone on the sedated bear and then place recording devices in the den."

He took a deep breath. "You must understand that we cannot guarantee the bear we sedate and wire will use the den we plant the recorders in. There is a good possibility she will, but we can't be sure. And of course the bear may be a male, which won't help us at all. But Mt. Dunaway was selected because over the years it had the highest percentage of female bears harvested during hunting seasons. To put it in a nutshell, the more dens we find . . . the more bears we sedate. . . the better the chance for success.

"Our goal is five units operating after the bears den. Which translates roughly into ten bears sedated and wired, near ten wired dens. Because half of all 'wires' will malfunction. Are there any questions?"

The wind had started to blow. It was growing colder. The sun was no longer visible even though it was still at least an hour before noon.

No one said a word.

"That's enough for today. Let's get back to the cabin and eat."

The walk back was like a guided tour in natural history. The guide, Moe Douglas, ranging on either side of the hikers, pointed out "signs." He was a powerfully built man, medium height, who wore several flannel shirts rather than a parka or a vest. His hair was almost white and stood up in a stiff crew cut.

Douglas pointed out coyote sign, deer sign, bobcat sign. He spoke knowledgeably about skunks, possums, porcupines, weasels.

But, as interesting as Moe's lectures were, Didi started to shut his voice out. She was weary now and had to concentrate on putting one foot in front of the other in a more or less straight line. The guide's voice now seemed like a dull hum . . . like the drone of a bumblebee.

Didi wished Renner would lighten the pace; he seemed to be picking up speed, though, and she had to keep up because she was second in line. Was this his idea of a quick conditioning march for his staff? Probably. Or maybe he was in such superb shape that it never occurred to him that others were not.

He had an effortless stride. The only parts of him that seemed to be moving were his legs and his battered old backpack, which bounced and jounced with his every step.

Didi smiled in spite of herself when she focused on his backpack. It seemed a harmless affectation to carry such an ancient item—as if Renner were displaying a badge of honor—a trophy won for past expeditions. As if he were telling the world that he really was an old mountain man.

Even sillier were the gaily colored pieces of yarn he had tied to the back buckles, which contrasted so markedly with the dull army surplus style canvas of the pack itself. Didi had seen that kind of ribbon before. Old people with bad eyesight often put them on their luggage when they travel by plane, so that the bags can be readily identified when they come around on the luggage carousel.

Harris Renner stopped suddenly, and Didi, so focused on the backpack that she had taken her eyes off the owner of the bag, banged into him.

She apologized profusely. All Renner said was, "I didn't know you cared."

They were waiting for Kurt Trabert, who was reloading his cameras.

The sun came out again in a dazzling autumnal fashion. The light played on the gaily covered pieces of yarn tied to the backpack.

Didi saw that each piece of yarn was tied into small knots—a modest decorative touch.

She smiled again because she recognized the type of knot. It was the old-fashioned surgeon's loop; the one all vets had once used to sew up wounds—before all the high-tech sutures and staples were available.

This Harry is an interesting character, she thought. He reminded her of her old dairy farmer friend, Dick Obey, who had been murdered during her first sad year after coming home to practice in Hillsbrook. He had the same kind of contradictions in his personality; one side absolutely modern, another side quite primitive.

"This may be Sherwood Forest," Rose said out loud, half to herself and half to others. She stared at the tall, lanky industrious photographer who had resumed his shooting. She moved closer to Didi and whispered, "And this Kurt Trabert might be Robin Hood himself."

"As long as you don't end up being Maid Marian," Didi cautioned.

Rose arched her brows. "Yes, dear. We all have to be careful, don't we?"

The merry band started the final leg. When they reached the cabin they flopped heavily on all available chairs. Moe Douglas went into the kitchen to prepare the food and coffee, accompanied by Marsha Greeley, who, during the trip, had bragged that she could make prize-winning pancakes out of the seediest instant batter on any kind of stove.

"Our shakedown cruise was a success," Harris

Renner declared loudly, half in jest. "In the Catskills, it only takes a one-day acclimation period. Tomorrow you people will all be fit."

Oddly enough, Didi agreed with him. And now she was looking for Rose, to see how she had weathered the conditioning drill. But Rose was nowhere to be found. Maybe the bathroom, Didi thought. She waited. No Rose. Suddenly worried, she got up and walked outside.

Rose was standing pressed against the cabin about three feet from the door.

She was rigid and pale as a ghost.

"Rose, what is it?"

"I miss my dogs."

"You'll see them in nine days."

"I worry about them. I'm frightened for them."

"You're being ridiculous," Didi scolded. "Trent Tucker is the best dog watcher in the county."

"No, Didi. It's not that."

"What is it?"

"I started to go into the cabin and I remembered the other morning. And suddenly I just couldn't go in. Because I knew what I would see. I would see another man who looked like a bear hanging there . . . and he too would be upside down—dead—and there would be bloody holes in his stomach."

"There's no one hanging there now, Rose."

"And then I couldn't breathe. I couldn't move."

"It's just an anxiety attack, Rose. It'll be okay in a minute. I'll stay here with you."

"Do you understand what I'm saying, Didi? I know that Trent Tucker will take good care of my dogs. But I still miss them. And I miss my barn."

Didi took her dear friend's hands and rubbed them. The flesh was ice-cold.

"I feel like a fool," Rose said.

Didi felt like a fool, too. Because on the entire hike she had not given one thought to Sylvester Glass. He seemed to have vanished from her consciousness the moment she left the cabin. That was foolish. And it was embarrassing. As her old professor used to say, "Keep your priorities in order."

Didi's grip on Rose's hand tightened. She could understand her friend's terror, the fear of entering the cabin again.

"Do you understand?" Rose whispered again.

Didi closed her eyes. The memory was now vivid, harsh, sad—that huge man swinging by his legs from the beam.

"Oh, my God!" she suddenly exclaimed. It was such a wrenching call, and so unexpected, that it snapped Rose out of her catatonia. "What? What?

What is it, Didi?" She pulled Didi's hand closer to her.

"Nothing. It's nothing," Didi said. "Let's go inside. I'm cold."

The two women entered the cabin hand in hand. Didi was now as pale as her friend.

She had realized that the knots she had seen tied in the pieces of yarn on Harris Renner's backpack were the same "surgeon's loops" that had been tied in the ropes fastening Sylvester Glass's feet to the ceiling beam.

Chapter 5

Allie Voegler sat glumly in his unmarked police cruiser on the dirt access road that led to Rose Vigdor's perpetually unfinished barn dwelling in Hillsbrook.

The way was blocked by her three dogs—two German shepherds and a corgi. They had just sat down and wouldn't move. They looked, in fact, distinctly unfriendly.

Particularly the young shepherd named Bozo, who kept curling his front lip.

Allie cursed under his breath. He didn't want to interrogate Trent Tucker—it might get back to Didi. And she would not appreciate it at all. She would accuse him of overzealousness. Or acting simply on his dislike of the "elves" she had inherited from her mother. Allie had never hidden his dislike of them; he considered them sponges on her generosity. But this visit had nothing to do with that. It was his job to follow up all leads, all possibilities. Robbery is robbery. And in his opinion, Tucker was a suspect in the Agway robbery.

Allie leaned on his horn and waited. Just sitting on Didi's friend's property made him think of her. He missed her and she had been away for only two days. He missed her even though he rarely saw her. He wondered how much he would miss her if they ever became lovers and she went away on a trip without him. He would probably go crazy.

Allie wondered if he would ever get rid of this infatuation. He was continually making a fool of himself. The only way out was to meet another woman. The only way to end this ridiculous spectacle of totally unrequited love was to fall in love with someone else.

So what else was new?

He stopped leaning on the horn and opened the window when he saw Trent Tucker walking toward him.

"Get those dogs under control," he yelled.

"They are under control," the younger man yelled back.

Allie climbed out of the car, keeping an eye on the dogs.

"What can I do for you?" Trent Tucker asked. His tone was not friendly.

"You living here while Miss Vigdor is away?"

"Yeah."

Bozo, the young shepherd, started to nip Huck, the corgi. A moment later all three dogs forgot about Allie. They ran off barking.

"You remember the last time I spoke to you?" Allie asked.

"Yeah. A couple of months ago. During the summer."

"Remember where?"

"Agway. What is this, a quiz show?"

"Right," Allie said. Trent Tucker was only nine years younger than he, but Allie felt old enough to be his father. The kid had that chronic unresolved adolescent "I don't give a damn" look. And he walked and stood around like no tragedy could ever befall him. He could drive a car drunk at 110 miles an hour in the wrong lane and everything would be all right. Allie knew the breed. He had been one himself. And the breed was always trouble. Sooner or later. Later or sooner.

"You were looking at those Winchesters. Remember?"

"Yeah."

"Did you ever buy one?"

"No."

"Why not?"

"No money."

"Want to hear something funny?" Allie asked.

Trent Tucker spat on the ground and looked around to find the dogs. They were nowhere in sight.

"Sure. I could use a good laugh."

"A couple of those Winchesters you were drooling over in the summer were stolen from Agway very early this morning."

"And you think I did it?"

"I didn't say that."

Tucker grinned.

Allie felt his neck tense. He really didn't like this young man. Was it simply because he was a suspect in a robbery? No, Allie knew it wasn't only that. All of Didi's elves disliked him and spoke against him to Didi because they knew he considered them a bunch of kooky spongers. Trent Tucker was part of the conspiracy against him for Deirdre Quinn Nightingale's hand and heart.

The realization of his personal animosity embarrassed Allie. He was a professional. He had to be very cool; he had to conduct a professional inquiry. After all, the kid was definitely suspect. He fit the "puppy dog" scenario that every cop knows: If a poor, lonely kid is seen staring into a pet-store window at a puppy . . . and the next night the window is shattered and the puppy is stolen . . . nine times out of ten the kid stole it.

"Did you stay here last night?"

"I stay here every night until she gets back."

"What time did you get in last night?"

"Late."

"Why late?"

"I had a few beers at Jack's."

"What time did you leave there?"

"Two or so."

"That's kinda late for just a few beers," Allie said. He looked around. "I don't see your pickup."

"Charlie borrowed it."

"What time did you get to Jack's?"

"About ten."

"And you left when?"

"I told you. About two."

"Well, I'll check it out."

"I'm sure you will," the younger man said nastily. Then he put two fingers into his mouth and produced a shrill whistle. The dogs came bounding toward him. Allie headed for his car.

Didi watched her colleagues eat the large sardine, onion, and tomato sandwiches that had been prepared in the tiny kitchen. They washed the food down with bottled water or beer.

Her own sandwich lay untouched on her lap in a paper plate.

The fire was going strong. The afternoon was moving rapidly into evening. The equipment for the morrow—the first official trek of the expedition—was neatly stacked against one wall of the cabin.

Rose had totally recovered and seemed to be flirting with the photographer, who was showing her some intricacy involved with his video camera.

Marsha Greeley and Moe Douglas were talking about the sardines in the sandwiches. She was astonished that they were the same sardines that would be used for the sedated bait. She wasn't offended—just astonished.

Harris Renner was fiddling with the fire. He seemed to love taking responsibility for it. When the fire was going fine on its own, he busied himself with stacking the kindling and tidying up the hearth with a broom.

Didi, who was now sitting in a patched wicker rocker, watched him.

She was confused . . . distressed . . . incredulous. There was no question that the knots on

Glass's leg ropes were the same as the knots of Renner's backpack.

But so what? Did that mean that Renner murdered Glass and tied him up onto the beam? No. There was no proof whatsoever of that. There was no hint of it. There was no hint that the two even knew each other. Worlds separated them. And Renner was in transit when Glass was killed. Or was he? Could he have had a motive to murder Sylvester Glass?

Besides . . . was the ability or inclination to use a surgeon's loop knot so uncommon? Maybe everyone in the cabin knew how to tie one. Surely *she* did.

Renner called out to her then, "If you're not going to eat that sandwich, give it to me."

Didi handed over her plate and watched the wildlife biologist down the meal. He consumed it voraciously but fastidiously.

She simply could not evaluate this man so far. She had no idea what he was about. One moment, watching him stoke the fire, it seemed quite possible that he was a demented murderer. The next moment, watching him attack that sandwich with such zest, he seemed totally incapable of anything more violent than uprooting a radish.

Someone turned on a portable radio. The signal

was dim, but the jazz quickly mellowed the cabin and seemed to bring the night on faster.

"What did you think of today's outing?" Renner asked her after he finished the sandwich.

"It wore me out," Didi admitted.

"I thought large-animal vets were always in shape."

"So did I."

Renner thought her response very funny and he strode over and placed his hand on her shoulder, as if paying tribute to her sense of humor. But it was more than that. He kept his hand there too long. Didi shook it off and stood up. Renner said good night and walked away.

Men can be treacherous sometimes, she thought. She wrapped a scarf around her neck and stepped outside.

The night was pitch-dark. It was cold. It was quiet, very quiet. No sounds in the underbrush. No sounds from the mountain slope behind the cabin.

As her eyes gradually adjusted to the night, she could make out her red Jeep.

Right behind the Jeep was a Mitsubishi 4x4 Montero. That was Renner's vehicle, she knew.

I should search his car, she thought. And then she was astonished at how casually she had conjured up such a course of action. She reminded herself: I am here in my capacity as a veterinarian.

Didi blew on her hands. She pulled the scarf tighter and pressed her lithe back against the wall of the cabin. The wind blew her short black hair against her head.

Maybe, she thought, this whole trip was the wrong trip at the wrong time for the wrong reason. Surprisingly, she already longed for Hillsbrook, for her practice, and even for her fractious elves—Charlie Gravis, Abigail, Trent Tucker, and Mrs. Tunney.

She even longed for her morning yoga discipline out in the backyard while Mrs. Tunney was preparing her staple—oatmeal. Which Didi loathed and never ate.

Didi walked briskly off the porch and onto the ground. She stopped. Is it arrogance? she thought. Sure, she had played a major role in helping the police solve several Hillsbrook crimes. But that was because in dairy farmer country the vet always knows things other people don't know.

This part of the state was not her turf. Not at all.

She wavered. Just a peek, she thought. What harm could it do?

Didi walked quickly to Renner's vehicle, opened the driver's side door, and slipped in. She was almost ecstatic at her ability to enter so quickly and with such stealth.

She ran her hands along the top of the dashboard. Nothing. She groped under the front seats. Nothing. She opened the glove compartment. An owner's manual and a small, open bag of potato chips. She took one and chewed it. Too salty.

Then she twisted in her seat and stuck one hand into the cramped back where the seat had been let down so that Renner could transport his supplies to the cabin. All the equipment had already been taken in.

She moved her hand slowly along the flat surface. Her fingers felt something odd. It was hair.

She pulled her hand back into the front seat, reopened the glove compartment, and inspected the hair under the small compartment light.

For the first time she felt that she was doing something illicit . . . even dangerous.

It was definitely dog hair.

Long and black with just a trace of brown. Maybe from a Gordon setter or one of those Swiss mountain dogs.

Hadn't the park ranger and the state trooper found dog tracks along with human tracks leading from the cabin up the slope of Mt. Dunaway?

Yes. She remembered that clearly.

Calm down, Didi cautioned herself. It could be the most mundane of coincidences. He could have been transporting his own dog or a friend's dog before he made this trip.

She climbed out of the vehicle and slammed the door behind her. She winced at the noise and her own stupidity. She watched fearfully. But no one from the cabin seemed to have heard the sound.

She brushed her hands of the dog hair and walked slowly back to the cabin. Proceed with caution from now on, she admonished herself. A healthy cow in a sick herd always appears at first sight to be as sick as the others. And vice versa.

The moment she stepped inside, Rose, who was seated in a chair by the banked fire, began to wave frantically. All the others seemed to be in their bunks.

"I was waiting for you," Rose confided. "Where've you been?"

"Checking up on the Jeep."

"You missed the local news. It was all about Sylvester Glass."

"What did they say?"

"The medical examiner reported that Glass had been beaten before he was killed. It's horrible, Didi.

63

It makes you loathe humankind. They hung him up. They beat him in the stomach with a rifle butt. Then they shot him."

Didi sat down in the chair across from Rose. She wanted to tell her about the knots and the dog hairs. She wanted to confess to Rose her suspicions of Harris Renner. But all she could say was, "We still haven't seen a black bear."

"Does she live there?" Abigail asked incredulously, pointing to the rather grotesque and very large stone house, which looked like a transported Norman castle.

"No. She has a cottage in the back," Charlie replied. "After her husband died, she sold the farm to a drug rehabilitation place. For rich people. They built that. It's really a wood house with a stone front. Part of the deal was that Cleo could stay on the property until she dies. And gets buried on it."

"Were they dairy farmers, Cleo and her husband?"

"Sure were. A big operation until it went bad, like all the others. Until the squeeze. The barns used to be there."

Charlie pointed to a huge greenhouse complex

just off the road, about five hundred yards from the house.

"It's ugly," Abigail said, but she wasn't looking at the greenhouses.

"What's ugly?"

"The house."

"Maybe. But the land is the best in Hillsbrook. Look at those hills. And there are good wells."

"What's inside the stone house?"

"I guess it's like a hospital. Once in a while you see the patients walking on the road."

"Charlie pulled the pickup into a carefully manicured space marked with a STAFF ONLY sign.

"We have to walk round back to the cottage," he explained. They exited the vehicle and started walking. It was hard going for Charlie, who was lugging along a canvas bag. They were traversing an old cow pasture that was in the process of reverting to new growth forest. Low trees were savagely whipping their now leafless branches in the wind.

When they saw the cottage, which was small and white and peeling, Charlie called for a rest.

"Where do the people come from?" Abigail asked.

"What people?" he responded, a bit testily. He was too old for these kinds of questions and these kinds of hikes.

"The patients."

"From all over the world. Including, I hear, Siam."

As they approached the cottage, an old woman wearing a tattered black sweater stepped out.

"Is that you, Charlie Gravis?" she called out.

Charlie and Abigail stopped about five feet from her. God! thought Charlie. Do *I* look that old?

"Yes. It's me, Cleo," he answered, and he realized that it was probably a good ten years since they had laid eyes on each other—even though they lived only five miles apart.

"What brings you here, Charlie?" she asked suspiciously.

"Your dog."

"Red?" The old woman was obviously confused.

"Yes. You called Dr. Nightingale."

"Is she Dr. Nightingale?" Cleo asked, pointing at the silent, willowy Abigail.

"No. We both work for Dr. Nightingale. But she's on vacation, Cleo."

The old woman gave him a sharp look. Then she folded her arms defiantly and said, "I'm out of sugar."

Charlie was totally perplexed by the comment. He tried to think what the old lady's statement could possibly have to do with anything, but in the end he gave up. Then, suddenly, he understood—Cleo was a bit dotty. Too many winters alone in the cottage.

"I want to help Red," he said, bringing the conversation back to the real matter at hand.

"Very well. Come in. By all means, come in!"

Chaos reigned inside the cottage. Everywhere Charlie looked there was a pile of clothes or a stack of magazines or a paper bag overflowing with cans.

Red lay on the floor, on a raft of towels. He looked like a hunting dog—a Blue Tick or a Platt—one of the breeds they use in the South to run boars.

"He can't walk much anymore, Charlie. It's his back. And the last couple of nights he has been groaning in a terrible way."

"If you don't mind, Cleo, I'd like to see him move."

The old woman sighed and called to Red. At first the dog just flapped his tail on the towel. It sounded like someone kneading dough.

Cleo called him again, more forcefully.

The big, short-haired dog rose painfully from his little bed, in sections, and walked stiffly over to

Cleo. She scratched his ears lovingly and cooed her sympathies for his pain.

"It's lumbago for sure," Charlie pronounced, "and a bad case." He rocked a bit on his heels, looking first at Cleo and then at Abigail. Neither of them seemed to take any note of his diagnosis.

"That's why I called Dr. Nightingale," Cleo Dopple finally said, holding Red's face tenderly against her stomach.

Charlie opened his bag and pulled out a small brandy bottle that was filled with a thick greenish liquid punctuated by white and gray spots. A piece of cloth was fastened over the opening of the bottle with a shoelace.

"What do you feed Red?" he asked Cleo.

"A little canned dog food, a little dry food, and once in a while an egg . . . and sometimes, when I make it, spaghetti and meatballs."

"Okay. Now you just put three tablespoons of this in his bowl every time he eats. Just three table-spoons, whenever you feed him. Clear?"

Then he handed the bottle to Cleo. She held it up as if it were dangerous.

"What is it, Charlie?"

"Medicine. A kind of broth made of parsley, boiled nettles, seaweed, and comfrey. You're holding the best lumbago medicine in the world."

"How much does it cost?" she asked almost fearfully.

"Don't worry about that now. Let's get Red fixed up first."

Cleo Dopple shook the bottle. "Does it fizz?"

Chapter 6

The research project staff broke into two groups the following morning—about two hundred yards up the slope where the trail forked.

Didi, Renner, and Moe Douglas were in one group. Rose, Marsha Greeley, and Kurt Trabert in the other.

It was a gray morning. The two groups split silently. Rose waved to her friend. They lost sight of each other within twenty yards of the splitting point.

Moe Douglas found a promising den very quickly. It was carved out of an enormous, long-dead beech tree trunk.

"It was used last winter, for sure," he noted. "And a bear's been here not long ago. Checking it out."

Harris Renner inspected the den and happily

confirmed the guide's analysis. He turned to Didi. "Are you ready to go to work?"

"As ready as I'll ever be," she replied. Didi felt nervous and excited. She knew a bear was close. She knew she would be examining a black bear soon. It was different from being a vet in the circus—much different—even though the animals there were for the most part larger and more dangerous than black bears. But even the Bengal tigers in the circus could no longer be considered "wild."

Moe Douglas quickly set up a camouflage blind. It consisted of a simple canvas wall painted over to mimic the coloration of the local trees and vegetation. About five feet long and three feet high, the blind was only a couple of inches thick, with plenty of slits for viewing.

Didi watched while the guide quietly and efficiently stowed all the equipment behind the blind. Then he laid out a small rug. He assembled a bolt action rifle and laid it on the rug, bolt open. He placed six bullets down beside the rifle. There were obviously two types of bullets.

Moe, sensing her curiosity, answered Didi's question before she even asked it. "There are bear repellents on the market in spray cans," he said. "When push comes to shove I think they're worthless." He picked up one of the bullets. "If the bear just wants to play—a plastic bullet." He put it down and picked up an example of the other type. "If the bear wants to chew—a real bullet."

Renner began preparing the bait buckets. The smell of sardines in the cold air was almost heady.

"What kind of sedative will you be using?"

"Pills. Stuck down the mouth of the sardines. A sort of valium cocktail. Good old diazepam. The bear is never really out."

After the bait buckets were fixed, Renner laid out the tiny microphones and recording devices that would be placed on the bear and in its den, if it was a pregnant female.

Didi checked her own field kit. It was unimpressive by any standard but it did contain the essentials. A stethoscope to locate fetal heartbeat. A tongue depressor and flashlight for throat examinations. Cotton swabs to take smears from eyes, ears, and other orifices. A cloth ruler to measure wounds. A notebook with magnetic pencil attached. A pair of scissors. A knife. Needles and thread. Surgical staples. Two bottles of antiseptic. A small bottle of distilled water. A small bottle of rubbing alcohol.

Harris Renner left the blind and placed the bait buckets near the den.

Then he put the predator call to his lips and blew. In the cold morning air it was horrifying: a squalling, screaming crescendo of pain and despair.

He waited about thirty seconds and then blew it again. Perfect pitch from some creature in hell. Then he pocketed the call and rejoined the others behind the blind.

The bear came in fast . . . from seemingly no-where . . . moving with great speed . . .angry . . . alert. Behind her was a yearling cub.

The sight of the animal froze Didi. She had never even imagined that the Catskill Mountain black bear was so large, so powerful, so swift. And the thick coat was black as pitch, not the charcoal shade Didi had expected to see.

Moe Douglas laid his hand gently on the rifle.

There was something so vital about the bear that Didi felt her own strength drain away. She felt to-tally incapable of acting.

The bear calmed down. She had discovered the bait and was knocking the buckets over. Mother and child began to eat with a diligent fury.

Five minutes later they were sprawled on the ground—happy, almost goofily languorous.

"Not yet, not yet," Renner whispered.

This is what a soldier must feel, Didi thought.

Prior to combat. It was totally unlike any veterinary experience she had ever had.

One of her legs cramped. *What is he waiting for?* she thought.

Renner kept up the patter: "*Not yet not yet not yet.*"

When he finally said "*Now!*" Didi was already moving.

Allie Voegler ordered a bottle of beer. Then he spun on his stool and looked around. It had been at least six years since he had drunk a beer in Jack's. In those days it was called "Jack's Or Better" and it had featured bands that came down from New York City on weekends. Jack's Or Better had evolved into a wild pickup scene and young people from all over Dutchess County came there.

At twelve noon it was hard to tell what now happened at Jack's at night . . . but Allie knew it had changed. They had a jukebox now; no more live music. And everything about the place seemed to speak of a kind of fatigue . . . the walls, the posters, the lights. Time had passed them by.

"Want a glass?"

Allie spun back on the stool as the bartender placed a bottle of Budweiser in front of him. But this bartender was different from the one he had placed his order with. This one was a woman.

"Want a glass?" she asked again.

"No."

"I was powdering my nose," she said bluntly, intuiting Allie's confusion.

Then she walked to the bar register, punched it open, and began to count the cash in it.

Allie watched her count. She seemed to be humming a tune as she worked. About forty, Allie surmised, maybe a bit younger, and not from around Hillsbrook. She was plain-looking and plain-dressed, except for her light brown hair, which seemed to be coiffed into a modified form of dreadlocks. She wore an apron with a watch pinned to one of the straps. Her face was Slavic blunt.

He kept staring at the hair. Other than on television, he had never seen a white woman wearing dreadlocks. But the style seemed to suit her . . . it seemed correct. As she counted and hummed she shook her head and the dreadlocks did a sort of dance.

Allie called out, "Miss!"

Without looking at him, she raised one hand, signaling that she would be there shortly.

Allie drank from the bottle.

Two minutes later he called out again, "Miss!"

She gave a mighty sigh, slammed the register shut, glared at him, and then walked over.

Allie opened his leather identification wallet and held it out so she could see the police ID card and photo.

She snatched it out of his hand.

"Hey!" he protested.

"Oh, sorry! You only wanted me to *look* at it," she said wickedly. "I thought you were giving me a tip."

Then she held the wallet up to the nonexistent light. "It appears to me that you are an officer of the law."

"That's right."

She handed the ID back to him. Her face collapsed. "Then it's all over for me . . . right? I can't hide anymore. Yes, I did it! I killed him! I shot the bastard three times in the head. But I couldn't help it. Believe me. It was the devil who pulled that trigger. The lactose devil. I could never handle milk products."

It took Allie a few seconds to understand that her confession was a joke.

"You didn't think that was funny?" she queried.

"Not very."

"So it goes. By the way, if you're a cop where is your uniform?"

"I'm a detective. With the Hillsbrook Police Department."

"I'm much impressed, Detective Voegler. I understand that Hillsbrook has been in the grip of a horrible crime wave lately. You must be very busy—rescuing chickens from cow flop."

"That's not funny either."

"What about your name?"

"What about it?"

"It says on your ID card that you're an Allie Voegler. That sounds like an imported sports car."

"No. You're thinking of an Alfa Romeo."

She grinned and wiped the counter in front of him. "Actually," she said to him in a mock whisper, "I was thinking of Alpha Centauri."

"That's a star," Allie noted.

"I thought it was a dog food."

"This is getting stupid."

"Good. Now I can get back to my register. Drink your beer, Detective Volkswagen, and be reflective."

"Wait!"

"Yeah?"

"I need some information."

She held out her hands as if ready to get cuffed.

"Do you know a young man named Trent Tucker who drinks here?"

"No."

"He claims to have been here last night . . . from about ten to two."

"What does he drink?"

"Beer."

"What kind?"

"I don't know."

"What does he look like?"

Allie described him.

"He looks like half the kids in here at night."

"So you can't make a firm identification."

"No."

"Well, thanks."

She looked at him mockingly. He squirmed. "You seem to like making fun of people," he said.

"That's my trade."

"What do you mean?"

"I do stand-up."

"You mean you're a comedian? No kidding?"

"That's right."

"What are you doing here?"

"I bombed in Binghamton."

"How long have you been doing it?"

"About ten years. I started late. I didn't recover from adolescent malaria until I was twenty-eight. What's your excuse?"

Allie laughed.

"My name is Mary," she said. "Let me buy you a real drink."

She poured a shot of Jack Daniel's and pushed it in front of Allie.

"Who did this Trent Tucker murder?" she asked.

"No one."

"Damn!" she exclaimed in mock disappointment. "I thought you were investigating a real crime!" And she made as if to pull the whiskey glass back.

"I like you," Allie blurted out.

It had been a long, cold, depressing morning for Rose and her group. She sat on a rock outcrop and chewed a piece of hard cheese. Marsha Greeley was out of sight. Kurt Trabert was smoking a cigarette a few feet from her. He was shivering.

"You are going to die of pneumonia if you keep dressing like that," Rose cautioned. He was wearing only a down vest on top of a sweater.

"Probably," he said morosely, and then grinned.

Rose liked the way he looked. She always liked either younger men or older men. He was definitely older . . . much older. She always liked raffish men of any age. And he was definitely raffish.

"I don't understand why you came with us. This is the second team. The photographer should go with the first team."

"Ah. You don't understand the psychology of scientists," he replied. "Give me a piece of that cheese and I'll explain."

Rose broke off a piece and tossed it to him. He caught it and continued, "Scientists are petrified of looking like fools. And, my dear, during the first day or so on a project like this, things always go wrong. So Harris Renner doesn't want me around today."

"Well, at least you shot me."

"I shall make you immortal. By the way, what the hell are you? A veterinarian?"

"No, Didi's the vet. I'm her assistant. Actually, I'm only here to get my karma readjusted."

Trabert chuckled. Rose enjoyed the sound of it.

"What kind of accent do you have?" Rose asked.

"I came to this country when I was about twelve. From Czechoslovakia."

"I thought it was German."

"My family was ethnic German. But we lived in Czechoslovakia."

When he had finished Rose's cheese, he took out a huge apple and bit into it. She watched him as he chewed. His hair was long and speckled with gray. He looks like a movie director, she thought. Or maybe a depraved industrial designer. She closed her eyes and thought of her dogs.

"Nothing at all!" Marsha Greeley came into view then. She was leaning heavily on her walking stick. "Nothing!" she repeated. The botanist spoke as if she had just seen something really distasteful. In fact, the group had found only two dens the entire morning, both long-abandoned, of no interest to the group. But Marsha had marked them diligently on the map.

"The iron butterfly," Kurt quipped under his breath. And then he began to reload and check his cameras. Rose watched him work. He was often flippant and a bit wacky, but when it came to his work he was quite serious and relentless. She liked that about him. In fact, there was a whole lot to like about him. When Rose realized this she almost burst out laughing. There she was, in the glorious wilderness, searching for bear dens, and she was thinking about things she shouldn't be thinking about.

A sudden gust of wind sent something into Kurt Trabert's eye. He cursed, flung the remains of the apple to the ground, and tried to remove it.

"There's one more area that looks promising," the botanist said to Rose. "And then we'll call it a day."

The two women watched Kurt manipulate his eyelid. Finally he blinked it away.

"Are you okay?" Rose asked.

"Fine."

"According to the map there's an old logging road not far from here. Roads mean tree falls. Tree falls mean dens. Specially if there's some beech or oak around. And I see both beech and oak."

Kurt hoisted his cameras. "I like beech and oak but I like birch trees better. Yellow birch. And I positively adore blue spruce." He winked at Rose and continued, "For me, photographing a blue spruce is an erotic adventure."

Marsha Greeley gave Rose one of those "listen to this fool" looks. Rose winked back to Kurt.

And then off they trudged toward this old road and the white ash stand. The botanist was in the lead. Rose behind her. And the photographer a meandering third.

They hadn't walked more than ten minutes when the terrain began to change dramatically.

There was no road . . . abandoned or otherwise. There were no beeches, no oak. In fact, the trees seemed to have vanished.

The ground was littered with a sandy gravel. It was just a large, ugly empty space . . . like a patch.

"Well," called out a laughing Kurt, "I have finally reached purgatory."

And then the ground just vanished. Not with a roar—more like a slurp. It simply fell away.

Rose found herself sliding abrasively through the earth.

She tried to scream but couldn't.

"Where is Abigail?" Charlie Gravis asked as he sat at the long kitchen table and sipped his traditional evening cocoa.

"Miss Quinn's horse was acting up. Abigail is in the barn," Mrs. Tunney explained. She was doing something by the sink.

"You'll never guess who I saw today," Charlie said.

"Who?"

"Cleo Dopple."

Mrs. Tunney wiped her hands on a towel. "You didn't! My God, Charlie, I thought she had passed on."

"Nope. She still lives in that cottage on her old property."

"Well, bless her. That woman has seen heartache."

Mrs. Tunney joined Charlie at the table. She stirred her cup of cocoa.

Charlie grinned into his cup. He had brought the subject of Cleo Dopple up only to test if Abigail had kept her mouth shut. She had. Mrs. Tunney knew

nothing. But Charlie knew his strategy was dangerous. Because now that he had brought up Cleo
Dopple, Mrs. Tunney would probe. As sure as God
let down milk from udders. He would have to be
cagey.

"Did she recognize you, Charlie?"

"She did. But it took a little while. Her eyes are
bad."

"Oh! She was a pretty woman. Is she still pretty,
Charlie?"

"Not like you," he said, and the moment he
said it he knew he had made an error. Mrs. Tunney did not trust flatterers as far as she could
throw them.

She sipped her cocoa, narrowing her eyes. "What
were you doing out there, Charlie?"

He had prepared a cover story. "I was in the hardware store . . . you know . . . Art Peters's place in
town. He told me Cleo Dopple had ordered some
cleaning supplies delivered. But his truck had broken down. So I told him I'd deliver them."

"That was very nice of you, Charlie."

"Well, I admit I was a bit curious. I hadn't seen
the woman in at least ten years. Probably more. And
you know that Jed Dopple and me were old drinking buddies. He was a good man."

"That's not what I heard."

"We all have our faults."

"That's for sure. What kind of cleaning supplies, Charlie?"

"Rug polish and furniture polish, mops and brushes. Stuff like that."

"Why would Cleo Dopple buy furniture polish in a hardware store? You don't buy it in a hardware store. You buy it in one of those discount stores. They have everything."

Charlie Gravis got nervous. This was a turn he had not anticipated.

"Well, she's an old lady now. I guess old habits are hard to break," he explained.

The door opened and a gust of cold wind flooded the kitchen. Abigail slammed the door shut and joined them at the table.

"Have some cocoa," Mrs. Tunney suggested.

Abigail shook her head and just sat there dreamlike with her arms folded.

"Is the horse all right?" Charlie asked.

Abigail nodded and smiled. She started to undo the muffler around her neck, then decided not to take it off.

Mrs. Tunney sighed, walked to the stove, and began preparing a mug of cocoa for Abigail even though it seemed she didn't want it. When the elaborate ritual of mixing water, cocoa, cinnamon, coffee, sugar, and milk culminated in a finished mug, Mrs. Tunney carried the treasure back to the table and placed it down, authoritatively, in front of Abigail. The young woman grasped the mug, but did not drink the contents.

Mrs. Tunney seemed to have become so abstracted by the making of the cocoa that she forgot about Cleo Dopple completely.

Charlie Gravis, however, had the distinct feeling that there was trouble ahead with Mrs. Tunney. But at least he had confirmed that Abigail was loyal and discreet. She could keep a big secret. Not a little secret . . . but a big one. He leaned back on his kitchen chair. For a moment he felt very much the lord of the manor.

Then Mrs. Tunney suddenly slammed her cocoa spoon down so hard on the table that it sounded like an explosion.

"What? What?"

"I just remembered that Cleo Dopple had a nephew."

"I don't think so."

"Yes. His name is Walter. He owns a farm near Kingston. I remember him clearly."

"So?" Charlie was becoming uneasy.

"He was a handsome man. And his farm did good."

"When was the last time you saw him?"

"1972 or 1973, I think. At the church sale."

"That's a long time ago. He may be dead. He could have lost the farm. He could be in Arizona."

"It wasn't a dairy farm," Mrs. Tunney said, as if only dairy farms went bankrupt.

Charlie didn't reply. He waited for the other shoe to drop. It did.

"This Walter may be perfect for Miss Quinn."

"But he's probably thirty years older than her . . . if he's alive," Charlie retorted. He looked at Abigail for help against Mrs. Tunney. But no help was forthcoming. Abigail was inspecting her cocoa.

"A very handsome man he was. And polite. And hardworking. I remember he was wearing a red flannel shirt and a beautiful tie . . . with a bird on it."

"It's going to be cold tonight," Charlie said, trying to change the subject, "and it'll be colder where Miss Quinn is."

But Mrs. Tunney would not be deflected from her dream match.

"Tomorrow, Charlie, you will take me to see Cleo Dopple."

*   *   *

Moe Douglas stood in front of the fire sucking on an unlit pipe. Harris Renner angrily paced, cursing in whispers.

Didi sat in the ancient wicker rocker.

Rose, Kurt, and Marsha Greeley had never showed up at the rendezvous point. They had never showed up at the cabin. They were now missing for five hours.

The authorities had been notified and a search was in progress.

Didi was in a most peculiar state. On the one hand she was worried that something terrible had happened to her friend and the others.

On the other hand she was still enthralled with the events of her day.

The brief, almost primitive examination she had made of the sedated black bear had affected her greatly.

It had turned out to be the first truly mystical experience Didi had had since she was a child.

Initially the event had simply been embarrassing. After all, she prided herself on being a scientist and since she had become a vet she had examined all kinds of creatures—Asian elephants, Bengal tigers, black Angus bulls, just to name a few—without any mystical experiences.

Never before, as an adult, had she felt this

strange sense of . . . well . . . it was difficult to describe. It was part ecstatic danger, part joy, and part intimacy with the creature.

Never before, as a veterinarian, had Didi sensed so strongly the physical presence of the patient. It was as if her fingertips and the bear's body were in deep communion.

She had felt a numbing fear at first, but then the fear became something else . . . and then something else again . . . and then this mysterious joy.

Above all, she had found herself succumbing to the smell of the bear—a rather delightful musty odor of wet coat and tree bark and just plain wilderness.

Didi rocked in her chair. Her mother, who saw visions on a weekly basis, would have considered such an experience quite normal; like a head cold. But her mother had been a devout woman. Didi was a skeptic. She rocked faster. She tried to think of poor Rose, now in harm's way. But her thoughts kept pulling her to that sedated, half-conscious, pregnant black bear—blinking and staring at her.

Didi closed her eyes as she rocked. She remembered a course she had in college on The Religious Experience. The professor had said in one of his lectures that mysticism had no outside object or subject. It was about itself. It was its own object and its own subject. It is like a swimming pool, he explained. You are either in it or out of it.

Are you a swimming pool, mama bear? she thought. But she must have been thinking aloud.

"What?" Harris Renner shouted over to her. Didi realized she had uttered the nonsense question out loud. She didn't know what to say now.

"Are you ill?" Renner followed up.

"Just talking to myself," Didi said.

"A vehicle is coming," Moe Douglas announced.

"I don't hear a damn thing," Renner replied. Nor did Didi.

The guide stared at his empty pipe. He didn't defend his statement. He didn't have to. Thirty seconds later Fay Whitely's Bronco screeched to a stop at the cabin.

The park ranger entered first, then the exhausted members of the missing group. They were silent and pale. Didi got up and helped Rose into the chair. Her friend looked dazed and there were abrasions on her hands.

"Thank God you're safe," Didi whispered.

Harris Renner exploded. "What the hell happened to you people? Where were you? Why didn't you contact me?"

Fay Whitely made a silent gesture with her right hand; that this wasn't the time for recrimination; that he should shut up. And Renner did.

Moe Douglas went into the small kitchen and brought back mugs of hot soup, using a tin pie plate as a makeshift tray.

The three rescued campers drank the soup greedily. Fay Whitely didn't have any. Marsha Greeley looked particularly bad with her walking stick over her knee like an old man with a cane. She hunched way over on the chair to drink the liquid.

All Didi could think was: What kind of soup was it? She realized she was still in some kind of mystical haze. Her old friends in Philly would have said that the bear represented some kind of goddess or a long repressed return of "the Mother." This is getting me nowhere, Didi told herself. Her friend from Hillsbrook was in trouble. She began to massage Rose's back gently.

"Oh, that feels good," Rose said. Didi noted scratches on the back of Rose's neck.

"It just fell away. The ground just vanished," Rose intoned.

Then Fay Whitely opened the snaps of her down vest with such force that it sounded like firecrackers. "I want to say a few words to all of you." But she was looking directly at Harris Renner. "You people came close to disaster. You don't want another tragedy."

Renner shot back. "What are you talking about? What *other* tragedy?"

"Sylvester Glass," Fay Whitely said.

"That murder, or whatever it was, has nothing to do with our project or anyone connected with the project. Don't tar us with that brush. It was a local thing. Or are you really saying that one of us was involved?"

"Calm down, Dr. Renner. Let's forget Sylvester Glass for the moment. I want you to know a few things. I want you all to know. We're in hunting season now. Not, however, on Mt. Dunaway. We closed it to hunters and hikers because of your project.

"But even if we hadn't closed it there'd be only a few hunters here. Know why? Because everyone— except you people—knows that Mt. Dunaway is a very dangerous place. It is crisscrossed with ravines like Demon's Gorge and dotted with equally dangerous abandoned quarries."

She looked at the three survivors. "You people hit an old bluestone quarry. Those stones built the sidewalks of New York in the nineteenth century. Then the quarries shut down. About fifty years ago the state let out contracts to fill the abandoned quarries with sand and gravel. A lot of crooked firms just covered the logs."

Then Fay wagged a finger at Harris Renner. "You're the leader of this project. If you were sending a group out, you should have warned them.

"They all could have died there of exposure. The only reason I found them is that we routinely check the worst sites every week or so. It was sheer luck that I checked that site at that time."

"They had a map with a safe path laid out," Renner replied.

She brushed his comment aside. "And, in fact, it's best not to split up at all."

Fay Whitely then rebuttoned her vest and stalked out.

No one said a word as the Bronco roared off.

Moe Douglas brought out more soup and a fistful of vitamin capsules which he distributed to Rose, Marsha, and Kurt.

"OK," Harris Renner said wearily, "all's well that ends well. I think we should all turn in. Tomorrow we'll stick together on the trail."

Didi watched Renner go to his bunk, take out a small notebook, and begin to write.

Rose said, "Guess what I fantasized about in that mine pit, Didi."

"I haven't a clue."

"An omelette. An enormous omelette made of eleven brown eggs from free-running chickens. The omelette was chock-full of chopped eggplant with tarragon."

"It could be worse, Rose."

"No," she said, the passion rising in her voice. "You don't understand, Didi. I hate eggplant. And tarragon makes me nauseous. I do believe, Didi, that my karma is already being rearranged."

Then her voice clutched. "So I probably led them into the pit! Don't you see?"

"Were you in the lead?"

"No. Marsha was."

"So don't be a fool. *She* obviously made the error. And what does it matter anyway? She was just reading the map wrong." Didi released her grip on Rose. "I'm going to get some coffee."

"Just a minute!"

"What is it?"

Rose gestured for her to come closer.

"Did you see them?" she asked.

"Who?"

"The black bears."

"Yes. Saw them. Examined them."

"Tell me! Tell me, Didi! Were they big? Were they

ferocious? Did they attack? Oh, tell me everything, Didi. I didn't get to see anything."

"They're big, Rose, and beautiful. And pregnant. Let me get a cup of coffee and I'll tell you everything."

Didi walked into the kitchen and poured a half cup of bitter black coffee from the perpetual pot. It was morning coffee and smelled like it. She stared out of the tiny prefab window. It was dark and starless outside.

She walked back into the main room of the cabin. Rose's chair was empty. Didi looked around, a bit bewildered.

Then she saw Rose standing at the back of the cabin, beyond the bunk area. Kurt Trabert was next to her, fiddling with his cameras.

Rose's right hand rested on the photographer's shoulder. It seemed a casual enough scene at first glance. But Didi, even from a distance, picked up on the undertone of intimacy.

She sat down quickly in the wicker rocker. The last of the mystical interlude was now gone. She wondered what had happened in that abandoned quarry between Rose and Trabert. Her friend Rose, the nature girl, was often quite reckless in affairs of the heart.

Didi felt a quick stab of jealousy. She was watching two people who were about to become lovers, if given the chance. It intensified her loneliness. There was no one for her . . . there had been no one for a long time. Allie Voegler wasn't the answer. It just wasn't going to happen with him. She liked him. But something was missing. He was too stolid. Too familiar. He just couldn't be her Prince Charming.

She winced at the persistence of her adolescent fantasies. She had found her Prince Charming once. He had bedded her, betrayed her, and left her. And he had turned out to be a criminal, to boot.

Didi could see Rose's hand applying slight pressure. The photographer looked up and smiled.

Yes, Didi thought, they will become lovers soon. No doubt.

There was a language of touch. But Harris Renner had put his hand on *her* shoulder and she had recoiled. So many ways to interpret a single touch.

She started to rock and her eyes caught the overhead beam again.

Oh, that damn beam! That stolid, ugly lynching beam.

She folded her arms and squeezed them, suddenly ashamed of her speculations about love and her fanciful bear flights.

She was sitting under a murder beam. And her friend Rose had almost died today. Along with two others.

Didi looked across the cabin again. Rose was now on her bunk. Trabert was climbing into his. Marsha Greeley was already asleep. Renner was still writing in his notebook. Moe Douglas was stretched out on his bunk, arms behind his head. He could have been asleep or awake.

Didi dozed off in the chair. When she awoke, everyone else in the cabin was in his or her own bed. It was like the proverbial night before Christmas: not a creature was stirring.

The whimsical Christmas thoughts amused her for a minute, but then she was reminded of their real-life connection to what was going on up here.

Why, for example, had the state troopers not interrogated each member of the expedition about Sylvester Glass?

And why had no one tried to find out *why* Marsha Greeley had led her party right into an abandoned quarry?

Just a simple little inquiry. Oh, the park ranger had read them the riot act. Everyone had issued dire warnings about the dangers of Mt. Dunaway . . . but no one had investigated how three people fell into what was essentially a mine shaft.

Didi squirmed in her chair. She was tired and wanted to sleep. But what was emerging in her mind was too troublesome. The unreality of the whole silly thing. As if everyone were marching blithely toward doom . . . marching toward death. It wasn't the night before Christmas . . . it was the night before Armageddon.

She saw the knapsacks piled in one corner. She could make out hers and Rose's. Renner's was easy to spot, too, because of those telltale knots. She knew Moe Douglas's—it was very large and red. The photographer, she knew, carried no knapsack at all.

Her eyes fell on an unfamiliar bag. That, she thought, must be the botanist's.

She stared at it. The answer to why Marsha Greeley almost led herself and two others to their death was in that backpack, Didi surmised. A map. Like Harris Renner had said. The whole thing had to be a terrible mistake . . . because the botanist had a map delineating the safe path.

Didi stared nervously into the bunk area. It was one thing to sneak into Harris's car in an outside parking lot while everybody was inside. It was quite another thing to rifle a backpack in the same room

where its owner lay sleeping. It was highly dangerous. And maybe not even necessary?

She sat in the chair and thought. Was it necessary?

What if the map wasn't there? What if the map
meant nothing?

Someone in the bunk area was talking in his
sleep. It sounded as though the sleeper was calling
out a name. Perhaps "Johnny."

Then there was silence again.

Didi stared at Marsha Greeley's backpack. It had
to be hers. It was fairly new. A handsome bag with
leather and brass supports.

Who could get hurt? There was a need to know.

Someone had to find out what was going on. If
indeed something *was* going on other than a random
murder and some lost sheep.

There were two outside pockets. Didi could see
the snaps. No Velcro. No noise. The map would be
there if it was anywhere at all. If, indeed, it existed
at all.

She waited another ten seconds, then sprang
silently from the chair, crossed the room, and
crouched beside the bag.

She looked back. The bunk area was quiet.

Didi opened the left-hand pocket and reached in.
Her hand felt a piece of paper, folded.

I am a thief twice over, she thought. The cabin was cold but she shivered and she sweated.

Then she walked quickly and quietly back to the fire and spread the paper on the floor to utilize the firelight.

Yes! It was a map. A simple map like the kind issued by hiking clubs. The map showed trails, elevations, natural landmarks, and place names.

With one finger, Didi traced the path Rose's group had probably taken. Renner had been right. The trail was clearly marked on the map.

She sat back. Perhaps the map was in error. As simple as that.

Harris Renner must have obtained the map from a hiking club, then given it to Moe Douglas for his modifications. Maybe Moe trusted the club maps so much he didn't even check it out.

Didi felt relief. A great deal of relief. She started to bring the map back to its source.

Halfway across the room she stopped.

There was a funny residue on her fingers. But, away from the firelight, she could not see what it was.

She wiped her hands on her sides, replaced the map, and went into the kitchen to use the sink.

The water emerged from the faucet very slowly, almost painfully, and it was only lukewarm. Didi thrust one hand under the water and stared at the other one in the kitchen light.

There were tiny spots of white on her hand, like pinpricks of chalk.

She stared uncomprehending at the little flakes . . . they seemed to dissolve and re-form.

Then she realized exactly what they were. She had done too many research papers not to know. Wite-Out, or Liquid Paper, or any one of a dozen other correction fluids for typewriter, pencil, or pen.

Suddenly something else was as plain as the nose on her face. The map had been altered . . . changed.

She shut the faucet and switched off the light. She stood in the kitchen and stared out at the bunks with their sleeping occupants.

She was frightened . . . excited . . . anticipatory. But she hadn't the slightest idea what to do next— other than to be careful.

She didn't know who to tell. She didn't know who to trust.

Everything about the research project now had DANGER stenciled on it. I am going to walk very softly, she told herself. Then she went to bed.

*   *   *

Allie Voegler swung his legs off the bed and onto the floor. He couldn't sleep. The clock read 10:30 in the evening. It was going to be a long night. He walked into the kitchen and peeled a banana, eating it as he peered out his kitchen window and onto one of Hillsbrook's streets. Allie lived on top of a bookstore and stationery store in the village proper.

There was nothing to see. He finished the banana, drank some milk, buttered a piece of bread, and ate that.

If not on duty he liked to go to sleep very early and get up very early. But this night was a bust. He had fallen fast asleep at 9:00. Here it was only an hour and a half later and he was wide awake. He cursed the night.

Then he picked up the phone and called Wynton Chung, because he was damn lonely.

Chung wasn't around. No answer at all. The word was that the new cop had a girlfriend. Maybe he was out with her. Why shouldn't he be? That's what rational people are supposed to do.

Allie switched on the TV to an opening season college basketball tournament. He watched for about five minutes, then shut it off.

He walked back into the kitchen and found two barbecued chicken legs in the refrigerator. He ate one. The apartment was cold. He sprawled on the sofa and tried to read a hunting magazine.

At eleven o'clock he did twenty push-ups, and then crawled back into bed.

No dice. No sleep. He sat up. He got up. He dressed. Agitated.

Why in hell did I dress? he asked himself after he had pulled on his shoes.

He sat down heavily onto the sofa.

"All dressed up and no place to go," he said out loud.

He stared at the blank wall. There used to be a picture there. He didn't remember what happened to it. It was a kindly watercolor, of a small village somewhere in the world, but not in America.

Allie stood up and started to pace.

Why not Jack's? he suddenly thought.

No progress had been made on the Agway robbery. But Allie still believed that Trent Tucker was involved.

Maybe, Allie thought, Trent Tucker was drinking at Jack's right now and shooting his mouth off.

If he wasn't there, maybe another kid was, somebody who had heard Trent crow about how he had bagged a new Winchester.

Allie strapped his ankle holster on, slipped the weapon into the holster, and left the apartment.

He was halfway to Jack's before he woke to the sheer self-serving fakery of his premise.

He knew damn well that he wasn't going to Jack's to find Trent Tucker or any of his friends. He wasn't going there to conduct a further investigation into a robbery.

He was going to Jack's to see that lady bartender. Mary.

The truth made him squirm behind the wheel, but he didn't turn back.

Chapter 7

Moe Douglas set up two blinds because they had all hiked up the slope together.

Didi waved at Rose, who crouched behind the neighboring blind with Trabert and the botanist. A dozen times on the walk up, Didi had started to tell Rose about the altered map. But she could never say the words. She didn't know why. And if she did tell what she knew . . . why only Rose? And why only about the map? What about the dog hairs in the back of Renner's vehicle and those knots on his backpack?

It was late morning. A warmish sunny day.

Renner had used the call about ten times but no bear was in sight. The den was a peculiar one, almost a shallow trench carved in crumbling rock. Bait buckets formed a semicircle around the entrance, like toy soldiers.

Renner made a motion to the guide—a sort of shrug—that seemed to signify it might be time to move on and find another den.

Moe Douglas shook his head vigorously. Then whispered, "No! I feel bear."

Renner didn't reply. He brought the call to his mouth again.

But before a single sound was elicited, a bear came into sight.

"Trouble!" Moe said hoarsely. "Old. Male."

The bear had appeared so quickly and with so little fanfare that Didi couldn't even determine the direction from whence he came.

This one wasn't particularly big, and he was the first bear Didi had seen whose coat wasn't in top shape. There were several bald patches at the shoulders.

Didi felt a sudden pressure on her leg. It was Moe's hand, tapping for attention. When she looked at him he brought his hand to the back of his neck and then pointed at the bear.

She studied the bear's neck. He was now in front of the bait cans and clearly visible. His nose was up, sniffing.

Didi saw the shaft of the arrow. It was embedded in the rear of his neck. Only about six inches of it remained visible. The rest had broken off. It was obvious that the archer had shot way off the mark; a shot like that would neither kill nor cripple a black bear. But bear archery was still in its infancy in the northeast and the hunters who tried it had cut their archery teeth on whitetail deer. Not black bear.

The bear was looking around, almost shyly.

Why doesn't he take the bait? Didi thought.

He didn't seem to be in any pain from the broken-off arrow in his neck. The wound had apparently closed a long time ago.

Nor did he appear hungry. He actually seemed to want to play with the buckets.

She looked away from the bear and toward Rose, behind the neighboring blind. Her friend was wide-eyed, entranced by this first encounter with a real-live black bear.

Suddenly the bear swatted one of the buckets and sent it flying. Then he flung another one up in the air so that it rained sardines.

A change was coming over the bear and Didi could sense it.

The bear stood up in full stature on his back feet. His nose was sniffing furiously . . . his ears pointing forward.

Then he fell back on all fours, wheeled, and trotted toward Didi's blind.

Renner made a violent motion with his hands—

signaling that they should all crouch as low as possible. Didi quickly dropped into the lotus position, the same one she used each morning for yoga exercises. Her heart was beginning to pound in her chest.

Moe Douglas slapped one of the plastic bullets into the chamber of the rifle.

The bear was no longer in sight. But they could hear him on the other side of the blind, sniffing the light, thin composite material of the blind.

Then he charged toward the other blind and swatted it with one paw.

Rose screamed.

The bear stared at the three humans his swat had revealed.

Moe stood up and fired the rifle. The plastic bullet struck the bear's rump. He screamed, wheeled, and glared.

Moe levered another bullet in the chamber. And aimed.

The bear charged him. The second plastic bullet struck high on the forehead. The bear roared and rose up to full height, reaching out with his paws like a boxer.

Moe levered a real bullet into the chamber. And aimed.

The bear dropped down on all fours. He began to

whimper, then simply ambled away, as if nothing had happened.

He even ate a sardine or two before he vanished into the thick brush.

Among the group there seemed to be the common perception that what had just happened wasn't real. That it was a dream they had all had at the same time. But they also understood that that was just wishful thinking. The fear had been real. The bear had been real. The danger had been real.

Renner broke the silence after a while. He told the guide to get a fire started and make some coffee. Didi realized it was just a way to return to normalcy, to give them all something to do—there was still coffee left in the thermoses.

Rose was pale and silent. She held on first to the photographer and then to Didi. Then she just stood with her hands on her hips, staring at the fire builder.

"I got most of it! I got most of it!" Kurt Trabert kept repeating in a low voice, holding up the video camera for emphasis, like a trophy.

Moe distributed mugs of coffee. Everyone sat down in some fashion. Renner handed out small squares of chocolate.

Soon everyone was talking, and talking at once. It was a babble. Trabert even did an imitation of the bear. Renner showed the scars on his leg, sustained when a bear had mauled him five years ago. Rose did a kind of bear dance. Marsha Greeley predicted snow and then put her head down between her knees as if she were nauseous.

Didi just ate her chocolate and wondered what else would happen on this expedition.

Renner then declared an hour break in the work schedule to take effect immediately.

"Let's all loosen up . . . relax . . . take a walk . . . meditate. Or write a letter home. Just watch your step. Don't fall in any quarries. Got it? We'll all meet back here in sixty minutes."

Moe Douglas curled up right in front of the fire. The day was getting colder. It began to look like snow.

Renner cleared up the bait cans that the irate bear had flung about.

Didi's legs were beginning to cramp, her back hurt, her stomach was doing occasional flip-flops. She needed a long, slow walk to unravel. She looked at Rose, hoping for company, but her friend was whispering to the photographer.

So she wandered off alone, making sure to lock the surrounding landmarks into her memory, visually.

It got warmish again and the sun came out. The

weather on Mt. Dunaway was wildly unstable . . . changeable. It seemed like a completely new weather pattern emerged every half hour.

She headed west, climbing a steep rocky trail. It felt so good to stretch out. What with angry bears and altered maps, her musculature was like a violin string.

At least, she thought, all that mystical nonsense had vanished. The only thing she felt when that black bear was on the other side of the blind was fear.

Didi took off her ski hat and unbuttoned her pale blue down parka as she walked.

Would she be on the PBS special—if it was ever aired? she wondered.

Had Trabert photographed her in the lotus position behind the blind?

She laughed deliciously to herself. She could hear the narrator now, describing how the Hillsbrook veterinarian used yogic breathing techniques to overcome panic in the face of a terrifying black bear attack.

What would the vet society of Dutchess County make of it all?

Her fantasy was broken by an odd spot of blue in the terrain. Just off the trail, in a small damp, rocky hollow.

She stopped and stared.

Had a hiker during the past summer dropped a trinket? A clip of some kind? Or a handkerchief? Whatever it was, the coming snows would bury it for another year.

"Just lovely," she said out loud as she approached and saw it was two wildflowers, just past their prime, struggling to survive a bit longer.

Without thinking, she plucked them from the rocky earth and brought them inside her parka.

She had no idea what they were, but she knew it was a rare find. It was too late in the autumn for wildflowers.

Excited, she wanted to announce her beautiful prize.

But to whom?

Rose was flirting with a tall, dark stranger.

Douglas and Renner were occupied with the mechanics of the project.

Oh! she thought suddenly. How stupid! The botanist, Marsha Greeley.

She rushed back down the trail toward the clearing.

I feel like a child again, Didi thought. Like when I found a patch of raspberries in the woods.

Marsha Greeley was seated on her backpack. She was consulting a small spiral notebook.

Didi approached without saying a word.

Marsha looked up from her notebook questioningly.

Didi pulled out the two flowers and thrust them triumphantly toward the botanist.

Marsha took the flowers. She looked at them critically for an instant.

Then she lay them gently on the ground.

"Aren't they beautiful?" Didi asked, exasperated. She had been looking for a passionate response.

"It's a bit late for these kinds of flowers," the botanist said.

"Yes, I know! That's what's so wonderful."

Marsha Greeley picked one up and twirled it ever so slightly.

"*Aster novi-belgii*," she intoned. "In the sunflower family. Twenty to forty violet-blue rays spreading out from a yellow or reddish disc flower."

"How interesting," Didi replied sarcastically.

Then she took the flower from the botanist's hand, picked up the other flower from the ground, and walked away.

Rose was alone, close to the fire.

"Look!" Didi said, holding the two flowers up.

Rose's face lit up.

"Where'd you get them?"

"A secret."

Rose took one of the flowers and held it in her teeth in a Carmen-like pose.

Didi did the same.

"We are known in art and legend," Rose pronounced huskily, "as the bear maidens of the mountain."

Then she got serious. "Why don't you let Kurt get a shot of them!"

"Where is he?"

"He went for a stroll. There he is!"

"I'll catch up to him," Didi said, taking the flowers and starting out.

But after only twenty yards Didi realized that the photographer was walking fast, very fast, away from the campfire, up a twisted trail.

What is going on with this man? she asked herself. Where is he running to? The wildflowers were beginning to lose their allure.

Then he totally vanished from sight.

She hesitated. Should she turn back? No. Not yet. She decided to follow him a bit longer. He had to slow down sooner or later. And he had to keep near the trail.

Didi kept walking at a moderate pace but Kurt Trabert seemed to have vanished off the mountain.

She stopped on a rise. A fear . . . a chill . . . was

beginning to afflict her. What if he had fallen into another quarry?

Didi rotated on the spot where she stood, searching for some sign of the photographer off the trail.

Just as she was about to retrace her steps back to the base camp to report a possible tragedy, she saw his head, like a turkey's, bobbing off to the right, in thick brush.

She left the trail and headed toward him. It was rough going at first but then the brush thinned out.

Kurt Trabert's head kept appearing and reappearing, mysteriously. He was behaving in a most peculiar fashion. When she got closer, the reason became clear. Every few steps he would crouch near the ground with a branch in one hand and his 35mm camera in the other.

He used the branch to clear small areas of the ground as he walked. He seemed to select the place to clear randomly.

Didi followed, fascinated. Once in a while, he would take a picture of something on the ground. Then he would begin the process all over—walk, clear, shoot.

Finally he stood up straight and stretched his arms upward, as if the crouching had hurt his back. Then he crashed through the brush to the trail and headed back in the direction of the camp.

Didi had been only twenty yards behind him, but the photographer was so engrossed by his peculiar activity that he never noticed her. And she, for some inexplicable reason, never called out to him. She just followed and watched, holding the two wild-flowers in one hand, having forgotten totally the point of the whole trip.

When he was out of sight, Didi began to examine the area he had been exploring.

It was hard to see the ground because after Trabert had cleared a space, he had recovered it with brush.

That in itself was most peculiar, Didi realized. She simply kicked the brush away but found nothing except stony earth.

Directly to the east, she could see the foreboding rock structure of Demon's Gorge—a deep, natural crevice . . . literally a subterranean canyon against which the park ranger had warned them several times.

Had the photographer known he was so close to danger?

Well, she knew the danger. It was time to return to the trail.

She began to retrace her steps.

She stopped suddenly. To her right was a small

bare patch of ground that Trabert had obviously cleared and forgotten to recover.

Didi knelt to look.

Yes. There was something here.

She studied the ground. It seemed to be some kind of hieroglyphic. It was incomprehensible.

She stood up, circled the patch of ground to get a different perspective, and then knelt again.

This time she brought her hand involuntarily to her mouth in shock. She suddenly realized what she was looking at: the partial paw print of what had to be a monster bear.

The pickup truck was damned crowded, what with Mrs. Tunney all decked out in her church finery and sandwiched between Charlie Gravis and Abigail.

"Watch the bumps, Charlie!" she kept calling out. Mrs. Tunney did not like moving vehicles of any kind.

Charlie wanted to ask her why she had gotten all dressed up to visit a dotty old woman who wouldn't even remember her. But he had decided against posing that question. He could already be in enough trouble to last him a lifetime, if Tunney found out about his herbal scheme. To irritate Mrs. Tunney even more would be suicidal behavior.

He had already taken Abigail aside and warned her against any mention of the medicine or the dog's lumbago once they reached Cleo Dopple's cottage. Deaf and dumb, he instructed her. You see nothing. You hear nothing.

"My, they've done a beautiful job," Mrs. Tunney noted as Charlie wrestled the pickup truck into the parking lot of the rehab center with its imposing stone front. "It doesn't look like the Dopple farm at all," she added.

Abigail laughed suddenly and without explanation.

They left the vehicle and began the trek through the old cow pasture toward Cleo's cottage.

Mrs. Tunney, walking in the middle, held on tightly to both Charlie and Abigail. She was unsteady in her dress shoes on natural earth.

When they finally reached the cottage, Mrs. Tunney said, "This is all so sad."

"What's sad?" Charlie asked. He had an idea that she wasn't talking about the cottage's peeling paint.

He didn't get a chance to find out, because at that moment Cleo Dopple stepped outside.

She was wearing the same tattered black sweater. Her hands seemed to be locked behind her back.

Charlie greeted her effusively.

"Hello, Cleo! It's good to be back. I brought an old friend along"

Cleo didn't seem to be interested. She brought her hands out from behind her back.

In one of her hands was a dark and fierce-looking object. Charlie stared at it. He had seen it before, somewhere.

Cleo grasped the object with both hands and thrust it forward.

Now Charlie recognized it. Cleo was pointing Jed Dopple's World War II .45-caliber pistol. Big and brutal, it could knock down a barn door.

"Run!" Charlie shouted. "Run!"

Abigail bounded off like a frightened deer.

Charlie grabbed Mrs. Tunney's hand and started to run back into the cow pasture. It was not really running—more like the chug-chug-chug of two ancient freight trains.

They ran out of steam after twenty yards. Abigail ran back to help them but Mrs. Tunney refused to move until she caught her breath.

Charlie looked toward the cottage. The crisis was over. Cleo Dopple had lowered the weapon.

"What did you do to that woman?" Mrs. Tunney demanded.

"Nothing at all," Charlie replied.

"You had to have done something!" was Mrs. Tunney's retort. Half a gasp. Half a scream.

Charlie raised his hands innocently.

"Look!" Abigail said.

Charlie looked. A man with a white clinical jacket and ridiculous Wellington boots was approaching them. He had a muffler with reindeer on it, and a clipboard in his hand. Charlie feared and loathed men with clipboards. Every dairy farmer knows that when a man shows up in the cow barn with a clipboard, there is big trouble ahead.

"Are you hurt?" he asked, looking them over.

"Don't appear to be," Charlie said.

"Are you Charlie Gravis?" the stranger asked.

"He is!" Mrs. Tunney affirmed.

"I wanted to warn you but I had no idea where you lived. She said she was going to kill you."

"A crazy woman," Charlie explained.

"She says you drugged her dog," the stranger noted.

"A real crazy old woman," Charlie reaffirmed.

"She says you gave her dog a high-powered amphetamine cocktail."

"It was a damn herbal mix! It was for Red's lumbago!" Charlie blurted out.

The stranger made a dismissing motion with his hand. "Well, whatever you gave him, the dog jumped through a half-open window in the cottage, bit one of our patients in the thigh, and ran off into the woods."

He started to walk back to the big stone house. He stopped once and yelled back, "I would keep away from Mrs. Dopple if I were you."

Charlie didn't know what to do. He could feel Mrs. Tunney's eyes boring into the back of his neck. They were like daggers.

Didi had waited until Moe Douglas went alone into the storeroom. He was wrestling a keg of detergent when she entered.

"Can I talk to you for a minute?"

"Sure," he replied, leaning against the keg.

"In confidence?"

"What the hell does that mean, lady?"

"It means our words go no further."

She detected a dislike of her in his whole demeanor. She hadn't picked up on this before.

"I don't talk much," he said laconically.

This was getting nowhere, she realized. It was time to get to the point.

"I saw something very strange this afternoon . . . near Demon's Gorge."

"What?"

"A bear print."

"There are bear around. What's so strange about finding their tracks?"

"It was a very big paw print."

"How big?"

She spread her hands apart about twelve inches. Douglas laughed.

"What's so funny?"

"No black bear in the Catskill Mountains ever left a track that size," he announced.

"I saw it!" Didi retorted, the anger rising.

"What you probably saw was a track left by Smokey the Bear wearing snowshoes," he said derisively.

"Why would I make such a story up?"

"Look! It was a rough morning for all of us. That bear almost mauled us. It wouldn't have been pretty. Everyone is a bit rattled."

"Then you think I'm hallucinating? You think I'm still in shock?"

He didn't answer. He started to wrestle with the keg again.

Didi stomped out, slamming the storehouse door shut behind her.

She looked around the cabin. Everyone seemed to be busy with small tasks. There was no one here she wanted to tell her story to, other than Moe Douglas. And he had laughed at her. She didn't trust the others. And she couldn't tell Rose. After all, Rose might already be in bed with Kurt Trabert. Too much was going on with too few explanations.

The only one she really wanted to speak to now was Fay Whitely.

Without a word to the others, she slipped out of the cabin and drove her red Jeep eight miles to the park ranger station.

Fay was dozing in the small, overheated shed, surrounded by communications equipment.

"Any problem up there?" she asked Didi while preparing the ubiquitous cup of bad coffee.

"No. But I saw something very strange on the trail."

"What?" she asked, handing Didi the cup.

"An enormous print of a bear paw on the ground."

Fay narrowed her eyes, grinned wickedly, and then said in a mock fearful whisper, "Don't tell me you're on the track of the mighty Kong."

Didi squirmed under the mockery. "Who is Kong? What is Kong?"

Fay Whitely stared at her hard, as if trying to evaluate her brain.

Then she said, "I didn't mean to make fun of you. But every region has its Loch Ness monster or its Big Foot. And we're no exception."

"Kong?"

"Exactly. After King Kong. There's a persistent apocryphal tale about an enormous black bear in this area."

"Has anyone ever seen Kong?"

"A few people. He is supposed to be missing one ear, shot off by a hunter. According to the tale, Kong himself is a killer, with an insatiable appetite for lambs, calves, and dogs."

"Do you believe he exists?"

"Frankly, no."

"But I saw the print."

"You saw *a* print. Reading bear tracks is a very inexact science."

"It was *this* large!" Didi said, spreading her hands.

"You saw what you saw," Fay Whitely said wearily. It was obvious she wasn't interested in discussing it any further.

Disgusted, feeling like a fool again, Didi started for the door.

She stopped and turned. "Is there anything new in the murder investigation?"

"I'm a park ranger, not a homicide detective."

"I know that. But I thought the state troopers would keep you current."

"They do. And there's nothing new. It had to be a big man who murdered him. Someone strong enough to hoist Glass onto the beam. And they believe he was murdered with his own rifle."

"No suspects?"

"Probably every one of his drunken friends."

"What do they make of the fact that he was beaten?"

"Boys will be boys. And tanked-up boys get ugly."

Didi opened the door.

"You want another cup of coffee before you go? The roads are dark up here."

"No thanks."

"You know, I tried to get into vet school. But in those days few women were admitted."

"Times have changed," Didi said. And walked out.

When she got back to the cabin a worried Rose was waiting for her by the fire.

"Where have you been, Didi? I've been worried sick. You can't just vanish like that. I didn't know where you were. Or what happened."

"I went for a drive to clear my head."

"Sit down, sit down," Rose urged her. Didi sat.

"I have something to tell you, Didi. Something wonderful!"

Didi rocked. "I'm waiting."

"I'm in love."

"What else is new?"

"No, you don't understand. I mean 'knock down drag out no holds barred' love. I mean the real thing. I mean moonlight and mandolins. I mean champagne, Didi."

"With whom?"

"Kurt Trabert."

Didi looked at her friend's flushed face.

"It would be a very dangerous proposition to fall in love with that photographer," Didi said in a measured tone.

"Are you going to act like an old prudish Aunt Didi? Are you going to warn me against social diseases also?"

Didi didn't reply. She rocked. It was obvious that Rose had misinterpreted the cautionary warning.

"Look," Rose said in a quiet, urgent voice, taking hold of Didi's hand. "I know you don't like him. I see that. But you don't know him. He's under a lot of pressure to produce. Kurt was once a famous photographer, Didi. He was! He had all kinds of exhibits in New York and L.A., and even Munich. Then he had a nervous breakdown. He's taking small jobs like this to work his way back. To get on his feet."

Didi didn't respond.

Rose sighed, kissed her friend, and said, "Everything is going to be all right. Be happy for me!" She vanished into the bunk area.

Didi stared into the fire, trying to quash her growing excitement.

The information that Rose had blurted out about Kurt Trabert now made a rational scenario possible.

She constructed it in her head, in the same manner she would make a diagnosis . . . starting with the onset of the disease.

The down-and-out photographer shows up early at the camp.

He finds Sylvester Glass.

They talk. They become friendly. Kurt learns about the giant of a black bear called Kong.

Sylvester claims that Kong is now in the vicinity of Mt. Dunaway. And he is going to hunt down and kill the murderous bear.

Kurt realizes that Kong can be his ticket back to photographic stardom.

But he needs a live Kong photograph.

He beats the information out of Sylvester. Once Kurt knows where Kong can be found, he murders Sylvester Glass.

Then, once in the field, he hides all traces of the prints after he identifies and photographs them.

It was a seductive scenario and by the time Didi

finished constructing it, the chair almost tipped over.

Then she slowed down and calmed herself as she came up with logical objections to her own scenario.

First of all: Why would Kurt alter the trail map and almost get himself and the others killed? They weren't anywhere near where Didi had found Kong's paw print. And if someone else altered the map—why? Who were they trying to hurt?

Second, Kurt was a tall man but he was thin. How could he have hoisted Sylvester Glass onto the ceiling beam?

The fire was going out. Darkness was enveloping the inside of the cabin. Fear was enveloping her. There was at least one murderer in the cabin. Rose was at risk. Everyone was at risk.

I need help, she thought. I will call Allie Voegler in the morning.

Chapter 8

The first ring of the phone woke Allie Voegler. He sat up in bed, dazed, still half asleep.

He didn't know where he was or who he was.

He turned. There was a woman in bed with him. She was naked. She was fast asleep.

Second ring. He remembered: He was Allie Voegler. This was his apartment. The naked woman was Mary, the funny bartender from Jack's.

Third ring. He picked up the phone.

A voice asked, "Allie?"

"Yeah?"

"Did I wake you?"

"No," he lied.

"I need some help."

And then he realized it was Didi Quinn on the other end of the line.

He stared at the receiver and then at the naked woman next to him.

Of all the people on earth, Didi was the last person he wanted to speak to now.

A wave of shame, of betrayal, of confusion, washed over him.

"Allie! Are you there?"

What had he done? What the hell had he done? Why? Who was the woman in his bed, really?

"Yes. I'm here."

"Get a pencil, Allie."

He searched for a pencil. He found one, and a pad. She gave him a name: Sylvester Glass. She needed information on him. She gave him a place— the Glide Gas & Service Station on Route 23. It was only seventy minutes driving time from Hillsbrook, she said. She gave him a time to meet—in six hours.

"Maybe we have a bad connection, Allie. I can't hear you."

Allie put the receiver down gently. Very gently. He covered Mary with a blanket.

The clock read 6:32 A.M. A digital clock. Hadn't Didi given him the clock as a gift? Yes! For his help in that terrible situation at the traveling circus— where the elephant had trampled the dancing girl to death.

Allie turned abruptly from the face of the clock. Digital clocks spooked him.

He walked into the kitchen, realized he was stark naked, grabbed a shirt hanging on the back of a kitchen chair, and tied it around his waist.

He filled a kettle with water and put it on the stove top.

The apartment was warm. That was always a problem—either too much heat or too little heat.

When the pot began to whistle he poured boiling water over a heaping teaspoon of instant espresso coffee.

Two packets of sugar. No milk. An inverted kitchen knife to stir it.

He sat down and sipped. The coffee was terrible.

Allie yearned for a fresh made cup of brewed coffee and, for some reason, two medium boiled eggs. With a side order of bacon.

If he had a wife, he thought, the only thing he would ever ask her to do was make breakfast for him. Or go out with him for breakfast.

He sat up, suddenly angry. Why was he thinking about medium boiled eggs?

There were serious things to think about!

Fish or cut bait, Allie Voegler, he said to himself. Go out with other women or wait for Didi. You don't have the constitution to do both.

He took another sip of the miserable brew.

But what if he waited forever? In vain.

What kind of clown would that make him?

Mary was standing in the kitchen doorway, wearing only the big smile on her face.

"What's so funny?" Allie said.

"It has been so long since I've been a one-night stand—the problems inherent in them had slipped my mind. That's what's funny."

"What problems?"

"For one, I forgot your name, Mr. Lawman."

Renner was carefully preparing a series of bait cans laced with sedatives.

Didi waited until there was a pause in the preparation and then announced, "I'm not feeling well."

He looked at her with a squint, obviously annoyed. The blinds had already been set up.

"I'd like to go back to the cabin for a while," she added.

Didi could see that this comment made Harris Renner even more unhappy.

He fiddled with a bait can. Then he said, "Sure. You know your own limits."

What the hell does that mean? Didi thought angrily.

But all she did was wave, turn, and head back toward the cabin.

She walked slowly, swaying a little, as if she were unsteady on her feet. When she was out of sight of the others, she moved quickly off the trail into the bush and doubled back.

Didi headed toward the spot where she had found the partial paw print of a monster bear. Of Kong.

In her knapsack was Rose's small camera, borrowed without permission; a measuring tape from her veterinary kit; and seven sheets of white paper.

Her object was simple—to find the print and record it as accurately as possible . . . in any way possible.

It was hard going and her breath came in short bursts.

As she reached the perimeter of the clearing where she had found the print initially, she began to move with great caution.

She was close, she knew, and the print was fragile.

But it was not there! It was not anywhere!

She looked around.

Had she come to the wrong place?

No. This was the place. Her geographic sense was always accurate.

Maybe the brush had been moved. Maybe the ground had been disturbed. Maybe some other animal had inadvertently covered the track.

Breaking off a thin branch, she began to move slowly forward, sweeping the ground gently.

No monster bear prints. No prints at all.

A fury rose in her. She walked faster, swept harder.

Her back began to ache.

She saw the rim on Demon's Gorge, confirming that she wasn't lost.

This was the place.

On she searched, but she found nothing.

Disgusted and exhausted, she flung the branch away and pressed on slowly, her eyes glued to the ground, ever mindful of the dangerous chasm close by.

She passed a sign that read:

DANGER!
NO HUNTING, HIKING, OR
TRAIL RIDING.

She walked almost half a mile more just west of the rim but found nothing except for some more DEC warning signs.

Then she sat down on the ground and rested.

It was no use to look farther. She had struck out and it was time to meet Allie Voegler at the gas station on Route 23.

Didi started the long walk back.

Some chilling thoughts accompanied her.

Kurt Trabert had revisited this site before she had the chance to return.

He had obliterated all the tracks because he now knew that she knew. About Kong. About the murder of Sylvester Glass.

And if Trabert had hung a huge man like Glass to a beam by his feet—he would have no trouble whatsoever hanging one young lady vet to a beam by her neck.

The wrath of Mrs. Tunney fell upon Charlie Gravis like Ezekiel's chariot.

She had condemned him—as a jackass beyond compare—for giving herbal remedies to one of Miss Quinn's clients.

—As a sneak, for doing it without Miss Quinn's permission—which never would have been forthcoming anyway.

—As an ingrate and a Judas, for exposing all of them to a possible lawsuit, not to mention a bullet in the back.

Last but not least, she had suggested that he might start considering an old age home.

It was obvious to Charlie that he had to find Cleo Dopple's dog—and fast.

So he called a strategy and planning session.

"We have to use logic," he announced to Trent Tucker and Abigail at the counter of the Hillsbrook Diner.

His young companions nodded in agreement. Then Trent Tucker began to demolish a rice pudding with cherry sauce and whipped cream.

"Where would I go if I was a big old dog with lumbago?" Charlie asked, posing the central question.

Between spoonfuls, Trent Tucker quipped, "I thought you had cured his lumbago."

Charlie ignored the slur. The boy was young.

"I'd go to the old land fill. It's just behind Mrs. Dopple's property," Abigail said.

"Why there?" Charlie asked.

"A lot of stray dogs go to that old garbage dump. Everything seeps up from the ground. Cans. Carcasses. Everything."

Charlie's face lit up. Abigail was brilliant! Sometimes. When she talked at all.

Trent Tucker pushed the empty dish away. "Park the truck by the edge of the dump," he said. "Open the doors. Put some of the old lady's clothing on the seat. If the dog's there, he'll come."

"How am I supposed to get a hold of Cleo's clothing?" Charlie replied.

There was silence. An impasse had obviously been reached.

Finally, Trent Tucker came up with a solution. "I make a call to the old lady. Tell her I'm from UPS. Tell her to meet me by the roadside to get her package. She goes out. You go in, get some stuff, leave. She'll never know. And she probably never locks the door unless she goes into town."

"That is trespassing," Charlie said. "Maybe even breaking and entering."

There was silence again.

Charlie stared into his coffee cup.

He sighed heavily.

On the one hand there was crime.

On the other the wrath of Mrs. Tunney.

A man his age shouldn't have to deal with such a choice.

It was unfair.

Allie Voegler's unmarked police cruiser pulled up right next to the red Jeep in the back of the gas station. The station itself had a toylike two-pump quality set against a magnificent backdrop.

They stared at each other through their respective car windows.

Then Didi made a motion that he should join her.

Allie nodded, left his vehicle, and climbed into the front of the red Jeep beside Didi.

The moment he was in the Jeep, Didi could see that something was wrong. He was pale, very pale, and grim.

Without thinking, she reached out and touched his cheek—in greeting, in compassion.

He reacted violently, as if her hand had been a match, jerking his head away from the touch with such force that he banged his head into the roll bar on the back of the seat.

"Oh, my God! Allie! Are you OK?"

He grimaced in pain but made a motion with his hands that she should leave him alone.

"I just touched your cheek, Allie. You looked ill. I was happy to see you."

Allie felt for blood on the back of his head. There was none.

"What I got for you on this Sylvester Glass isn't much. I could have told you over the phone."

Didi squirmed a bit. It was obvious he hadn't wanted to come.

"Any information is appreciated," she said. She wondered what was the matter with him. He seemed to be in some kind of mental anguish. Like he was unable to solve a puzzle or remember a name or find an object.

"Well, it looks like this Sylvester was your classic old-fashioned handyman. He did everything from digging septic tanks to poaching firewood. He had a lot of friends and relatives scattered throughout the Catskills. But he was closest to his brother, Albert. Brother Albert now lives in Phoenicia but he used to own a small dairy farm in Greene County, until a crazed black bear slaughtered his stock, about six years ago."

Didi slapped the wheel with her hands. "That confirms everything," she said, elated. "That bear was Kong."

"Kong? What the hell are you talking about?"

"I'm frightened, Allie. That's why I asked you to meet me here."

He turned quickly toward her, as if to embrace her, as if her being frightened were unbearable . . . but at the last moment he pulled back.

"Just tell me what's going on, Didi."

She told him, briefly, in chronological form.

How she and Rose found the gruesome corpse.

How she discovered that the knots on Renner's backpack were the same as those on the ropes that held the corpse to the beam.

How Marsha, Kurt, and Rose almost died in an abandoned quarry.

How she discovered that the map had been altered.

How she had followed the photographer and found the enormous paw print.

How she had learned of Kong . . . or at least the myth of Kong.

How she became sure that Kurt Trabert had murdered Sylvester Glass.

How the paw print had vanished.

After she was finished, Allie said, "And everyone in Hillsbrook thought you were on a scientific expedition."

Didi laughed. "That, too."

"Why don't you contact the state troopers?"

"Because they don't believe that Kong exists. And I couldn't find the print to photograph or trace it. Besides, I have my doubts that they would find my theory credible. They wouldn't believe the motive."

"So what are you going to do?"

"I don't know. But I'd like you to hang around awhile."

He didn't answer. He drummed his fingers on the dash.

Didi persisted. "Only for twenty-four hours or so. Please, Allie. There's a motel down the road. I think it's called the Blue Line Inn. You can get a room there. A lot of hunters have left the area already. They'll have a vacancy."

"Why not?" he replied wearily.

His drumming fingers caught something. He picked up two lifeless stems from the top of the dash.

"Your windshield wipers?" he asked.

"My wildflowers. Dead and gone. But they were beautiful, Allie."

"My mother told me even I was a beautiful baby."

"They're called Belgian waffles," Didi said and then burst out laughing at her corruption of their technical name—the one Marsha Greeley had used in identifying them.

Didi twirled the poor dead flora in her hands.

That whole episode had been strange, she remembered. The botanist's response had been strange—so bloodless, so scientific, so precise. When Didi diagnosed an illness for a layman she never used the scientific name. She never said, "The prize bull you just purchased is suffering from pneumonic pasteurellosis." She said "shipping fever."

It was as if Marsha Greeley were trying to impress her. To display her knowledge.

Didi rolled the dead wildflowers in her hand.

What if she wasn't a botanist, in fact? What if she wasn't Marsha Greeley?

What if no one in the project was who they said they were?

She turned suddenly to Allie. "Can you check out a few license plate numbers after you get into the motel?"

"Sure."

"I'll read them out to you when I get back to the cabin. Wait for my call."

Allie opened the door.

"I appreciate this," she said.

He started to leave.

"Wait!"

"What?"

"Rose Vigdor has fallen in love with that character."

"With Kong?"

"No. The photographer."

"Things happen," he said.

"Yes. They do."

She watched him walk slowly back to his car, his hand gently touching the back of his sore head.

Then Didi drove back to the cabin, copied all the vehicle license plate numbers on the back of a bill, lay down on her bunk, and set her travel alarm for a half hour hence.

She fell fast asleep. The brazen jangling from the tiny clock woke her in exactly twenty-eight minutes.

Didi washed her face in the tiny kitchen, drank half a cup of black coffee, called Allie in the Blue Line Motel, and gave him the numbers.

Then, recovered from her "illness," she headed back up the slope to rejoin her comrades.

She stopped after not more than fifty feet.

Because a very strange procession was coming down the slope.

At first she saw only four figures in a square pattern, carrying what looked to be a log.

They came closer. Didi could make out the faces.

Rose and Harris Renner were in front of the square.

Moe Douglas and Marsha Greeley were in the back of the square.

Their faces were strained. They seemed to be moving as fast as they could.

And it was not a log they were carrying.

It was Kurt Trabert. On a makeshift stretcher.

Chapter 9

They waited for an ambulance inside the cabin.

Didi alternately tended to Kurt Trabert's wounds and consoled Rose.

Only one of the wounds was serious—a deep, savage bite through the shoulder. But the bleeding had stopped.

"I gave him morphine on the slope," Harris Renner told Didi, making a motion with his fingers to signify that the drug was in a syrette.

Didi turned to Rose again. Her friend seemed calmer. But there was Kurt's blood all over the collar of her parka and up one sleeve.

"Tell me what happened," she said to Rose.

"It was terrible. It was grotesque. The fury of it, Didi. And then Kurt screaming—" Rose brought her hands to her ears, then down again.

Didi realized she would get no rational story from

Rose at this time. She looked around the cabin. Moe Douglas looked available. He was sucking his unlit pipe.

She walked quickly over to him. "How did it happen?" she asked.

He grunted. "A bear bit him."

"Obviously," Didi replied.

Moe removed his pipe, grinned, and gave her a little dig, "But it wasn't Kong."

Didi didn't reply. She waited.

Moe explained, "A lady bear. Very young. Things just went bad."

"Did she take the bait?"

"Sure did. She gobbled down all the doped sardines. She sat down. She looked wiped out. She looked sedated as hell. Renner gave us the signal. We started toward her, the photographer, as usual, in front, shooting the bear. Then turning and shooting us approaching."

He paused and inspected his pipe as if it were functioning.

Didi stared at him, realized she was staring, and then looked away. There was something about this man that was starting to disturb her and perplex her. He was a mass of contradictions. One moment he sounded like a backwoods fool and the next moment a sophisticated and rational observer.

"The bear wasn't out. She was wide awake when we got there. She grabbed the photographer. It was ugly."

"What about your plastic bullets?" Didi asked.

"I didn't have the rifle with me."

"Why not?"

"The situation looked very safe."

"What happened then?"

"The bear chomped on him a few times. Then she just lumbered off. Like a puppy dog with big feet."

The emergency vehicle arrived. Everyone gathered around as Kurt Trabert was tied onto a gurney.

"I'm going with him," Rose declared.

"No one's going with him," Renner contradicted in an angry voice. "We all have some decisions to make. Right now."

"Don't tell me what to do!" Rose shouted.

"Get your associate under control," Renner cautioned Didi.

Rose's fist was clenched around the gurney. Didi covered it with her own hand. "They're professionals, Rose. Let them take care of him. He has lost a lot of blood and he's in shock—but he'll pull through."

Rose stared wildly at her friend for a moment and then unclenched her fist.

Kurt was wheeled out to the waiting ambulance.

"Maybe it's best we all just relax for a while," Renner said. "Do what you want—but we'll meet in front of the fire in an hour. Understood? All of us. There's a lot to talk about. It may be time to cut this project short. You can't fight bad luck. You just walk away from it."

Rose went to her bunk and lay down. She didn't want to talk.

Didi sat on the edge of Rose's bunk. Her theories had been sent reeling. Or, at best, turned on their head.

Nothing had happened to disprove that Kurt Trabert murdered Sylvester Glass. Nothing had happened to disprove the existence of Kong.

But now it was obvious that someone was out to murder the photographer. And that someone had almost succeeded in an ingenious way.

There was no doubt in Didi's mind that someone had either removed the pills from the sardine heads or substituted placebos.

Harris Renner, of course, controlled the sedation process. He had the best opportunity. But it could have been anyone. The real problem was: Why?

Was one of the group an old friend of Sylvester Glass seeking vengeance?

Was someone in the group also looking to find and exploit Kong?

Was it some other motive?

If the sedatives were tampered with, Didi reasoned, it had to be attempted murder. Because the photographer was always the first person to approach the bear.

She was very tired. She got up, walked to her own bunk, and lay down, her hands behind her head.

There was another possibility, she realized. That it was just a fluke.

She knew the vagaries of the drug, diazepam, in humans. She knew that there were many documented cases of the phenomenon called "paradoxical rage."

A sedative or tranquilizer or muscle relaxant is prescribed and administered. Instead of the textbook reaction, though, the drug induces a violent reaction in the individual. In fact, this paradoxical rage had been used as a defense in court in domestic violence cases.

Perhaps, she thought, that is what happened to the bear. Why not?

She fell fast asleep.

Rose shook her awake fifty minutes later.

She whispered in her ear, "The Lord High Executioner is ready to hold court."

They walked over to the fire.

"We have a decision to make," Harris Renner announced imperiously. He looked around at each of them before he continued.

"I've been on too many of these projects to be naive. Some of them get off to a good start and end badly. Some start bad and end well."

He slammed one hand into the other for emphasis.

"But I've never come across such bad luck. First a corpse. Then a near catastrophe in an abandoned mine. And now the mauling."

He turned to Moe Douglas, who was stoking the fire.

"Did you ever see anything like this?" he demanded of the guide.

"No. Nothing this bad."

"And for some reason I get the feeling that things are only going to get worse. One of us is in the intensive care unit. I don't want any of the rest of us to end up in a body bag."

He looked around again, as if to measure the response to his words.

"So, I think we should abort the project right now. Go home. Try again next denning season. That's what I think."

He waited. No one said a word.

"Of course, I'm going to make the final decision. But I want your imput."

Didi looked at Rose. Rose looked at Marsha Greeley. Everyone looked at Moe Douglas.

No one said a word.

"Come on! What do you think?"

"I think you're right," Rose blurted out. "I think we should go home."

"And you?" Renner asked Didi.

"Keep it going," she replied. Too many unexplained things would be left dangling if they just walked away.

"You don't believe in bad luck?" Renner asked sardonically.

"I'm a vet. I believe in sick and well. Not bad and good. Unless you're talking about absolute evil."

"We are not having a philosophical discussion."

Then Moe Douglas said, "I think we should keep going. A lot of people put in a lot of work to start it up. Why quit now?"

"And you, Marsha?" Renner asked.

"I agree with you. End it. Too many omens."

"What the hell is an omen?" Moe asked.

Rose shouted at him, "Kurt, with half his shoulder ripped away. That's an omen."

"Let's calm down," Renner said.

Did looked across the room and saw the backpacks. She could make out Renner's pack with the knotted pieces of cloth. She felt cold.

Rose took an apple out, stared at it as if contemplating a bite, apparently thought better of it, and put it back into her pocket.

Didi smiled. She remembered that Rose had once declared, "Biting into a large Hudson Valley apple cures instantly a great many mood derangements." But she had never listed or named them.

Moe said, "Another thing. The DEC is gonna be very unhappy."

"Why?" Marsha asked.

"Why? They funded the damn project. And they made a big effort."

"I don't see any DEC people here," Marsha noted.

"That's not their job. They did their job. With money. My salary, at least. And they closed the mountain to hunters and hikers, just so we could operate."

"You have a point, Moe," Renner noted.

"It's a small point," Marsha retorted. "Remember what that park ranger told us after we fell in the quarry. No one hunts or hikes Mt. Dunaway anymore. It's too dangerous. She said everyone knows that. Let's face it: The DEC just made legal what was already a reality."

"OK. OK," Renner said. "This is getting us nowhere. I see we're split fifty-fifty on this. So, as I said, I'm making the decision. We'll all have a meal—a good meal. Then get a good night's sleep. Then have pancakes. Then pack up and go home. I am officially terminating this project—as of now."

No one seemed to know what to say or do next.

Finally Moe Douglas walked into the small store-room and started to throw cartons around, as if registering his disgust with Renner's decision.

"We can go straight to the hospital after we check out in the morning," Rose whispered.

"I don't see why not," Didi responded, also in a whisper. Why am I whispering, she thought.

"Do you really think he'll be OK?" Rose asked, still in a whisper.

Didi didn't get a chance to answer. Harris Renner loomed up in front of her. Rose walked into the kitchen.

"Are you sad?" he asked in a low, almost intimate voice.

"About what?"

"My decision."

"I'm sure you think you made the correct one."

"What an academic evaluation!"

"Well, I went to college a long time to become a vet," Didi replied, smiling.

"Can I call you in a few weeks?"

"Regarding what?"

"A social call. We can have that philosophical conversation. About absolute evil. Or some such thing."

"I'm in the Hillsbrook phone book," Didi said sweetly.

He nodded and walked toward his bunk.

"Oh, Dr. Renner," she called after him.

"What?"

"Do you have a dog?"

"Several," he replied and kept on walking.

Didi walked to the fire, picked up the poker, and rammed it into the embers. Sparks flew out. She felt the heat against her face.

This whole adventure, if one could call it that, was ending absurdly. Just pack up and go home. Forget the murder and attempted murders. Forget everything.

Didi rammed the poker harder. A shower of sparks flew up.

Then she pulled the poker out, replaced it in the rack, and sat down in the wicker chair.

She rocked. She stewed. She listened to the sounds about her. It was growing dark outside.

In years to come, she thought, the only thing I

will remember about all this is the damn wicker rocker. Rock-a-bye my vet, to a perplexing melody.

"Did anyone take the towel I left on my bunk?" someone called out.

It was Marsha Greeley's voice, Didi realized. There was no response to her query.

But that woman's response to Renner's query had surprised her. She had thought a professional botanist would never want to terminate an expedition. Field work, Didi knew, was important in those academic careers.

Didi stopped rocking. Was she thinking right? Was it the botanist's response? Or was it her actual words?

It was her words. Yes.

And it wasn't surprise; it was more a kind of confusion.

Didi started rocking slowly. What had Marsha Greeley actually said? Nothing much.

The main thrust of her response was to denigrate Moe Douglas's comment that the DEC had gone to great effort and expense on behalf of the project. Particularly in closing Mt. Dunaway to hunters and hikers.

The botanist had merely restated what everyone knew: No one hunted or hiked Mt. Dunaway anymore, whether it was closed by the DEC or not. It was just too dangerous, what with the abandoned quarries and Demon's Gorge.

So what was confusing about what the botanist had said?

Then she realized it wasn't what the botanist said that confused her; it was what she herself had *seen*. The botanist's words had merely highlighted what she had seen.

The signs along Demon's Gorge.

The clear warnings against hunting and hiking.

Didi sat up straight in a now motionless rocker.

Why would the DEC put up obviously new signs like that on a mountain that was already abandoned by hunters and hikers?

And why would they put them up along Demon's Gorge rather than at the base of the mountain?

Didi looked around suddenly, furtively, as if frightened that someone was watching her thinking.

No, she was alone, unnoticed.

She felt a rush of almost manic intellectual triumph. But she realized there was not much time left. And she could no longer act alone.

Charlie parked the pickup truck just next to the incline of the landfill. The road was only fifty feet away.

Everything had gone perfectly so far. Like a brilliantly orchestrated jewel robbery.

Trent Tucker had made the call. Cleo Dopple had left the house to collect a mythical package by the side of the road.

She had left the door open. Abigail slipped in and out within sixty seconds, carrying not only one of Cleo's coats and her black sweater but an old bowl filled with Red's favorite dog food, both dry and wet.

Charlie had praised his associates for their good work, but he knew the hard part lay ahead and he was the only one capable of actually collecting Cleo Dopple's dog.

Trent Tucker had said that it would be too cold and too long a wait in the pickup truck for a man Charlie's age. But Charlie had squelched that fast.

Here he was. Alone. The doors of the truck had to remain open so that Cleo's clothing on the seat was visible and smellable. The motor had to stay on as well as the lights to elicit attention. The dog food had been placed just outside the truck on the ground.

For the first hour he just thought how nice it would be to smoke a cigar. And he remembered all the cigars he and Jed Dopple had smoked and all the whiskey they had drunk and all the war stories they had told each other.

The night became colder and darker. The heater was on but negated by the open doors of the truck.

Every fifteen or twenty minutes the truck stalled out and Charlie had to restart it. There were sounds drifting up from the landfill toward the road. Strange sounds. Once in a while he thought he heard the yapping of dogs.

Maybe I should sing, Charlie thought as the third hour of the vigil began. He was getting very tired and cramped. His legs kept falling asleep.

He decided that he would sing, but the only rousing song he could think of was pornographic. As for sad songs, well, he knew "Annie Laurie," but what good was that?

A hymn, he thought. That would be perfect. And Thanksgiving was approaching. "*Now thank we all our God with hearts and hands and voices.*" He uttered the words but he just couldn't sing the tune.

Charlie's head kept getting heavier and heavier. It kept falling down over the wheel.

How he longed for a large mug of Mrs. Tunney's cocoa.

Then he fell fast asleep.

He dreamed he was back on Iwo Jima. He was bringing a canteen of iced cocoa to a Japanese prisoner. The prisoner turned out to be an old man. He handed him the canteen. The old man threw it back at him.

Charlie woke up wiping the cocoa from his face. He was confused, disoriented. He kept on wiping. His face kept on getting wet.

Then he realized a dog was licking his face.

It was Cleo Dopple's hound, Red, seated beside him on his mistress's sweater, slobbering all over him.

"It's about time you showed up," Charlie said, pushing the dog's head away.

He saw that Red was not alone.

On the floor, between the seat and the dash, was some kind of matted, mottled sheep dog.

And behind the seat, on the ledge where Charlie kept his raincoat, was a terrier-type dog that looked like a cross between a Jack Russell and a pit bull.

"Sorry, Red," Charlie announced, "but your friends have to go."

He leaned forward and started to shoo the sheep dog out of the pickup first.

The dog snapped at him with such speed and ferocity that Charlie banged his head on the wheel trying to avoid being bitten. It hurt like hell. He cursed the sheep dog.

Then the terrier from hell on the ledge began to yap.

And Red began a very low, very deep growl in his big chest that culminated in the curling of his upper lip.

"I was just kidding, Red," Charlie apologized, nursing his bruised hand. "Your friends are my friends."

Now what do I do? Charlie asked himself.

He couldn't just stay there. They might never leave. And if they did leave, Red might go with his friends.

No. There was only one course of action . . . one logical course. Bring the whole flock to Cleo Dopple and hope for the best.

The tiny alarm clock inside her shirt made pathetic little bleeps.

Didi sat up, pulled the clock out, and shut it off.

It was 10:30. She looked around. Everyone was fast asleep in their bunks.

She rose silently and walked stealthily to the small kitchen.

Inside the kitchen, she flicked the light on and wrote the following note on a sheet of 8-½ x 11-inch lined notepaper:

Dear Dr. Renner:

I just received word of a possible
swine flu outbreak in Hillsbrook.
Please make sure that my
associate, Rose Vigdor, gets safely
back home. It was an honor to
work with you. I am sorry the
project was not completed.

Sincerely,
Didi Quinn Nightingale

Then she placed the note on the side of Renner's
bunk with Scotch tape and left the cabin with her
backpack.

She drove quickly to Allie's Voegler's motel. The
office was still open. Mr. Voegler was in room 51,
the clerk said.

Didi parked the red Jeep flush against Allie's car,
then she softly knocked on the door of room 51.

There was no answer. She knocked harder. No
answer.

Finally, she banged.

And the door opened.

Allie stared at her, goofily. He was wearing his
pants, but no shirt and no shoes.

A small light from the lamp by the bed illuminated his body. She realized this was the first time she had ever seen him even partly nude. He was a big, powerfully built man.

"Aren't you going to invite me in?" she asked.

Her question seemed to dumbfound him even more. Didi looked past him, to the bed, and saw a six-pack of beer.

"I just can't leave you alone for even a minute," she quipped, pointing to the beer.

She stepped inside and slammed the door behind her.

Allie grabbed her and kissed her.

She was so astonished she just stood there. He kissed her again, on the lips.

Then his hands were all over her.

Didi fought her way loose and screamed at him, "What are you doing!"

He backed away.

"Are you crazy? Are you drunk?"

He didn't answer. He held up his hands in a kind of apology.

"I thought . . . I mean . . . I saw you and . . . " He wasn't making sense.

"You mean you thought I came here to sleep with you. Is that it, Allie?"

He sat down on the edge of the bed.

"You know I love you, Didi."

"This isn't the time or the place. Don't you understand? I came here because I need your help."

The phone rang. Didi's body was trembling. The phone kept ringing.

"Damn you, Allie. Pick it up!"

Allie finally answered the phone. He listened. He began to write something on a pad.

Didi tried to get herself in control . . . to get focused again. She picked up the six-pack of beer and flung it across the room. Then she sat down in the one chair in the room.

Allie hung up the phone.

"That was feedback on those license plate numbers you gave me."

"Anything interesting?" Didi asked, trying to speak in a measured voice.

"Very interesting," he said. Then he started walking toward her, saying, "Look, Didi, I'm sorry . . . I'm very sorry."

She put her hands over her ears. "Let's deal with important matters now, Allie!"

He stopped in his tracks. "OK," he said. He sat back down on the bed.

"Marsha Greeley is not Marsha Greeley. At least the car she drove is registered to one Janet Bright.

She lives in Otsego County. She's a pilot, runs a small flying school in that airport near Oneonta."

Didi sat back in her chair. So, her intuition had been right. She was posing as a botanist. The technical nomenclature was part of the scam. But why?

"Is there a real Marsha Greeley?" Allie asked.

"I think there is."

"Then what happened to her?"

Maybe Janet Bright murdered her. Or more likely she notified her that the expedition was canceled and she showed up instead. All it would take is a fake telegram from Harris Renner. "Are you sure all the other plates checked out?"

"Yes."

Didi stood up.

Allie asked, "Do you still need my help?"

"More than ever, Allie. Just put your clothes on and let's go."

They drove off together in the red Jeep, Didi, as usual, at the wheel. She took the road back to the cabin, but kicked in the four-wheel drive about half a mile before the cabin and drove into the brush.

The Jeep jounced them like two jelly beans in a spinning jar.

"Slow down, Didi!" Allie demanded.

She did slow down.

"Where are we headed?"

"Up Mt. Dunaway."

"For what?"

"To read signs."

"Did you say 'read tea leaves'?"

"No. *Signs*."

"You mean like Indians? Are we searching for this Kong? For his tracks?"

"No. Road signs. Trespassing signs. Letter signs."

She slowed down even more, reached over, opened the glove compartment, pulled out an advertisement for a Chinese take-out restaurant newly opened just outside Hillsbrook, and thrust it in front of his face.

"Signs!" she said angrily.

"OK. OK." Allie took the menu and replaced it in the glove compartment.

"It's hard to explain," Didi admitted, a bit apologetically.

"Everything is hard to explain," he noted.

They rode in silence for fifteen minutes. Then Didi stopped the Jeep, turned off the engine, and savagely pulled on the emergency brake.

"We leave the Jeep here," she declared.

There was a three-quarter moon, but it kept disappearing and reappearing.

"Look there!" Didi ordered.

Allie followed her point out his side window.

"I don't see anything."

"Look harder. There! That small dark patch."

"OK. I see it."

"That's the cabin where we're all staying."

Didi had parked the Jeep about a thousand yards above the cabin, on a steep slope. They left the Jeep and started the hike. She carried a full backpack. He had nothing to carry.

After five minutes of hiking, Didi had to slow her pace. Allie was obviously out of shape. His breathing sounded like a bear.

She kept turning her head and asking, "You OK?" Which seemed to infuriate him.

"Just keep going," he said.

God save me from macho men, she thought and slowed imperceptibly.

The night was still and cold. The shifting moon made the trees seem like grasping octopi. She wrapped her muffler around her face to keep the branches from lashing.

The first sign came into view so suddenly that she stopped abruptly in her tracks. Allie stumbled against her.

"Sorry," he said. When he regained his balance he stared at the sign.

"Is that it?" he asked.

"One of them."

He made a disgusted face. Then said, "A long march to read a NO HUNTING OR HIKING sign."

"It's not just any old sign, Allie," she said.

"It sure looks like one to me."

"There's no reason for it to be here, Allie. We're very close to Demon's Gorge. No one hunts here. No one hikes here."

Didi began to circle the sign. Then she touched it. Then she ran her hands along the face of it, then down the post.

There was nothing uncommon about the structure of it . . . or the material . . . or the placement.

"What are you looking for?" Allie asked.

"I don't know," she replied in an angry whisper.

She stopped circling and stared at the sign. "It shouldn't be here, Allie. Don't you understand? Something is peculiar."

He didn't say a word.

Didi rested one hand on the top of the sign. She knew she was doing something wrong: She was thinking wrong. She was missing something very important.

"What if it's a code?" she asked out loud, somewhat desperately.

"What kind of code? You mean the words mean something else?"

No, she realized that was ludicrous.

"What if it's a path? A series of markers leading somewhere?"

"Yeah," Allie replied mockingly. "Follow the signs right over the edge of Demon's Gorge."

"Then what if the sign itself is a sign?" she asked excitedly.

"You lost me."

"I mean it's a pointer."

"A pointer? What are you talking about? Pointing to what?"

"Like those highway lights the state troopers put out to tell motorists about a road cave-in."

Allie stomped one leg down on the ground just beside the sign. "Didi, there's no cave-in here."

Didi unwrapped the muffler from her face.

"Did you hear me, Didi?"

"Wait!" she said anxiously.

"What? What it is?"

Rather than answering the question, she asked excitedly, "Did you bring a shovel, Allie?"

"No."

"Neither did I. What a fool I am!"

She dropped her knapsack to the ground, opened it, and pulled out an aluminum canteen cup.

"Thirsty? A drinking problem?" Allie joked.

Didi ignored him, crouched down at the base of the sign, and began to dig.

"What are you doing?"

"What does it look like I'm doing?"

"Digging."

"You got it, Allie."

The ground was not as hard as it should be. She could feel that immediately. It excited her. It meant that someone had recently been there before. And not only to excavate a hole for the sign.

She dug faster with the canteen cup, excavating a larger and larger circle around the base of the sign.

After five minutes of furious digging, her arms cramped. She rested.

Allie crouched down beside her without a word, took the aluminum cup, and began to dig.

"Thank you," she said.

He made only three powerful scoops with the cup and then they both heard the thud.

"I hit something," Allie said.

Didi rushed to her backpack and returned with a small flashlight. She directed it into the hole.

The tip of a blunt object revealed itself.

"It's covered with plastic," Allie noted.

Didi shut off the beam, inverted the flashlight, and began to dig with it feverishly. Allie continued with the cup.

"Can you get hold of it now?" she asked.

Allie dropped the cup, grabbed the object with both hands, and pulled it out with such force that he fell over backwards.

Then he recovered, ripped the plastic off, and held it out so Didi could illuminate it fully with the beam.

It was a beautifully carved piece of wood.

"A rifle stock," Allie noted, turning it over admiringly in his hand.

"Look here!" he said, pointing at some letters carved in the wood. Only the last three could be made out—lli.

"Let's get the others," Didi said.

They went back to the hole and resumed digging. It went much more quickly this time because Allie pulled the sign out of the hole completely.

They retrieved two more objects wrapped in plastic.

Allie stripped the plastic off and lay them next to the first object.

They stepped back and studied the collage in the light from the flash.

"It's a disassembled weapon," Allie said, "stock, barrel, trigger housing."

"Can you put it together?"

"Sure," Allie said with supreme confidence. "Keep the light on my hands."

He crouched in front of the objects and began to assemble. But it turned out to be difficult. He cursed and fumbled and started over again and again.

Finally, it was finished and he held it up triumphantly.

"I never saw a rifle like that," Didi said.

"I never did either, except in magazines. That's why I had so much trouble putting it together. But it's not a rifle, Didi."

"What is it?"

"A very expensive over-and-under Italian shotgun." He hefted it admiringly. "You just never see them around these parts," he added.

"Because of the price?"

"Not only that. You don't use a weapon like this for deer or bear or even turkey or squirrels."

"What do you use for it?"

"Fast charging, dangerous animals that you hunt in dense terrain, where the visibility is very limited, where you have to stop an animal very fast, before you know what hits you."

"What about using it for a giant bear?"

"You mean this Kong you told me about?"

"Yes."

He thought for a while, shifting the shotgun up and down in his hands.

"You know, Didi," he gave his considered opinion, "I really don't think so."

"But surely Kong is dangerous."

"If he exists."

"I saw the track, Allie. He exists. Just deal with the issue."

"OK. Yes, Kong is dangerous, but you still wouldn't use this kind of weapon. There are many ways to hunt black bear, but you use a high-powered rifle with a scope. You usually take your first and last shot from about three hundred yards. Especially in this terrain."

"I don't get your point about the terrain, Allie. There's plenty of dense brush on this mountain."

"Some . . . agreed. But it's low brush. There's plenty of visibility, in all directions. No way a bear is going to come charging at you, unseen, from eight feet away."

He laughed. "Anyway, why bury the weapon? The whole thing is mysterious."

"Agreed."

"Almost crazy."

Didi didn't reply to that. She was getting colder as the sweat from digging dried.

"What do we do now?" Allie asked.

Didi dug into her knapsack and pulled out her

backup muffler. It was incredibly long, one of her "preppy" affectations as an undergraduate.

"We have two more signs to dig up," Didi said, and handed the muffler to Allie.

"What am I supposed to do with this?" he asked, holding the muffler.

"Wrap it around your head," she said.

He followed instructions. Didi flicked off the light. They trudged on.

They dug the second hole working as a team. Didi used the cup for about five minutes, then Allie took it, then Didi. Tag-team digging beneath the sign that went very fast but turned up nothing.

"One more," Didi said, and they trudged on.

"We're only about fifty feet from the rim of the gorge," Didi cautioned as they reached the third sign.

"Which way?" Allie asked.

"There!" Didi pointed.

"I see nothing."

Didi laughed, a bit harshly. "Yes. You'll see nothing until you fall over it."

Allie took the canteen cup from Didi, knelt down beside the sign, and began to dig. He looks like a terrorist, Didi mused as she watched him. Her preppie muffler wrapped around his head gave him a very sinister appearance indeed. She wondered what she looked like.

"Something's here!" Allie called out.

Didi crouched beside him as he kept digging. The moon vanished. Didi flicked on her flash. She saw the outline of a plastic-covered object. It was much larger than the objects in the first hole.

Allie put down the cup, Didi lay the flash down, and together they pulled the object out.

"There are others in there," Allie noted.

"Let's deal with this one first."

Allie stripped the plastic off. A strange, sweet odor was immediately discernible.

Didi said, "It looks like a haunch of meat."

Allie turned it over.

"You're right. It's the left hindquarter of a white-tail deer. I'd say fresh killed. And just dressed. Maybe a few days ago."

"How can you tell that?"

"Just the way it looks. You can still see the flecks of blood."

"Let's get the others out," Didi suggested.

Within five minutes, four other plastic-covered objects lay on the ground.

Once stripped of their covering it was obvious what they had found—a completely dressed and quartered whitetail deer.

Didi stared for a long time at the strange trophy. Then she took two chocolate bars out of her knapsack, gave one to Allie, and began eating the other one herself.

"Why would someone bury venison?" she asked.

"Old Indian trick. To age it."

"Yes. I've heard of that."

"Maybe it's just a hunter who got his deer up here and didn't want to lug it down alone. So he dressed, quartered, and buried it until he could get some of his friends to help. That makes sense."

"And he buried it under the sign so he could locate it quickly?"

"Right?"

"Then you don't think, Allie, that there's any relation between the weapon we found buried under the first sign and what we found now?"

"No. I told you. You don't hunt deer with that kind of weapon."

"I think they're related."

"How?"

"I think everything is related: the signs, the buried objects, the murder, the mauling, the botanist who isn't a botanist, everything."

"How?" he persisted.

She walked around the packets of meat on the ground.

"I have a feeling this meat is bait," she said slowly.

"Bait?"

"Yes. Just like Harris Renner baited cans with those sardines that were full of sedatives."

"You mean, this meat is doped?"

"Not necessarily. But it *is* bait."

"For what? For who?" he asked. Then he laughed. "Oh, I see where you're going, Didi. Bait for Kong . . . for the mysterious Kong."

"Maybe."

"And where is Kong now?"

"I don't know."

"Let's get back, Didi."

"No, not yet, Allie. Soon."

She went to her backpack, removed two blankets, and folded them carefully on the ground.

"What are you doing?" Allie asked.

"Making you comfortable," she said, and gestured for him to sit on them.

Then she started gathering small pieces of wood.

"What are you doing now?" Allie asked.

"Making you a fire so you can roast some venison and stay warm."

"You sound like you're going somewhere and leaving me on this goddamn mountain."

"Yes. I am."

"Where?"

"I'll be away for only an hour or so, Allie."

"I asked you where. You better start trusting me, Didi, or I'm bailing out right now."

"OK. I'll tell you."

She got the fire going and then said, "Demon's Gorge."

"Are you serious?"

"Yes."

"Why?"

"A hunch."

"I'll go with you."

"No."

"Why?"

"Because you're too big and too slow and make too much noise."

"I'm a hunter," he said angrily, his pride hurt.

"You used to be, Allie."

"And a police officer," he added.

"Who rides around in a car all day long," she said.

Allie didn't respond. He knelt beside the fire, palms toward it.

Didi said, "Do you recall the joke you made when I speculated that the signs might be some sort of path?"

"No."

"You said that path would send you right over the

rim of the canyon. Well, Allie, I think you were right. Now, I think so."

"You're putting yourself in harm's way, Didi."

"I don't think so. I looked at the maps. There are several trails down, along the rim."

"They have to be treacherous."

"Not if you're prepared."

"And you are?" he asked sardonically.

"Of course," she lied. "I brought along some of those mountaineering stakes. I forget what they're called. And rope. Drive the stake into the ground near the rim of the gorge, fasten the rope, and just go easy down the trail."

"Easy?" Rope or not, any trail into that gorge has to be at least a forty-five-degree incline."

"It's not really a steep gorge, Allie. What makes it treacherous is the floor of the gorge. Falling rocks, holes, twisted old trees, even a swamp or two. From what I understand, the people who died in the gorge broke legs or ankles, then died of exposure."

"Six of one, half a dozen of the other."

"I'll be back in an hour."

"It's your show, Dr. Nightingale. If you're not back in an hour, I'll come looking for you."

Didi picked up her backpack, shouldered it, and started off. She stooped suddenly and walked back to where Voegler was warming himself. A wind blew up and sent debris swirling around them.

She was standing over him. She rested one hand lightly on his shoulder. He didn't look up.

"I'm very grateful for your help, Allie," she said.

"Sure," was all he said in reply.

Didi started off. She had lied to Allie about everything. She had no sure knowledge of the trails leading from the rim of the gorge into the gorge itself, but she knew they existed.

And she had no sure knowledge that the gorge held the key to all the mysteries.

But everything seemed to be leading there. Didn't it? She walked faster. Like the knot on the rope which led to a corpse. Knot after knot to the base. She was marching toward the base—the font. Maybe Kong was there. Nothing else made sense . . . but Kong did. What about the shotgun and the venison? She couldn't deal with that now. The gorge—Demon's Gorge—would deal with it. If the answer wasn't there, it was nowhere. The project was over. In the morning everyone would be gone. Hopes for solutions would end.

Oh, yes, Demon's Gorge was the place to go. It was the end of the line.

Didi reached the rim of the gorge and turned

north, keeping close to the edge, her eyes alert for any sign of a trail down.

She was no longer cold and no longer tired. For the first time on the expedition, she felt at ease in her surroundings. She felt as wild and as strong and as primeval as the gorge beneath her and the terrain about her.

She cautioned herself against her propensity for mysticism—like her strange feelings when examining her first black bear.

This, she told herself, is simply an inquiry into a strange geographical locale. Didi chuckled at her own delusions. Just an inquiry? A report? It had better be more then that.

She reached a dip in the rim. Yes, it was a trail. But much too steep, more like a slide. She'd never get down safely, and if down, she'd never get back up.

Didi stared down into the gorge. It must have been a mighty river that cut so deep a swath.

Her eyes had grown accustomed to the night. I can see like an owl now, she thought. But a jumble of rocks and twisted trees lay over the gorge floor, making it impenetrable. It all seemed a malevolent warning.

She walked on, the backpack now biting into her shoulder. The mild pain was somehow pleasing.

She reached a second trail. Yes. This was definitely a navigable incline. She followed it with her eyes. Even better! About halfway to the bed of the gorge, a large rock broke the descent, and then the trail split into two—one on either side of the rock.

"*Didi be nimble! Didi be quick!*" she laughingly intoned. She dropped her backpack.

The first three or four steps were difficult because her boots were not catching the loose gravelly earth on the path.

Then she switched to a heel-first type of descent and she felt better.

On either side of the trail were stunted, twisted trees, like naturally formed bonsai, and she used them for support.

When she reached the rock table she rested and contemplated which of the two tributary paths she should now take.

Squatting on that rocky outcrop, her light-headedness vanished. And then her courage. And then her confidence.

She grew cold.

What was she doing here? Wasn't this a mad wild goose chase?

Wasn't her presence in this bizarre place a classic example of first being stumped, then being so chagrined at being stumped that she had to act as if she knew what was going on?

What *was* she looking for?

Suddenly she heard a strange sound. Low but audible.

The sound vanished. Had it been the wind? Or rolling rocks? Or trees splintering.

Then she heard it again. And again. It sounded like a person coughing. It seemed to come from the side, not from the bed of the gorge.

She kept turning on the rock ledge, trying to locate it.

It vanished again.

The moon vanished.

Then a large shadow crossed the rock over her head.

She jumped back.

It was gone.

She started to shiver.

It had been a very large shadow. Of a living creature. Large and soaring.

Then she heard the bloodcurdling scream. Like all the demons of the gorge had been let loose. Like nothing she had ever heard before.

She turned and ran back up the trail, panicked, slipping and sliding, clutching and clawing.

When she finally reached the rim, she rolled over the top and lay there breathing heavily.

That shadow. she knew, had not been Kong. That scream, she knew, was not that of any bear. It was the scream of an animal that had not been seen in the Catskills for more than a hundred and fifty years.

Lying there, her hands bloody, her body shaking from fear and cold, she had only two consolations.

First of all, her decision to enter Demon's Gorge had been correct.

Second, and more important, she now understood what had happened; what was happening; and what was about to happen.

At least, she thought she did. So she lay there on the ground, trying to recover enough strength to act.

She knew that the light at the end of this tunnel was indeed an oncoming train. But trains can be derailed.

Chapter 10

The ride from the landfill to Cleo Dopple's cottage should have taken five minutes.

But Charlie had to drive very, very slowly. So slowly that it took almost half an hour. He had been unable to close the passenger side door because when he tried, Red's two companions tried earnestly to take his arm off.

The pickup looked like a bird with a wounded wing as it chugged along, the open door swinging back and forth and creaking in the cold night air.

Charlie parked boldly not more then twenty feet from the cottage, hoping that Cleo would hear the vehicle.

He climbed out and waited. The cottage was dark and silent.

He walked to the front door. Then he realized that the dogs were still in the truck.

"Gentlemen!" he called out. "It's time!"

They didn't move.

"Red!" he said. "Get over here."

Red groaned, sat up, stared, then climbed out of the truck. His bodyguard followed.

Charlie knocked on the door. No answer. He banged. No answer.

He stepped back and was about to shout when the door swung open.

A bleary-eyed, bathrobed Cleo Dopple stared at him.

When she realized who it was, she said angrily, "You! How dare you show your face here!"

Charlie didn't have time to reply.

Big Red pushed past him and climbed all over his mistress.

The two stumbled together back into the cottage.

Charlie and the two other dogs followed.

It was a wonderful homecoming scene. Red, on his hind legs, licking Cleo's face and neck, Cleo cooing like the happiest of mourning doves.

Then Cleo came to her senses.

She pushed the big dog off, waggled her finger at him, and said in a loud, scolding voice, "You were a bad dog, Red! You can't jump out of windows. You can't bite people. You can't run away from home."

Red rolled his eyes apologetically.

"Yes! Baaad dog!"

Now Red rolled over like a puppy.

Cleo looked around. For the first time she seemed to notice the other two dogs.

"And who are these?" she demanded.

"Friends of Red's," Charlie replied somewhat sheepishly.

"Well, take them and go," she ordered.

"It's not that easy," Charlie said, starting to explain.

The explanation never got off the ground.

The terrier decided to nip one of Red's legs. Red, who was on his way back, swung away from the nip, kicking the sheep dog in the nose.

The cottage exploded into a cacophony of barks and growls. The three dogs took off after each other—running, slamming, somersaulting through the house, knocking over objects like ten pins.

Charlie and Cleo stood silently, immersed by the spectacle, unable to do a thing.

Then, as quickly as the tornado had come, it went.

The three comrades lay on the floor panting happily. They had obviously enjoyed themselves immensely.

Charlie looked around at the carnage. He had the funny feeling that Cleo Dopple was about to get her gun and blow them all away. He started moving slowly toward the door.

Cleo heaved a sigh.

Charlie looked at her quickly. No. There was no sign of anger at all.

In fact, there was a look of almost beatific love enveloping her face.

"Oh, Charlie," she said, "aren't they like children? They were bad. And now they're sorry. And they want their milk and cookies."

She sighed again.

"Look at them, Charlie. They're adorable."

Then she went to get them their "milk and cookies."

Charlie walked out, shut the door softly behind him, and climbed into the truck.

He didn't start the engine. His mind was racing—but not with thoughts of the success of his mission. No. With thoughts of Red and the way the hound dog now moved. Charlie had experienced some other successes with his herbal lumbago treatment—but nothing like this. The dog had not only recovered from his lumbago, he seemed to have taken years off his age. So what if he had gone a little crazy and nipped someone. Dogs will be dogs.

The astonishing thing was that he had been worried about this particular brew. Because he knew he hadn't boiled the nettles enough.

Maybe underboiling the nettles was what made the brew into a wonder treatment.

Charlie leaned back in the seat and closed his eyes.

Yes, he could see the news report. Senior citizen develops and markets medical breakthrough. Hillsbrook citizen wins coveted Salk Award.

Yes, Charlie could see it all. He would rake in the cash. He would start his own chain of veterinary clinics, specializing in herbal treatments. He would travel around the world lecturing.

He sat up suddenly, opened his eyes, and started the engine.

Of course, he promised himself, I won't forget Didi Quinn Nightingale. She took care of me and now I'll take care of her . . . as well as all the others.

Less than fifty minutes after she left the small clearing and the fire, Didi returned.

Allie knew the moment he saw her, even in the moon-pierced darkness, that something was very wrong.

She was pale and walking very slowly. Her face was set in a strange blank mask. She didn't raise her arm to greet him or say a word.

Watching her, he was filled with an intense love for her—much different from his usual feeling. He wanted to hold her, comfort her; he wanted to take her into his arms so badly his hands began to shake. It was more than Eros.

He scrambled to his feet and started toward her. Then he suddenly stopped, as if his way were blocked by an invisible fence.

I can't! he thought If I touch her now she'll think it was like when I so stupidly grabbed her and kissed her in the motel. That can't happen again.

He stood his ground and watched her. She kept walking toward him, silently and slowly.

"Go to the fire," he said.

She dropped her backpack to the ground and knelt in front of the fire.

He watched her warm her hands. He longed to touch her—fiercely—he longed to console her, no matter what she had experienced. He vowed to himself that the first thing he would do when he got back to Hillsbrook—even before he took a shower—was to break off the affair with Mary. He knew it must be ended immediately. He would sink or swim with Didi Quinn Nightingale.

Then he wrapped one of the blankets around her and knelt also. It's so odd, he thought. It's like we're praying before the fire.

"You look like you've seen a ghost, Didi."

"No," she replied in a monotone, "not a ghost."

"Kong then?"

"No."

"Did you go into the gorge?"

"Yes."

Allie started to ask another question but she stopped him with a gesture of her hand.

Then she asked, "Can you make me some tea?"

He nodded vigorously, got up and retrieved the canteen cup they had used to dig up the signs, and washed it out with water. Then he boiled water in it and threw three tea bags in.

He waited, holding the cup, then sipped it, then handed it to Didi.

He waited and watched. She drank the tea greedily at first, then slowed down.

Finally, she placed it on the ground between them, like it was a chess piece.

"I want to ask *you* a question, Allie," she said in a calm voice.

"Ask away."

"Would you commit a crime for me?"

"No," he replied quickly.

"I didn't think you would."

"Then why did you ask?"

She ignored his response.

"Would you tell a lie for me?"

He smiled. God, how he longed to touch her face.

"Well," he said, "since like most people I tell a hundred small lies a day—to myself and others—I don't see why I couldn't accommodate you with a lie . . . at least one small one."

"The problem is, Allie—what constitutes a small lie?"

"You tell me," he said. He felt a bit ridiculous having such a conversation around a dying fire in the cold wilderness.

"I will tell you. I will tell you the specific lie."

But she hesitated. She was silent.

He held the cup in his hands and stared down into the depleted tea bags.

"I'm waiting," he said.

"OK. I want you to go back down the slope, climb into my Jeep, and drive to the cabin. They'll be sleeping. I want you to wake them all up, introduce yourself as a police officer, and tell them that I asked you to go there. Rose, of course, knows you and will confirm who you are."

She took the cup out of his hands and put it back on the ground, as if she were annoyed at him for picking it up.

Then she continued.

"I want you to tell them that Kurt Trabert has walked out of the hospital. Vanished. That he needs further treatment. That he may be deranged because he told a nurse he must find Kong immediately. Tell them that if he shows up at the cabin, they must persuade him to return to the hospital."

"That's not a small lie, Didi. It's a big lie. Or has Kurt Trabert really walked out of the hospital?"

"Not to my knowledge."

"Then why say so?"

"To flush out a killer."

"How is that going to do it?"

"It's a pail full of baited sardines."

"What?"

"Will you do it for me?"

"Now?"

"Yes. Right now."

Allie stared at her. He didn't know how to handle her request. He felt stupid. He felt incompetent.

"The whole thing will take only an hour or so, Allie. But you better go back to the motel first and switch cars. Don't show up at the cabin in my Jeep. It might make them suspicious. I'm supposed to be in Hillsbrook."

"Who will it make suspicious?"

"There are four people sleeping there. Take your pick."

The color was coming back into Didi's face.

"You know, Didi, I really don't want to do this."

"I can see that."

"Isn't there any other way?"

"No."

"How do I know you're not off on one of your wild goose chases?"

"You don't."

"Tell me what you saw in the gorge, Didi."

"Not yet."

"Then I'll be damned if I do this for you," Allie said angrily. A moment later he calmed down. He looked at her. He threw some wood on the fire. He made another cup of tea. She was watching him now. He could sense that.

"Why not?" he finally asked, rhetorically. "I stay here and I'll just get in trouble. Right?"

"Right," Didi agreed, smiling.

Allie Voegler hiked back to the red Jeep, drove it to the motel, switched vehicles, and drove to the cabin.

It was silent and dark.

He tried the cabin door. It was open. He pushed it back, but didn't step inside.

What is Didi up to? he thought. What am I getting myself involved in? Everything had happened so quickly. And he had been so swept away by compassion and love for her. He hadn't had time to think.

She had looked deranged when she returned from the gorge. Maybe, he speculated, this whole trip was a function of her temporary derailing. Maybe it's just a nonsense task she gave him.

"Who the hell are you?" a voice demanded from the darkness of the cabin.

Allie stepped inside. "I'm Allie Voegler. A detective with the Hillsbrook Police Department."

"You're on the wrong side of the river," Moe Douglas noted. He walked into the small kitchen and switched the light on. Allie stayed in the cabin proper but now they could see each other clearly.

The others stumbled out of their bunks. Rose was so happy and surprised to see him that she actually kissed him.

They gathered into a circle around him.

He started off, "Didi Nightingale sent me." And then he told the small lie exactly as instructed.

Only Rose and Harris Renner seemed to respond to it at all.

Rose caught her breath in horror and started mumbling: "I should have gone to the hospital with him . . . I should have gone to the hospital with him . . . I should have . . . ."

Renner rolled his eyes at Allie and grimaced, a bit

sarcastically. He seemed to be wondering why this information transfer couldn't have waited until morning.

But Allie wasn't there to explain. He was there to lie. He said good-bye to his audience, claiming a pressing problem elsewhere, and walked out of the cabin.

He hesitated for just a moment outside the cabin, happy that his ridiculous task had been fulfilled. It dawned on him that everything Didi had told him about Kong was bizarre.

Then he drove his car back to the motel, switched to the Jeep, drove it up the slope, left it, and hiked back to the campfire.

This, he vowed, was going to be his last hike for a long, long time. The closer he came to the campsite, the angrier he became at Didi . . . for using him like a messenger . . . for not confiding in him . . . for, ultimately, not loving him.

But the moment he reached the edge of the clearing, and saw Didi sleeping beneath the blanket by the fire, his anger vanished.

It was such a lovely scene, with the moon full out now, he just stopped and drank it all in.

Suddenly he saw a figure, about fifty yards away, just beyond the clearing line.

Like himself, the figure was watching a sleeping Didi.

Allie blinked his eyes. Was he hallucinating?

No. It was a human figure, in a ski mask. A tall person. A man built like a runner.

Allie had the funny feeling that if he moved an arm the stranger would move an arm.

Allie did not move. The man did not move. Allie wondered what Didi would think of all this . . . being stared at while sleeping by two men. And for all Allie knew, this stranger, also, was in love with her.

Then the stranger crouched. Allie also crouched. It was like a game, he thought.

Then the stranger stood up and walked into the clearing.

Allie did the same.

Only then did he notice that the stranger was now carrying a rifle.

He raised the weapon and fired three shots into a sleeping Didi.

For a second, too horrified, Allie was frozen stiff.

Then, with a scream, he sprinted across the clearing, smashed the stranger to the ground, and flung the rifle away.

Turning, still screaming, he raced to Didi and

stumbled to his knees beside her. He pulled the blanket back.

It wasn't Didi! It wasn't anybody under the blanket.

The venison they had dug out of the ground beneath the sign lay packet to packet, simulating a body.

"I'm OK," he heard Didi say.

He wheeled. Didi was standing next to the fallen stranger.

Allie's legs started to buckle.

"I'm OK," she repeated.

Allie fought to compose himself. He started to walk slowly toward Didi. The stranger on the ground tried to rise. Allie walked faster. The moment he reached the stranger, Allie ripped the ski mask away from his face.

It wasn't a man.

"Allie, I want to introduce you to Fay Whitely, a local park ranger."

The woman on the ground paid no attention to Didi's introduction. She stared straight ahead.

"Why did she try to kill you?" Allie asked.

"Not me. She thought it was Kurt Trabert under the blanket. Her partner in the cabin—that fake botanist—passed on your little white lie, Allie."

"Do you know what's going on, Didi?"

"Now I do."

"Why don't you enlighten me before I get the state troopers up here to arrest this lunatic."

Allie kept his eyes on the shooter. Her head was now between her legs, as if she were nauseous. He removed the weapon from his ankle holster and held it in the palm of his right hand. He had left the handcuffs in his car.

"I saw a mountain lion in Demon's Gorge."

"A . . . what?"

"A mountain lion."

"No you didn't, Didi. There are no mountain lions in the Catskills."

"He was a big one. About two hundred pounds. And I'd say about seven feet from the tip of his nose to the tip of his tail."

"OK. You saw one. Maybe it escaped from a zoo. What does it matter?"

"It matters a lot, Allie. And it didn't escape from a zoo. It was probably purchased from illegal trappers in California or the Southwest. There's been a population explosion of mountain lions out there. I think the buyer was Marsha Greeley, a.k.a. Janet Bright, the pilot from Oneonta. I think she flew it back East and then trucked it to Demon's Gorge, with our friend, Fay, here."

"Why would they do that?"

"Money. Big money."

"You've lost me, Didi."

"Do you hunt anymore, Allie?"

"Not much. Not this year anyway."

"Why not?"

"It's like anything else. You get tired of it. It doesn't provide the rush anymore."

"You're a deer hunter, right?"

"Mostly. I hunted everything—a little. But deer was the big thing. I guess that's the problem. You grow weary of stalking whitetail."

"Why?"

"I think it's because there's no danger involved. Whitetail don't attack."

"Then you'd hunt again if it was dangerous game?"

"Probably. I'd surely love to go on safari."

"What about mountain lion in the Catskills?"

"In a minute."

"And you'd pay?"

"Through the nose, Didi. Hell, there isn't a self-respecting hunter in New York State who wouldn't sell his car, house, and wife to hunt lion."

"Ten thousand?"

"Sure."

"Fifty thousand?"

"Any amount. If they can raise it."

"So there you have it, Allie."

"What do I have?" Allie asked incredulously, keeping his eyes on the suspect.

"The whole case wrapped up."

"How do you figure that?"

"Janet Bright flew the lions in. Fay Whitely contacted the hunters. Those who signed on to hunt lion had to follow a certain procedure—look like a deer hunter, carry a deer rifle. Then go up the mountain. Find the signs. Dig up the venison to lure the big cat. And the shotgun to kill it. All in Demon's Gorge. All very clean, exciting, and fast. In and out with a mountain lion trophy."

"It makes sense, Didi."

"But they ran into some problems. Sylvester Glass probably found out about it and wanted money to remain silent. The two women murdered him, after beating him to find out how much he knew. Then there was our expedition. It was a danger to their enterprise. They tried to abort it by altering maps. Then Kurt Trabert became obsessed with Kong. This was even more dangerous because he was looking for Kong near the gorge. So they doctored the bait pails and he was mauled. When you told them that Trabert had left the hospital they had to end the threat once and for all."

Didi pointed to the bullet-riddled blankets. Then

she pointed to Fay Whitely, who was now glaring at some distant point in the woods.

"I had no idea it was her," Didi said quietly. "She seemed like a woman who—" Didi paused, searching for words. "Like a brave, virtuous woman."

"In these mountains a few thousand dollars will buy a lot of virtue and tons of bravery," Allie noted.

"I guess so."

"And Kong, Didi?"

"What about him?"

"Does he exist?"

"I have no idea."

A gust of wind blew against them fiercely, crackling the embers of the fire. Then it died down. Allie sat down beside Fay Whitely, the gun in his hand. Didi sat down beside him. The three rested in silence.

Chapter 11

"Well, it's about time you paid me a visit," Rose chastised her friend as Didi walked into the perpetually unfinished barn.

"What are you doing on the floor?" Didi asked. Rose was stretched out on the ground, faceup.

"Penance!" she replied.

"To whom and for what?"

"To my dogs, for abandoning them."

"You were only gone a few days. And Trent Tucker told me they got along fine without you."

Two of the dogs seemed to take heart at the compliment and sat down on her chest.

"But you're right, Rose. I should have come sooner."

"A lot of calls when you were away?"

"Yes. There always are."

"But no swine flu?"

Didi laughed. "No swine flu. Thank God. That was only a subterfuge, Rose. I needed an excuse to leave."

"I know that. Now, at least, I know it. Oh, Didi, you were brilliant. Did it ever occur to you that you might be psychic?"

"I'm not psychic, Rose. Believe me. And I'm not brilliant. Events were controlling me—not the other way around. It was only when I was shivering in Demon's Gorge, a few feet from a mountain lion, that I understood, feebly, what was going on."

"What will they do to the mountain lion?" Rose asked.

"Trap it, I suppose. And send it back where it came from."

"What will they do to Fay Whitely and her friend?"

"Lock them up and throw away the key, I hope."

The dogs climbed off Rose. She sat up. One strap of her denim overalls had fallen off a shoulder.

"Have you heard from Kurt?" Didi asked kindly.

"No. Not yet. And I don't think I will."

"Why not?"

"It was a fling, Didi."

"I never understood exactly what that word meant."

"Maybe you ought to try."

"What *does* it mean?" Didi snapped. She angrily zipped up her parka and stared at the red Jeep parked about twenty yards off the road. Her veterinary assistant was in the passenger seat, waiting impatiently. When Charlie Gravis saw her look so briefly toward him, he rolled his eyes and blew on his hands.

Rose was about to snap back, "Ask Allie Voegler." Trent Tucker had told her that the Hillsbrook cop was carrying on with a bartender at Jack's named Mary. But the words never came out. She wasn't going to be the one to spread a rumor like that—not when her friend was involved. These so-called rural areas, Rose thought, are kind of treacherous when it comes to love.

Rose stood up, ostentatiously put on her work gloves, and pointed to the scaffolding high up in the barn.

"Time to get back to work," she announced. The dogs barked.

"See ya," Didi said and walked back toward her Jeep.

Rose watched her go.

Suddenly Didi stopped, wheeled, and shouted back, "I forgot to tell you. I've been invited on another scientific expedition."

"With Harris Renner?"

"No. This one is down south. In Georgia."

"Black bear?"

"No. Wild boar. And one in particular. He's a uni-boar."

"What's that?"

"The offspring of a boar sow and a male unicorn."

Rose started to laugh.

"Do you want to come along?" Didi asked glee-fully.

"Of course," Rose shouted back. "Don't even think of going alone."

Didi waved, and climbed into the Jeep. Rose started to climb up the ladder.

The three dogs formed their usual circle at the foot of the ladder, wondering, as usual, when the woman would come down.

Moe Douglas stared around the cabin. Everyone was gone. The state troopers had taken the two women away. The trappers had caught the mountain lion. The scientists had gone back to their universities and the veterinarian back to her practice.

He walked into the small kitchen and started a pot of coffee. His job now was to clean up after them. But they had all been gone almost twelve hours and he hadn't been able to do a damn thing yet.

When the coffee was done, he poured a cup and went back to the fireplace.

If there hadn't been murder, he would have found the whole mountain lion thing no big deal. Maybe even laughable. Hell, everyone knew that hunters were crazy; that they would pay anything to poach something exotic and dangerous and forbidden.

In fact, he and a friend had once illegally trucked some razorbacks a thousand miles. They had released the three tusked boars and two sows only about ten miles west of Mt. Dunaway. It was a young man's dream. Boar hunting in the Catskills. They never saw the hogs again.

As for this bear denning expedition, if there wasn't a paycheck involved, he wouldn't care that it had been aborted.

But there *was* a paycheck involved—his. And he had been depending on almost three weeks good wages. Not the three days he now would get.

"Bad break, Moe," he muttered to himself.

He squatted down in front of the fireplace and poked at the embers. Dead. Not a spark left. And there was no need to get the fire working.

He finished the coffee and spat the last half mouthful into the embers.

He looked around the cabin once more. "You

cleaned up, enough, Moe," he said to himself. "If the DEC wants it cleaner, let them hire a maid."

Moe shouldered his backpack and rifle, walked out of the cabin, and banged the sliding door shut.

Halfway to his vehicle he halted. He would be going home almost empty-handed. Three days' pay. Not enough to put stuffing in the Thanksgiving turkey—if there would be one.

No, he thought. He had to go home with more.

He dropped his backpack onto the ground. It was warmish. The wind seemed to promise snow or rain. It was a very good morning for hunting white-tail. He had no idea of the date; maybe the hunting season was over. But it didn't matter on Mt. Dun-away. A day early, a day late. What did it mean? Yes. He would bring home a whitetail deer for Thanks-giving. And he would make his great venison stew, with carrots and oranges and a little brown sugar.

Moe Douglas headed up the slope. The rifle was slung over his shoulder, soldier fashion.

When he reached the altitude of Demon's Gorge he headed toward the rim instead of away from it, as was usual.

He just wanted to look again at the "scene of the crime."

Staring down into the incredible thickness of

rocks and trees at the base of the gorge, he realized it was an absolutely ideal place for a big cat hunt.

Moe smiled. Those crooked ladies sure knew what they were doing. And the buried shotgun was a gem! It made the whole thing feel like a commando raid into enemy territory. Digging up powerful weapons by night. Silent. Swift. Oh, yes. Those ladies had known all the tricks. They knew how to sell excitement.

He turned away from the gorge and headed farther up the mountain. It was time to hunt.

Moe Douglas hunted whitetail deer every season and always bagged his limit.

He knew what he called "the three commandments."

One: Only fools stalk deer. The creatures either come to you or they don't come at all.

Two: The best way to wait for them is to sit against a tree in a small clearing adjoining a field or stand of woods.

Three: The deer never enter the clearing, but they always pass close, because clearings provide unobstructed scent pathways.

Moe found a small clearing about half a mile from Demon's Gorge. The perimeter was densely wooded. No standing trees within the clearing but several boulders. The place smelled of deer.

He sat down on the ground, his back pressed against a low boulder. His feet were stretched straight out to avoid cramp. He laid his rifle across his knees. There was a round in the chamber and the safety was off.

He settled in to wait. That was the fourth, fifth, sixth, seventh, eighth, ninth, and tenth commandments. If you can't wait, you can't hunt whitetail.

In the past he had waited as long as twenty hours. And as short a time as fifteen minutes. There was no way to tell when a deer would come. You had to sit and listen hard. Then act fast. There was never time for more then one shot.

As he waited he began to fantasize about the size and quality of the stew he would prepare. Moe grinned when he remembered that his father would never eat his son's venison stew, no matter how good it turned out.

Moe's father had believed that venison must be cooked with squirrel meat—to neutralize harmful elements in the deer meat, he said. But those harmful elements were never identified.

Moe grinned at the memory and pressed his back harder against the rock.

Then he heard a sound. He tensed.

It didn't come again. He relaxed. For a brief moment he thought that the gods had sent him a fat buck quickly to make up for the lost paycheck. Someone up there had to be looking out for Moe Douglas.

He drifted into a torpor.

Then the sound came again. Deer! he thought. Only deer made that funny rubbing noise in the woods.

He didn't move. The sweat began to roll down his face and steam in the increasingly cold air.

He waited. One more time, he thought.

The sound came again. Louder. Clearer.

Moe Douglas took a deep breath.

Then he exploded into action, leaping to his feet and jumping clear of the boulder, so that he had a clear view of the woods along the perimeter.

He planted both feet firmly and snapped the rifle to his cheek.

It wasn't a deer, though.

It was the largest black bear he had ever seen . . . a bear with half of one ear missing.

The beast was on his hind legs, running his claws up and down the trunk of a tree.

For the first time in his life, Moe Douglas experienced a disabling fear. He could not move. He could not think. His nostrils were filled with the odor of the beast—a thick, pungent distillation of vegetation and carrion.

Then the bear lightly dropped down on all fours.

The movement unfroze Moe Douglas.

I can kill him now, he thought. Through the eye, into the brain. I can kill Kong. One bullet. I can kill the largest black bear in the mountains.

His finger was on the trigger. The huge bear's left eye was in the crosshairs of the scope.

Suddenly, almost violently, he brought the rifle down, out of shooting position. His legs and arms were trembling.

He started to back away. I cannot murder Kong, he thought. Kong doesn't exist. There is no black bear on earth that large.

He turned and scrambled out of the clearing on all fours. Once in the brush, he lay with his face on the ground for a long, long time.

Allie walked into Jack's at just past nine in the evening.

He had wanted to get there earlier, but a school bus had hit a station wagon on Route 44 early in the afternoon. The entire Hillsbrook Police Department had taken part in the rescue operation. He and Chung had served as stretcher bearers.

The driver of the wagon had died on impact.

All the children had survived, although one was hurt seriously.

Allie sat down wearily on a bar stool. He was off duty now. He could drink.

Mary wasn't behind the bar.

In fact, Allie had never even laid eyes on the young man with blond hair parted in the middle who was furiously slicing lemons and limes.

"Is Mary around?" he asked, tired and angry that the young man had not even acknowledged his presence. Maybe, Allie thought, he thinks I'm too old to be a customer here. Maybe he thinks I'm making a delivery.

"No, she isn't," the young man said.

"I'll have a bottle of Heineken," Allie ordered, a bit too aggressively.

The young man took his own sweet time. But finally he delivered the beer.

"And a glass," Allie said, although he rarely used one.

The glass was duly delivered.

"Is she off?"

"Who?"

"Mary."

"She's gone."

"Gone?"

"She doesn't work here anymore. She went to New York City. To work in the Kitchen."

"Kitchen? She's a bartender, not a cook."

The young man laughed out loud.

"What's so damn funny?"

"The Kitchen is a club in Manhattan. She's performing there."

The young man went back to his lemons and limes.

Allie stared at his bottle. He didn't know whether to laugh or cry.

His presentation had been carefully planned and rehearsed.

He was going to tell Mary that he couldn't see her anymore.

He was going to explain that it wasn't a slight on her. She was a beautiful and smart and passionate woman. Much too good for him.

But he had this "thing" for another woman. A long-standing thing. And he couldn't deal with another affair. He couldn't deal with the guilt even though he had no idea why he should feel guilty at all. After all, the other woman continually ignored him.

Allie took a long swig of the beer. Yes. He had planned the presentation carefully.

But now he realized what a fool he had been. He had planned it so that Mary wouldn't be hurt by his decision.

It turned out that Mary didn't even care enough

about him to leave a note. He realized that he had indeed just been a one-night stand for her.

Allie closed his eyes and tried to relax. He could hear the bar filling up . . . with kids. It was quite obvious to him that when it came to women he was a dud. But he had always known that. Now it was becoming clear that he was a hopeless fool. He wondered if he was dysfunctional. That word always intrigued him. The new cops, like Chung, used it often.

He opened his eyes and spoke to the beer bottle: "You are being held by a dysfunctional lothario."

The bartender placed another bottle in front of him.

"I'm not finished with this one," Allie noted testily.

"Someone bought you a beer."

"Who?"

The bartender pointed to the far end of the bar. Allie peered through the light and smoke.

A young man raised his hand, as if admitting the crime.

Allie saw, to his astonishment, that it was Trent Tucker. He'd be damned if he'd let that young fool buy him a drink.

"Take it back."

"What?"

"Take it back."

The bartender stared at Allie, then shrugged, then took the beer back.

Ten seconds later Trent Tucker sat down next to him, a bottle in each hand.

"What's the matter, Officer Voegler? My money isn't good?"

Allie didn't' answer.

"You still think I had something to do with that Agway robbery, don't you? You think this is dirty money."

Allie slammed the bottle on top of the bar. "Go away, kid. I'm on duty. I don't take free drinks from anyone."

"You know, I can help you."

Allie turned and faced the young man. "You can help me? Are you kidding? First get a real job."

"There are no jobs around here anymore."

Allie stood up to go.

"Wait. I mean I can help you with Didi."

"Didi? Do you call her that to her face?"

"No."

"So don't call her 'Didi' in a bar."

"I know you really like her."

"That's no secret, kid."

"Well, I mean, I know something about women."

That was too much for Allie. He grabbed the kid

by his shirtfront and lifted him halfway off the ground.

A hush fell over the place and the customers began to move away from the bar, just like in an old Western. Embarrassed at the scene he was making, Allie released his grip. He knew he had to get out of there. But he just couldn't get his feet to walk. He felt as if he weighed a thousand pounds.

"Why don't you just keep your mouth shut," he whispered to Trent Tucker.

"OK. OK."

But the young man didn't return to the far end of the bar. He stayed next to Allie.

"Actually, I think she likes you a lot," Trent Tucker finally said in a quiet, confidential voice.

"Your opinion is noted," Allie said.

"But you have to court her. Don't you understand? She's a very old-fashioned girl."

Allie laughed. "Court. You mean like you do? In the back of a pickup truck. With a girl you found in this joint."

"I mean flowers . . . and wine . . . and books."

"Get away from me, kid."

"Court her!" Tucker exclaimed as if he were uttering some revealed truth.

I have to get out of here, Allie thought, or I'm

going to send one of Didi Quinn Nightingale's elves to the hospital.

He gathered his strength, dropped a ten-dollar bill on the bar, and pushed through the denizens until he reached fresh air.

He headed toward his car.

"Voegler!"

He turned. The kid had followed him out.

"Don't you understand what I said?" Trent Tucker shouted.

"Go back inside. You had one beer too many."

"Don't you understand what courting a lady means?"

Then Trent Tucker stumbled and fell hard. He rolled over in pain, one hand trying to grasp his ankle.

Allie went over to him.

"Are you OK?"

"I messed up my ankle."

"Is it broken?"

"I don't think so."

Allie helped him up.

"Where's your truck?"

Trent Tucker pointed to the rear of the lot.

"OK. Let's go," Allie said, supporting him as they slowly made their way to the truck.

"But I want to stay at Jack's," Trent Tucker said.

"There's always tomorrow night," Allie replied.

He helped the young man into the vehicle.

"Drive slow," Allie cautioned.

"OK, Uncle Allie," the young man said. But he didn't start the engine.

"I'm not your damn uncle," Allie said, heading back to his car.

As he drove off, he realized that the kid had made at least one intelligent comment. Allie Voegler didn't have the slightest idea what courtship meant.

Worse, he had no idea where to find out.

At least, he thought, he was a good listener. Who else could listen to her tall tales about a giant black bear named Kong and not laugh out loud?

He didn't drive home. He drove to Didi's house and parked on the road about fifty yards from the driveway.

What was she doing?

What was she wearing?

Was she thinking of him at all?

Two pinpricks of light suddenly appeared on the road.

It was a deer, heading toward the pine forest. Why did they always cross the road at night?

Maybe, Allie thought, it was a courtship ritual. He started the car again and drove into town.

Trent Tucker, meanwhile, had napped in the pickup and then hobbled back into Jack's.

"Where you been?" one of his drinking companions asked.

"Taking care of business," Trent replied. And all of his buddies nodded, as if they understood what he meant. After all, he worked for Dr. Nightingale.

When Trent Tucker ordered another beer, the new bartender asked him, "Who was that guy?"

"A cop."

"He doesn't like you."

"He thinks I'm a thief."

"Are you?"

"Do I look like one?"

The bartender didn't answer. He shrugged and wiped the bar. Then he gave Trent Tucker another beer.

"On the house," he said. Trent Tucker nodded his thanks. Things were looking up in Hillsbrook.

Charlie Gravis always went to sleep at ten in the evening and got up at five in the morning. It didn't matter whether it was hot or cold. It didn't matter whether he was tired or not tired. It didn't matter whether he had slept the night before or not. That's when he went to sleep and that's when he got up.

He never, never used an alarm clock. But this night, he stuck a very old travel alarm clock under his pillow and set it for 2:45 A.M.

Another thing that made this night different was that he slept with his clothes on.

The alarm woke him at 2:30. It was a very old clock, and inaccurate. He sat up in bed in his small room in the "servants' quarters" of the Nightingale home and waited.

At five minutes before three, he grinned. Mrs. Tunney was going to the kitchen for her tea. She never slept the whole night through. She always went into the kitchen for a cup of tea at this hour.

Charlie waited until he knew the tea was done. He got up. He walked into the kitchen.

"What are you doing up?" Mrs. Tunney asked, a bit sharp.

"I want to talk to you," Charlie said.

Mrs. Tunney gave him one of her arch looks. She didn't like the idea of being talked to, particularly at that time of night. "Why don't you have a cup of tea instead?" she asked.

"No," Charlie replied, "a talk." He sat down on a chair.

Mrs. Tunney was wearing a puffy robe and a muffler around her neck.

"Are you happy, Mrs. Tunney?" Charlie asked.

She stopped her cup in midflight. She looked as if she'd been hit with a pot. "That's one of the stupidest questions I've ever heard, Charlie," she said.

"Well, answer it."

She did. "We have a place to sleep, Charlie. We have food. We live where we've always lived. And Miss Quinn is wonderful."

"Yes, yes, I know," Charlie said. "But what if I told you there's a lot of money on the horizon, Mrs. Tunney. I mean a lot of money. I'm not talking about a thousand bucks."

"Go to sleep, Charlie," she said.

"You think I'm going crazy, Mrs. Tunney? Well, let me tell you something. You know I found Cleo Dopple's dog, don't you?"

"We all know you did a good job in finding him," Mrs. Tunney said.

"Well, let me tell you about Cleo's dog. When I went to see him, the dog couldn't even walk. When I brought him back, he was like Joltin' Joe DiMaggio."

"You'd be surprised, Charlie, what a little fresh air can do for an old dog."

"Fresh air won't help advanced lumbago, Mrs. Tunney."

She sipped her tea. She narrowed her eyes. She tugged at her muffler. Then she said, "I have a very funny feeling, Charlie, that you're treading on dangerous water."

Charlie smashed his hand down on the table. "I cured that dog!" he said.

"So he could go out and bite someone? So he could jump through a window?" she asked sardonically.

"You're throwing out the baby with the bathwater!" Charlie shouted.

"Don't you dare wake everybody in this household."

"OK. I'm sorry. I lost my head, Mrs. Tunney. I'm sorry. But I'm telling you the truth."

"Charlie Gravis, this was settled a long time ago. You will not make any more of your fool medicine. You will not dispense any more of your fool medicine. You will not sell any more of your fool medicine. Unless you want to see me, Abigail, and Trent Tucker out in the cold. Miss Quinn is a fine young woman, but she draws the line at that kind of nonsense. We all know that, Charlie."

"This worked," Charlie said in a quiet voice.

Mrs. Tunney put her hands over her ears.

"Please don't do that, Mrs. Tunney. I'm telling you, it worked. If you had seen the dog before and after, you'd know I'm telling the truth."

She kept her hands over her ears.

Charlie said in a louder voice, "Why don't you come with me to Cleo Dopple's like you went the first time."

Mrs. Tunney got up from the table, walked to the sink, rinsed the cup.

Charlie said in a kindly voice, "I'm not going to abandon Miss Quinn when this thing gets off the ground. I'll make her the goddamn CEO."

"Don't curse, Charlie."

"Why don't you just come with me to Cleo Dopple's again, Mrs. Tunney?"

Mrs. Tunney tightened the muffler around her neck. It was chilly in the cavernous kitchen. "Charlie," she said, "I am going to sleep now. You should do the same. This conversation never took place. And it's never going to take place again." She started toward the narrow hallway.

"Wait!"

Mrs. Tunney stopped.

"Don't we owe it to Abigail and young Trent Tucker to provide for them in their old age?"

"Miss Quinn will provide," she said.

"What about a vacation, Mrs. Tunney? What about eating out in restaurants twice a week—for a month. What about a new car, Mrs. Tunney? What about giving money to your church so they can buy an organ that works? Just plain old good money,

Mrs. Tunney. Earned honestly. We're getting old, Mrs. Tunney. There's a few things we ought to do. I know we're OK here, but there's a few things we ought to do."

Mrs. Tunney walked over to Charlie Gravis. She put her hand on his shoulder. "You're not that old, Charlie," she said.

"Oh, I'm very old, Mrs. Tunney," he replied.

"Good night, Charlie." She vanished down the hallway.

Charlie stood up, walked to the refrigerator, took out a piece of New York State cheddar cheese, and gnawed it. He was very angry. He didn't know what to do next. He had a million dollars' worth of miracle lumbago medicine lying in a vat three hundred yards from the main house and he was surrounded by fools. He sat down on the chair. He didn't know what to do. It is possible, he thought, that I am one of those late-blooming geniuses. It is possible that suddenly I have become a brilliant natural healer. Cows. Dogs. Parrots. Goats. Hogs. And maybe— maybe—even people.

I am a prophet without honor in my own village, he thought. But he knew, deep in his heart, he knew beyond a shadow of a doubt that one day Didi Quinn Nightingale, doctor of veterinary medicine par excellence, would understand just how valuable he was.

He heard a sound in the hallway. He turned and saw Mrs. Tunney coming back. For a moment his hopes soared. She sat down across from him, reached into her robe, and pulled out a deck of cards.

"You know, Charlie," she said, "I don't much favor card playing. But there is a time and place for everything, and it's obvious you need something to get your mind back on track."

She opened the deck and began to shuffle. "Casino, Charlie?"

"I don't play casino, Mrs. Tunney."

"And I don't play poker," Mrs. Tunney replied. "What about rummy?"

"Rummy it is."

Didi stood by the window in her mother's room, staring out over the field and into the pine forest. The moon was very full now. She looked at the clock. It was 3:15 in the morning. She had been up for an hour. She had heard noise downstairs, and knew it was either Mrs. Tunney getting her tea, or field mice mounting an attack.

The room was freezing. She put on a hooded sweater. She wanted to hear music, but she had misplaced her earphones and she didn't want to wake anyone.

The pine forest, as usual, gave her great visual pleasure. At night the trees seemed wavy. They seemed to sway, but she knew it was an optical illusion.

For some odd reason, she remembered a book report she had done when she was a student at Hillsbrook High. She had written the report on one of the editions of Scott's diary, which was found on his corpse during that fatal expedition to the Antarctic.

She had always loved books about explorers and she never understood why there were no women explorers.

The book report earned her a C+, and the mark had infuriated her, because it was an excellent report.

She smiled at the window. Now she could see her face there. She couldn't remember Scott's last lines exactly—it had been too many years since she read the book and wrote the report.

But she remembered it was something like " . . . had we lived, what a wondrous tale we could have told."

Yes, she thought, if Kong had lived, what a wondrous tale could have been told. But she knew that there was as much chance that Kong existed as there was of a mountain lion coming out of the pine forest to drink.

She suddenly burst out laughing. She had a spectacular idea: After the Thanksgiving bash, she was going to gather all her friends in Hillsbrook and ensconce them in one of the rooms that the diner rented out for special events.

She'd serve them coffee and cheesecake, then dim the lights and wheel in a TV and a VCR.

Then she would make a short speech. "Ladies and gentlemen, I'm sure you all want to hear about my adventures with Rosie in the primeval forest. Well, there was a videographer who came along with us. And he caught every dramatic episode. So here, for your pleasure and edification, is the video 'Didi Quinn Nightingale Enters the Bear Cave.'"

Then she would slip the video into the slot and the assembled would all watch King Kong ravish Fay Wray.

She walked back quickly to her bed, sat down, picked up a notepad, and scribbled on it "Get *King Kong* from the video store." She turned off the small light by the bed and lay back down.

The house was silent now. Either Mrs. Tunney had finished her tea or the field mice had retired.

Once in bed and lying down, she abandoned her frivolous plans.

She did have something serious to think about. About that stupid word "fling."

Was Rose right?

Should she have a fling?

One couldn't have a fling with Allie Voegler.

Maybe she should go to New York, buy a party dress in Soho, go to one of those hip bars, and pick up a tall, dark, handsome stranger.

His name would be Wallace.

He would be an about-to-be famous sculptor who worked with metal.

He would be an excellent cook. He would wear running shoes. He would have a dog named Luther, a basset hound. And he had not set foot in a cow pasture in his entire life.

This, she thought, is too ridiculous.

She fell fast asleep, the sleep of the weary, the sleep of the just.

At 3:20 in the morning she was awakened abruptly by someone knocking, knocking, knocking at her door.

She sat up. "Who's there?"

She heard Charlie Gravis call out, "It's me. There's trouble!"

"Come in."

Charlie opened the door and walked in. He was carrying a shotgun.

She rubbed the sleep from her eyes and barked at him, "I told you to get rid of that thing, Charlie!"

"We got trouble, miss," Charlie said.

"What kind of trouble?"

"There's a strange car parked in front of the house. It's just sitting there, and there's someone inside."

Didi got up, put on her boots without her socks, threw on a mackinaw over her pajamas, and clumped down the stairs, Charlie following her.

At the foot of the stairs were all the rest of her elves.

"Make sure you have the safety on that stupid thing," she said.

She opened the door and walked out into the cold night.

Charlie was right. There was a large, black Volvo station wagon sitting smack in the middle of the driveway. The yard dogs were circling it and whining.

"Just stay here," she called back to her elves.

She walked slowly toward the car and circled it from the rear. It had a Vermont license plate. She moved around to the front. The window was rolled down. A middle-aged woman sat limply behind the wheel. She was dressed bizarrely, as if she had thrown on anything at hand.

"Can I help you, miss?" Didi asked.

The woman stared at her. She laughed crazily. "Can you help me? I've just driven twelve hours to find you. Are you going to help me like you helped my friends Janet Bright and Fay Whitely? Are you going to get me arrested for murder also?"

Didi stepped back, shocked at the woman's venom. "Who are you?" she asked.

"I'm the real Marsha Greeley, Dr. Nightingale."

Didi stared at her. She didn't know what to say.

Marsha Greeley said, "I came down here to beg you, to hurt you, to plead with you, to find out what the hell is going on. The state police called me. They told me you were instrumental in having my friends arrested. They told me my friends had murdered a man—and tried to murder a few others. I don't know what to believe. I don't know what to do. The whole thing is crazy."

Didi said, "Why don't you come inside, Professor Greeley."

She replied, "I don't want to come inside."

Didi said, "I didn't know they were your friends."

Marsha Greeley laughed kind of wildly. "I met them both five years ago. In a ski lodge in Indian Mountain, Connecticut. Do you know where that is? It's northwest Connecticut. Good skiing. We became friends. After all, women over thirty in those kind of places have to stick together. The place is infested with teenyboppers. We stayed together for two weeks each year—the first two weeks in January—at the same lodge. They were two wonderful women. We skiied, we drank, we talked. And they used to joke all the time about making a whole lot of money and buying their own ski lodge so they could keep the damn teenyboppers out. And they had this scheme: to run a unicorn hunt. But it was just a joke!"

The woman paused. She seemed to be about to cry.

"What do you mean by 'a unicorn hunt'?" Didi asked.

"In our ski lodge," she said, "we hung up a fake tapestry. It was a silkscreen copy of that famous medieval tapestry, you know. About a bunch of men hunting a unicorn. And Fay and Janet always used to joke about how that's the way they would make their fortune—because men would pay anything to hunt a unicorn—to get that trophy on the wall. But a mountain lion . . . that's incredible. That they would do such a thing is incredible!" She banged her hands on the wheel for emphasis.

Didi asked, "You were invited by Harris Renner to participate in this study, weren't you?"

"Yes," she said. "Six months ago. It was all set up. About three months ago I called Fay and told her all about it. Because the study was going to be in the area that she patrolled as a park ranger. I didn't think anything of it. And then about a month ago I received a telegram from Haris Renner telling me that the expedition was canceled."

Didi replied, "That telegram never came from Renner. It came from your friends. And Janet Bright became you."

Marsha Greeley thrust one hand outside the car window and grabbed Didi's arm. "Do you know how crazy this whole thing is?" she asked.

"Crazy and sad," Didi said.

"They were my friends," Marsha Greeley said. "The whole thing was a joke, about the unicorn."

Didi grasped her arm tightly. "The mountain lions weren't a joke, Professor. The murder wasn't a joke. The attempted murder wasn't a joke."

Marsha Greeley pulled her arm away savagely, and then buried her face in her hands and wept.

From behind her, Didi heard, "Hot cocoa, miss. She needs some hot cocoa."

Didi wheeled, and saw a concerned Mrs. Tunney standing there.

"Let's help her in," Mrs. Tunney added.

Didi opened the car door and they walked Professor Marsha Greeley back around the house and into the kitchen, the yard dogs yapping at their heels.

Deirdre Quinn Nightingale, DVM, ripped off her examining gloves, rolled them into a ball, and flung them into the bucket.

"Well?" Lou Tisdale's question came out as an aggressive bark.

Didi didn't answer. She stepped away from the cow she had just examined and studied her.

She was a lovely little milk cow with very large ears.

But she had stopped eating; her milk production had declined; and her bones seemed to be turning brittle, almost fragile. She got and down very slowly. She moved slowly.

Oh, yes . . . this lady . . . and in fact her name was Lady . . . was a sick cow.

There were five other cows in the barn. Didi

walked past them slowly. They seemed fine. Their breath was like steam in the freezing barn.

"I know what's the matter," Lou Tisdale fairly shouted.

Charlie Gravis, Didi's geriatric assistant, couldn't let that pass. He retorted angrily: "If you knew what's the matter, why the hell did you get an old man like me out of a warm house on a day like this?"

"Who wanted you!" Lou snarled. "I wanted her! She's the vet. If you knew anything about cows, Charlie, you'd still be a dairy farmer."

Didi stepped between then before it escalated further.

"Gentlemen, please! Let's deal with the matter at hand." She was used to defusing situations involving angry dairy farmers. These days they were always angry. Milk prices kept going down. Feed prices kept going up. The squeeze seemed eternal.

Then she smiled in an almost daughterly fashion, and asked, "What is the matter with Lady, Lou?"

"Radiation," said the farmer. Then he took off his wool hat, shook it, and replaced it on his balding head in a different position.

Charlie Gravis guffawed. Didi signaled to him that he should keep his mouth shut.

She moved her toes furiously in her boots; the

cold was numbing them. Lady started to bellow weakly and roll her eyes. There was no steam coming from her muzzle now.

"What do you mean, 'radiation'?" Didi asked Lou.

"I mean that damn nuclear plant on the Hudson. Their poison is leaching into the wells. And I'm going to sue them."

Didi pulled her ski hat down farther on her head, but it couldn't cover her exposed neck. I should let my hair grow out in the winter, she thought.

Then she walked over to Lady and looked her over once more, feeling the front legs and shoulders.

She stepped back. "Tell me, Lou, what do you feed your herd?"

"The usual. Dried forage."

"Baled?"

"Yeah."

"Off the trucks?"

"Right."

Didi nodded. All year long, huge flatbed trucks came into Dutchess County from Canada and the Midwest, selling baled hay and other forage at discount prices. Dairy farmers and horse breeders depended on them.

"What kind of grains do you feed them?"

"None."

"None? How about protein supplements?"

"None."

"What about bonemeal or wheat bran or soybean meal?"

"No."

"Are you serious, Lou?"

Lou Tisdale didn't answer.

"Answer the doctor!" Charlie demanded.

Lou was silent.

Didi walked up to him. She spoke slowly and forcefully. "I don't think it's radiation poisoning, Lou. I think it's phosphorus deficiency. A vet doesn't see it so often anymore. Know why, Lou? Because every dairy farmer has been sent hundreds of notices over the years by county agents, farmer associates, and veterinary groups warning against feeding dairy cows just dried forage. You have to supplement the diet because the forage is marginal in phosphorus content."

The big dairy farmer thrust out his gnarled hands in a pathetic gesture.

"The wife works part-time in town," he said, "and I haul trash three times a week. Just to make ends meet. I can't feed any other way."

"Then you don't belong in this business anymore," Didi said. And a moment later she felt ashamed of herself for the comment.

"Can't you just give her an injection?" Lou pleaded.

"No. It's chancy. Excess phosphorous is even worse than a deficiency. Get some real bonemeal, Lou. Or wheat bran—that's even better. Do it now, Lou."

Didi and Charlie headed for the red Jeep.

He climbed into the passenger seat and dumped the bag into the back.

Didi went around the front of the vehicle.

She was so cold and angry that she didn't even notice the vehicle parked near hers.

But then she heard: "Dr. Nightingale, I presume."

She wheeled and stared at a kindly old mustachioed face in the open car window.

"Hiram! Hiram!" she yelled, and rushed over to his car. She stuck her head in through the window and kissed her old professor.

Then she stepped back.

"I can't believe it's you," she said, laughing.

"Well, it is," he replied.

Didi just stared at him happily, lovingly. Hiram Bechtold had been her favorite professor at the University of Pennsylvania School of Veterinary Medicine. He was the best . . . the smartest . . . the most kindly. He had retired from full-time teaching after she graduated, to "think," as he put it. Didi had kept in touch with him by phone, had asked him for help in diagnosis and treatment, but she hadn't seen him in almost five years.

"Well, follow me home, Hiram! I want you to see the house and the clinic and meet my elves."

He held up his hand.

"I can't, Didi. I have to get back. It's a long drive home. But I did get to see your house and meet your Mrs. Tunney. She was the one who told me you were here."

Didi was confused. Why had he made the long drive up, just to turn around and go back?

Hiram picked up on her confusion. "I did come here to see you, Didi. But it isn't a social call."

"What, then?"

"Clifford Stuckie was murdered in Philadelphia two nights ago. Horribly murdered."

At first the name didn't ring a bell. But then she remembered. "You mean, *the* Clifford Stuckie, Hiram? The millionaire? The one who owns Rising Moon Farm here in Hillsbrook?"

"And, Didi, a beef cattle operation in the Florida Panhandle, plus homes in New York and Colorado and God knows where else. Yes, Didi, that's the one."

"I didn't see anything in the Hillsbrook paper."

"It was all over the Philadelphia papers. But I learned it from a police officer. They came to my house five hours after the murder."

"Your house? Why?"

"It seems his Rolodex in the carriage house where he was murdered was open to my name and number."

"Did you know him?"

"No, not really. Of course, I knew *of* him. But I spoke to him only once, a few years ago. He told me he had an experimental hog breeding place in Hillsbrook; that he needed a good vet; and he asked if you were reliable. I told him you were the best."

"They do call me every few months. And they do pay their bills on time."

"The police found something else in the carriage house, Didi: a love letter."

"Well," she said, "he does have a girlfriend. I met her once at Rising Moon."

"It was written to you, Didi," Hiram announced.

Didi was stunned.

"To me! Are you serious?"

"Yes."

"But I barely know the man, Hiram. I met him briefly, maybe three times over the years. When I go there, I deal mostly with the foreman. I forget his name."

Bechtold didn't speak for a long time. He stared through the window at Lou Tisdale's crumbling barn.

"Are you okay, Hiram?" Didi asked.

"Didi," he said, "they think—they think you may be involved in the murder. Do you understand? They consider you a suspect in Stuckie's murder. They're coming here, to Hillsbrook."

"Hiram! What are you saying?"

"They think you may have killed him. Because of the letter."

"My God. You don't believe that . . . do you, Hiram?"

"Didi, I'm an old man. I don't know what to believe anymore."

"Hiram, this is me! This is your old student. Didi Nightingale. I'm a country vet, remember?"

But the old professor had rolled up the window.

He started the engine and drove off without saying another word.

Didi watched him go. The darkness was coming. She looked into the red Jeep. Charlie was dozing.

What is going on? she thought. What madness is this?

The wind was flaring up. But she didn't move.

Something was nagging at her, making her very uncomfortable.

When he had refused her offer of hospitality, she had wondered why he would make the long drive just to turn around and go back.

Now she wondered why he made the trip at all.

Why *had* Hiram Bechtold driven all the way from Philadelphia in the dead of winter to tell her this strange tale?

Why hadn't he just picked up the phone?

That would have been the rational thing to do.

Didi looked at old Charlie Gravis dozing in the Jeep.

Hiram was even older than Charlie, and feebler.

What if the whole outlandish story was just a figment of an aging man's deranged imagination?

Alzheimer's? Senility? Severe depression?

Yes, she thought, it was probably one of those. Her eyes welled up with tears. Poor Hiram! The moment she got home she would have to call his wife, who was probably worried sick over her wandering husband.

Didi climbed into the Jeep.

"Do me a favor, Charlie. Take me home, then take the Jeep to the post office before it closes and check for mail. I'm expecting a lab report."

By the time they arrived home, it was pitch dark.

She waited until he drove off and then headed toward the house.

"Didi!"

"Who's that?" Didi asked, peering at the two figures who were suddenly visible on her right.

"Allie."

"Oh, Allie. You scared me. How are you?"

Allie Voegler was, as usual, underdressed. No coat. Only a muffler hanging loose over his red flannel shirt. He looked very big in the darkness.

"I'm fine, Didi. I want you to meet someone."

Didi laughed and said, a bit flirtatiously: "You sound very serious, Allie. Are you trying to fix me up?"

Allie didn't laugh. The stranger next to him was still silent.

"Didi, this is Detective John Paul Pratt, of the Philadelphia Police Department. He wants to question you."

The stranger took a step forward and thrust out his hand to shake.

Didi kept her hands by her side.

She didn't feel like being friendly or hospitable.

All she felt was an inexplicable dread. As if she were a child again, lost in the pine forest as darkness closed in.

**And be sure to read
the first book in
the Dr. Nightingale series:
DR. NIGHTINGALE COMES HOME**

Deirdre "Didi" Quinn Nightingale needs to solve a baffling mystery to save her struggling veterinary practice in New York state. Bouncing her red jeep along country roads, she is headed for the herd of beautiful, but suddenly very crazy, French Alpine dairy goats of a "new money" gentlemen farmer. Diagnosing the goats' strange malady will test her investigative skills and win her a much needed wealthy client. But the goat enigma is just a warm-up for murder. Old Dick Obey, her dearest friend since she opened her office, is found dead, mutilated by wild dogs. Or so the local police force says. Didi's look at the evidence from a vet's perspective convinces her the killer species isn't canine but human. Now she's snooping among the region's forgotten farms and tiny hamlets, where a pretty sleuth had better tread carefully on a twisted trail of animal tracks, human lies, and passions gone deadly . . .

And the second book:
DR. NIGHTINGALE
RIDES THE ELEPHANT

Excitement is making Deirdre "Didi" Nightingale, D.V.M., feel like a child again. There'll be no sick cows today. No clinic. No rounds. She is going to the circus. But shortly after she becomes veterinarian on call for a small traveling circus, Dolly, an extremely gentle Asian elephant, goes berserk and kills a beautiful dancer before a horrified crowd. Branded a rogue, Dolly seems doomed, and in Didi's opinion it's a bum rap that shouldn't happen to a dog. Didi is certain someone tampered with the elephant and is determined to save the magnificent beast from being put down. Her investigation into the tragedy leads her to another corpse, an explosively angry tiger trainer, and a "little people" performer with a big clue. Now, in the exotic world of the Big Top,

Didi is walking the high wire between danger and compassion . . . knowing that the wild things are really found in the darkness, deep in a killer's twisted mind.

The third one is:
DR. NIGHTINGALE
GOES TO THE DOGS

Veterinarian Deirdre "Didi" Quinn Nightingale has the birthday blues. It's her day, and it's been a disaster. First she's knee-deep in mud during a "bedside" visit to a stud pig. Then she's over her head in murder when she finds ninety-year-old Mary Hyndman shot to death at her rural upstate farm.

The discovery leaves Deirdre bone-weary and still facing Mary's last request: to deliver a donation to Alsatian House, a Hudson River monastery famous for its German shepherds. Deirdre finds the retreat filled with happy dogs, smiling monks, and peace.

This spur-of-the moment vacation rejuvenates Deirdre's flagging strength and spirit until another murder tugs on her new leash on life. Deirdre's investigative skills tell her this death is linked to Mary's. But getting her teeth into this case may prove too tough for even a dauntless D.V.M. . . . when a killer with feral instincts brings her a hairsbreadth from death.

And finally:
DR. NIGHTINGALE
GOES THE DISTANCE

Intending to forget about her sick cats and ailing cows for one night, Deirdre "Didi" Quinn Nightingale, D.V.M., is all dressed up for a champagne-sipping pre-race gala at a posh thoroughbred farm. She never expects death to be on the guest list while hobnobbing with the horsey set and waiting to meet the famous equine vet, Sam Hull. But when two shots ring out, two bodies lie in the stall of the year's most promising filly.

The renowed Dr. Hull is beyond help, and the filly's distraught owner offers Didi a fee and a thoroughbred all her own to find this killer. Now Deirdre is off snooping in a world of bloodlines, blood money, and bloody schemes. The odds are against this spunky vet who may find that her heart's desire is at stake—and murder waiting at the finish line . . .

Who the hell did he think he was, suggesting Tom step down? His rank was so far beneath Tom's, he couldn't even remember what it was like to be in Agent Frenz's position. When this debacle was over, the first thing Tom was going to do was file an inquiry into Frenz's assignment to this case. It was insulting.

Tom strode into the interrogation room and found Natasha exactly where he'd left her, sitting straight-backed at the table, waiting patiently. He sat down across from her and got down to business. He was sick of messing around.

"Why is Yuri here?" he asked.

There was a moment of silence as Natasha savored whatever morsel she was about to share. She tilted her head, sighed, looked at him like he was pitiful—like he was missing something so very obvious.

"Why, Natasha?"

"He wants Gaia," Natasha replied.

Tom felt all the muscles in his body recoil. He turned his head and looked at the one-way mirror, somehow keeping his gaze steady. He knew that Vance had his hand on the doorknob right now to come relieve him before he could explode. He tried with all his might to convey his message to his superior: *Back off. I'm staying*.

"Why?" Tom asked, his jaw clenched.

"He's decided that Gaia would be the better candidate to take over the Organization," Natasha explained.

"Tatiana has been, for lack of a better word, passed over."

I don't believe this, Tom thought, his fists gripped together under the table. *He wants Gaia? He wants Gaia to take over his international terror organization?*

"If he wants to groom her to take his place, why instruct you to kill her?" Tom managed to ask.

"He did not order the hit," Natasha replied. "That was me."

Tom once again saw himself lurching over the table. Saw himself squeezing every last trace of life out of Natasha. Instead, he waited. He breathed. He gradually started to see straight again.

"I didn't appreciate his decision to demote Tatiana. She trained all her life. She deserved to take the helm," Natasha said. She flicked something off the knee of her orange jumpsuit and gazed at Tom.

"Why did he do it?" Tom asked her. "What suddenly made him decide to. . . choose Gaia?"

"Gaia was always the ideal candidate, but Yuri couldn't risk coming to the States," Natasha explained. "Not as long as Loki was operating here. It was too risky."

Tom gazed at the tabletop, his mind working. "So once Loki fell into a coma—"

"Yuri ordered you to be taken out of the picture," Natasha finished. "I didn't know it at the time—I was as shocked as everyone else when you were taken to the hospital—but that is what he was doing. He wanted you gone so he would be free to—"

"To approach Gaia," Tom said.

"Precisely."

Tom's mind reeled. This was unbelievable. In his wildest dreams he never would have imagined that this was the story behind everything that had happened. That Yuri was alive. That the Organization still functioned under his watchful eye. That Loki...

"Loki had nothing to do with my kidnapping," Tom said, almost to himself.

Natasha snorted. "Of course not. It was all Yuri. Even Loki's coma. It was all orchestrated to gain access to Gaia."

She said it like it was the simplest thing in the world. Like she hadn't just told him that his own daughter—his only child—was susceptible to the world's leading psychotic. How could she do this? How could she talk to him like he was an enemy, like he was the scum on the bottom of her shoe? How could she do this to him—to *them*?

"I want proof," he said firmly. "I want proof that Yuri is still alive. Proof that you're related to Katia."

Natasha sat back in her seat, suddenly bored. "Go to the safe house in Alphabet City. Under the painting on the wall is a safe. The combination to the safe is three, twenty-two, seventeen. There will be a box inside. There you will find everything you're looking for."

Tom was out the door before she finished the sentence.

I am the worst father in the history of the earth. I brought a daughter into this world, and from the moment she took her first breath I have failed her in every conceivable way. I protected her from nothing. Quite the opposite, actually. All I've ever done is *put* her in *harm's* way.

I lost her mother. I let my insane brother worm and scheme his way into her life. Let him influence her. I left her with George Niven—an alleged friend who turned out to be a traitor. And then I left her with Natasha, who not only tried to kill her, but who was working for a man who wants to take her and groom her to become head of one of the most evil institutions ever known to man.

My daughter grew up not only without parents, but having to face the worst possible threats on a daily basis. Not only did she have to deal with the normal anxieties of adolescence—boys, school, friends—but she had to fight off my enemies. She had to fight for her life every day and I wasn't there to comfort her, to guide her, to give her a shoulder to cry on.

I'm a sham.

If this turns out to be true—if Yuri is alive—I have to take him out. He will not have my daughter. I don't care if I have to move her to Alaska or Australia or the Amazon. But this time, I will protect her. I will do whatever it takes.

Even if I die trying.

"GET AHOLD OF HER, DAMN IT!
Grab her around the arms!"

Resignation

"She's freakin' strong, man!"

"She's just a girl, for Christ's sake!"

The muffled voices came through the dark shroud that had been yanked over Gaia's head. She struggled and fought against the viselike grip of the man who held her, kicking her legs out, flailing back and forth, but it was no use. She was being dragged backward toward the door, off her feet, the heels of her boots squeaking against the hardwood floor.

What the hell is going on? Gaia wondered. Were these the same people that had taken Dmitri? And kidnapped her father? How had they known she would be here? They had, after all, come prepared. They had black sacks for blindfolding and a precision uncommon to run-of-the-mill burglars and drug fiends that might prey on a recently deserted apartment.

Yep. This was planned. Planned, of course, for her. The resignation settled over Gaia's shoulders like a steel blanket. Someone was still after her and they had anticipated she would come looking for Dmitri. Whoever they were, she'd walked right into their grasp.

Gaia heard Jake sputtering and cursing and struggling somewhere in the darkness and she was suddenly thrown to the floor. Her spine was slammed against the hard surface and a foot pressed into her sternum.

"Jake?" she called out, coughing against her will. "Jake, where the hell are you?"

"I'm right here," Jake's voice replied. He was still standing—somewhere over her. And he sounded like he was trying not to sound scared.

"Not for long," one of the voices said with an obvious sneer. "Kill the kid. We don't need him."

Gaia took a sharp inhale as a rush of adrenaline burst through her veins. She reached up into the darkness, grabbed the ankle attached to the foot that pinned her down, and flung it left with all her might. The guy went down hard, kicking her in the jaw as he went, but the rest of the attackers were surprised enough to give her a few seconds.

She jumped to her feet and whipped the black sack off her head. Jake was pinned against the living room wall, his arms tied behind him, the barrel of a gun pressed into his forehead. Gaia saw the gun-bearer's thumb pull back the safety.

"Duck!" she shouted.

Jake hit his knees and Gaia, aware that there were three other men converging on her from all sides, tackled the gunman to the ground. The firearm skittered under one of Dmitri's massive bookcases and the attacker looked up at her, stunned. Gaia brought her fist down right in the center of his face, knocking his head back against the floor. His whole body went limp as he fell unconscious.

"Gaia! What the hell is going on?" Jake shouted.

Gaia turned around and saw all three of the other men advancing on her slowly, arms outstretched, like she was a rabid lion. At that moment she felt like one. These guys had messed with the wrong girl at the wrong moment on the wrong night. They were about to feel a lot of pain.

"Don't do anything stupid," the guy in the center said.

They were all wearing black ski masks with just the eyes cut out, but this guy's eyes were the kind of extremely light blue that was almost clear. The skin around them was pale and his eyebrows were so blond they were barely visible. He was scrawny. Too scrawny to take her unless he had some serious skills.

My first target, Gaia thought, nearly salivating.

She bent at the waist and rushed the guy, flying right past his two friends and tackling him onto the glass coffee table, which shattered all around them. She pinned him down with both hands to his neck and reached up with her back leg to kick one of the advancing attackers in the face. He flew back into a bookcase and didn't get up again. Then the guy beneath her lifted both legs and kicked her over his head, where she tumbled awkwardly into the side of

Dmitri's favorite chair before quickly scrambling to her feet.

"Gaia, I can help if you'd just—"

She whirled over to Jake, who had struggled to his feet, and whipped off his blindfold. He looked relieved to see her alive, but that lasted less than a second. His eyes widened and Gaia instinctively ducked at the same moment Jake did. A huge vase shattered against the wall right where their heads had been.

"My hands," Jake said, crouched to the floor.

Gaia tugged at the cloth that bound his wrists and, surprisingly, it came apart easily. When they stood up again, it was two on two. Scrawny Guy and his bigger buddy faced them down, but being against the wall, Jake and Gaia were at a distinct disadvantage.

Suddenly, Scrawny Guy let out a battle cry and rushed Jake. Jake ducked his punch yet again and Scrawny Guy cracked his knuckles against the exposed brick wall, crying out in pain. Gaia saw the blood out of the corner of her eye.

So maybe the wall *wasn't* a bad thing.

She and Jake exchanged a look and the battle began.

Gaia attacked the bigger guy with a flurry of punches, ducking and weaving anything that he tried to counter with. He was slow, but she could tell that if one of those right hooks hit home, she could be down for the count. Gaia concentrated her power on his head, hoping to knock him out the same way she'd knocked out his friend. But suddenly, there was a crash off to her left, and Gaia turned to see if Jake was all right.

Big mistake.

Jake was fine—it was the Scrawny Guy who was down and struggling to get up, having taken a potted plant to the head. But when Gaia turned around again, there was a fist coming right at her face.

Uh-oh, Gaia thought.

Her eye exploded in pain. Sparks seemed to flash across her plane of vision as she sprawled across the floor. Her cheekbone felt as if it had just been smashed with a tire iron.

Head pounding, Gaia flipped over onto her back and saw a boot coming for her gut. It was about to hit home when she rolled away, gaining as much momentum as she could. She slammed into the bookcases and grabbed a shelf to leverage herself up, but she was only halfway to standing when the same boot hit her squarely in the center of her lower back.

"Stay down, bitch!" the guy said.

She could hear Jake and Scrawny Guy, still duking it out behind her as she tried to catch her breath. Scrawny turned out to have more stamina than she'd thought. The bigger guy backed away from her to help his associate, seemingly satisfied that she would take his advice. That was when she saw it: the gun handle, sticking out ever so slightly from under the bookcase.

Gaia grabbed it and whirled around as she stood, still regaining control of her breathing. She pulled back the safety and aimed.

"Don't move!"

The big guy stopped in the middle of the living room and Scrawny Guy looked at her like a deer caught in headlights. Jake hit him with one swift elbow to the back of the head, knocking him out. Then he walked over, `crunching across the broken glass on the floor`, and stood next to Gaia, never taking his eyes off hers.

"Turn around," she told the last man standing.

He did as he was told, arms raised to shoulder height out at his sides.

"Don't do anything stupid, kid," he said, eyeing the gun.

"Who sent you?" Gaia spat. Her hand started to shake and she reached up with her other arm to steady herself.

"Like I'm gonna tell you that," he said.

"I think you will," Gaia said, taking a few steps toward him. She was starting to feel weak. Her head was getting groggy. It was coming and it was coming on fast.

No. Not yet, she begged. *Not until I find out what is going on.*

Her eyes stung with unshed tears as her hands continued to tremble with exertion. She thought it was over.

She thought she was free. Who the hell was trying to kidnap her now?

"Tell me!" Gaia said through her teeth, struggling to ward off the blackness.

"Gaia," Jake said.

"Look, you're gonna have to shoot me. Cuz I tell you, and I'm dead, anyway," the guy said, smirking.

"All right. Enough is enough."

Jake walked around behind the thug and took him down the same way he'd taken out Scrawny Guy. Gaia let her arms go limp. As her knees went out from under her, her mind was racing.

Who took Dmitri? Who's after me? Who. . . ?

Suddenly she felt Jake's arms around her, stopping her fall. He lowered her to the floor and sat cross-legged with Gaia across his lap. The darkness was coming more intensely now, enveloping her, dragging her down. She felt him slip the gun from her fingers and she tried to speak, but it was too late.

Right before she blacked out she felt the touch of his lips against her forehead.

TOM WAITED IN THE HALLWAY, HIS

back up against the wall as the tactical team swept the premises of **All True**

Natasha's safe house. His patience grew thin, even though he'd only been there no more than two minutes. He needed to get inside. He had to get inside.

He couldn't believe that any of the things Natasha had told him were true—not until he saw proof with his own eyes.

Kurt Handler, the squad leader, stuck his helmeted head out of the apartment and flipped up his clear eye-guard. "We're all clear, sir," he said.

"Get them out of there!" Tom told him. "I don't want anything moved."

Handler pressed a button on the side of his helmet and spoke into the built-in microphone. "Blue team, move out!" he said. Seconds later, half a dozen agents tromped out of the apartment and headed back down the stairs. Only Handler stayed behind, guarding the door with his M-16.

"It's all yours, sir," he said with a nod.

Tom's hands were clammy as he slipped past Handler into the small apartment. It was sparsely furnished, the walls painted a bland white, but he didn't take in much detail. A forensics team could comb the place later. For now, all he cared about was the safe.

He picked the framed poster off the wall and revealed a small door. As he worked the combination, his fingers were calm and sure, as they'd been trained to be for so many years, but he was barely breathing. This was it. The moment of truth.

The door swung open with a creak, and inside Tom found stacks of currency from countries all over the world, along with a dozen or more passports from various nations. He pushed everything aside and felt the back of the safe for the box. The box she'd said would be there. The box he almost hoped he wouldn't find.

His fingers grazed a sharp edge and Tom's heart froze. He grasped a small metal box and pulled it out, being careful not to disturb the other contents of the safe. When he opened the box his knees felt slightly weak. He walked over to the ratty couch and sat down.

There, right on top of a stack of photos, was a picture of two young girls, smiling with their arms wrapped around each other. One he recognized immediately. The blond hair, the wide grin, the dimple in one cheek, the gold lavaliere necklace hanging around her slim neck.

Katia. She looked so much like Gaia had at that age, she was like a double of her daughter.

And the other girl was undoubtedly Natasha. Her hair darker and fuller, her smile more reserved, her eyes mischievous. There was no doubt in his mind that he was looking at a younger version of the woman he'd interrogated earlier that night.

Also obvious in the photo was the resemblance between the two girls. The high cheekbones, the sloped noses, the set of their eyes. They had their differences, but they were clearly related. Cousins. No doubt about it. They could have been sisters.

Reluctantly, Tom flipped to the next photo in the pile and his mouth went dry. The same two girls, same day, but this time Yuri was in the picture. His face smiled out from between the heads of the two girls, his hands wrapped around their shoulders. A family.

It was all Tom could do to keep from crushing the photos in his hand.

From there, he knew what he would find. There were pictures of Natasha and Tatiana through the years. Pictures of Tatiana growing up, riding horses, practicing archery, firing a gun. And then, the very last photo was the one Tom was looking for but hoping he wouldn't find. His blood ran cold as he lifted it and held it up to the light.

Yuri. No doubt about it. He was older, grayer, and more frail but had the same cold, determined look on his face that Tom remembered so well. He had his arm around Tatiana, who gazed stoically at the camera, her palm pressed into the barrel of a rifle that stood in front of her. In the photo, Tatiana was only a year or so younger than she was now.

Yuri was alive. `Everything Natasha had told him was true.`

Tom dropped the picture back into the box, slammed the lid shut, and headed for the door. He had to find Gaia. He had to find her *now.*

JAKE SAT DOWN GINGERLY ON THE couch next to Gaia and pressed a bag of frozen green beans against her cheek. Gaia winced, a shot of pain streaming right through her temple, then reached up and took the bag, holding it in

Irrevocably Stupid

place. Jake pulled away and leaned forward to study her face, his brow creased. She couldn't even imagine what the bruise looked like, considering how tender and puffy it felt.

"You know, with the lives you Moores lead, you might want to stock fresh steaks in your fridge," Jake said with mock-seriousness.

Gaia scoffed and the pain radiated along her jawbone. She grimaced and closed her eyes. That guy packed even more power in his punch than she'd imagined.

"Sorry. I won't make you laugh again," Jake said, raising his hands. His perfect face was unscathed except for a small scrape on the underside of his chin.

Gaia was just leaning back into the couch, ready to collapse and really *focus* on her new obsession over who might be chasing her, when the door to the apartment burst open. Her father barreled in, his hair sticking up slightly on top, panic radiating from him like visible energy. Gaia sat up straight again and Jake instantly got to his feet. The moment Gaia's father saw them, his entire demeanor changed. His shoulders lowered from up by his ears back to their normal position.

"You're here. Thank God," he said. Then he came around the coffee table and saw Gaia with the frozen food package against her face. His Adam's apple bobbed up and down as he checked his emotions. "What happened?"

"We got jumped," Jake replied.

"By professionals," Gaia added, moving her jaw around to see if she could. It hurt a little too much so she closed her mouth again.

"Damn it," Tom said, turning away from them. He brought his hand to his face and Gaia looked up at Jake. What was going on?

"You know who did it, don't you?" Gaia asked, ignoring the little aching shoots around her cheekbone.

"I have my suspicions," Tom said. He hung his head for a moment and then took a deep breath. There was a heavy sense of foreboding in the air. Something bad was about to happen. Her father turned around again and looked her in the eye. "You're not going to like this," he said.

"Shocker," Gaia said under her breath. Jake sat down next to her, sitting a bit closer. For a moment Gaia thought he was going to reach for her hand again, but he didn't. Instead he pressed it into his thigh as if he was concentrating to keep it there.

Gaia's father sat down at her other side, a few inches away so that he could turn to face her. Gaia held her breath and pushed the frozen beans a little more firmly into her face, bracing herself.

"Gaia, Yuri. . . your grandfather. . . is alive."

Gaia blinked. "Mom's dad?"

"And this is a bad thing, I take it?" Jake put in.

Tom shot him a look that told him to keep out of this discussion. Gaia quickly decided to check her tongue as well. There had to be a good story behind this. Back when Yuri was alive he was a serious menace—a person her mother had gone to the ends of the earth to escape. Loki supposedly murdered him years ago. This revelation was just one more sud in the soap opera of Gaia's life, but it was a big one.

Tom quickly recounted the story—Gaia heard all about Natasha's confession and the information and the confirmation. She took it all in, going a little more numb with each word that was spoken.

"So Natasha wanted me dead because she thought I was going to take Tatiana's job," Gaia said slowly, when her father was through.

"Basically," Tom said. "But it's not just a job. It's a lot more than that. *A lot* more."

"Yeah, I get that," Gaia said.

"So there's some freak out there positioning himself

to kidnap her and train her to be the head of an international terrorist cell?" Jake asked.

How keen, Gaia thought sarcastically. She couldn't believe she was having this conversation. Couldn't she ever just have a talk with her father about the weather, her grades, the messy state of her bedroom?

"I took a few of the pictures," Tom told her, reaching into the breast pocket of his suit jacket. "Was this man there tonight when you were attacked? I doubt he'd come himself, but you never know."

Gaia took the picture from her father and her brow creased in confusion. "What's Tatiana doing with Dmitri?"

"Dmitri?" her father asked. "Who the hell is Dmitri?"

Gaia's mouth went dry. She had a feeling she knew what was coming, but the very idea, the very *thought* made her feel so indescribably, indubitably, `irrevocably stupid,` she wished there was some way to shut her ears against hearing it. But she couldn't, so instead, she closed her eyes.

And then, her father said the words she wanted least to hear. "Gaia, this man's name is not Dmitri," he told her. "It's Yuri."

Why can't things be different? I know. . . I know. . . everyone in the world wishes things were different, but I don't understand. I don't understand what went wrong.

Well, that's not exactly right, is it? I do understand what went wrong. I had a disease. I had treatments. I developed a disorder. And that disorder was responsible for atrocities I will never be able to reconcile myself with. That atrocity killed people. It killed a lot of people. It killed the woman I loved. And yes, these things are hard to bounce back from. Nearly impossible. To ask someone to forgive what I've done. . .

But that's just it. *I* didn't do those things. It wasn't me. It was him. It was all him. And if there's one person who should understand that, it should be my brother. He was there. He saw it all—what I went through as a young boy, how I changed as I grew into a man. He of all people should know that I have no control over Loki's actions. He of all people should *know*.

I wish he would die. I wish he would just wither and sputter and die.

Not my brother. No. Not Tom. Of course. But Loki. Why won't he die? Why won't he go away and leave me alone? Why do I have to live with this? What did I do? Where did I go wrong? Am I being punished for some crime in a past life? Is this some kind of test? Twins are born, one perfectly normal and blessed, the other mad and cursed? Is this my test?

At least Gaia knows. At least Gaia can forgive. And she's the last person I would have expected it from. She's just so young. How can she understand? How can she forgive the person who murdered her own mother?

But it wasn't me. Not me. Not me. Him.

I need my family back. I need them. Don't they see that I need

them? I need someone to ground me.
To stay with me. To talk to me
and. . . and. . . to *see* me. See
me and not him. If they won't let
me. . . if they won't come. . .
then how can . . . how can I. . .

   This struggle. It's too much.
How can I. . .

   But it wasn't me. It was him.
It wasn't me.

   Why won't they let me in? Why. . .
why. . . why. . . ?

He couldn't stop thinking about the fact that she was out there somewhere **guys** **like** **him** with that Jake jerk, possibly doing things that he didn't even want to think about.

ABOUT HALFWAY THROUGH THEIR
second set, Sam decided it was
time to bail on the Dust
Magnets. He hadn't imbibed as
much alcohol as his buddies
had, and his judgment was still
intact. To him, the Dust
Magnets' music sounded much
like the soundtrack the
devil might play in
hell.

The Female Spectru!

Sam walked toward the subway, his thoughts gradually turning toward Gaia and her new boyfriend—if that's what he was. He definitely didn't seem like Gaia's type. Sam thought Gaia went for the more intelligent, laid-back, scruffy-around-the-edges type. Guys like him.

But then, he knew firsthand that it was possible to be attracted to two very different people at the same time. Look at his own track history: He'd moved right from Heather Gannis to Gaia Moore. Those two occupied completely opposite ends of the female spectrum.

So maybe she does still have feelings for me, Sam thought as he approached the entrance to the F train. *If she does, I know I can still win her back.* The problem was, he couldn't stop thinking about the fact that she was out there somewhere with that Jake jerk, checking up on Dmitri—Dmitri, who was *Sam's* friend. Sam should have been the one helping Gaia. Jake had nothing to do with it and yet he'd run out of the club with her as if it was his place—his job.

As if he was Gaia's boyfriend.

Sam's heart turned as he tried to blot out the mental images that threatened to take over—Gaia and Jake holding hands, Gaia and Jake kissing, Gaia and Jake going back to her apartment. . . .

He had never felt quite this jealous in his life.

It was time to get home and go to bed and put an end to this awful night. In the morning, the situation would look brighter. In the morning, he could come up with a plan to get back into Gaia's life. Sam was about to descend the steps to the subway station when he heard his cell phone ringing. He grabbed it out of his jacket pocket and checked the caller ID screen, smiling when he saw Gaia's name and number.

See? She can't stay away, he told himself.

Stepping away from the subway entrance so a pack of people could squeeze by, Sam hit the talk button and lifted the phone to his ear.

"Hey, Gaia. What's up?" he said.

"Sam, are you sure Dmitri didn't tell you where he was going?" Gaia demanded. Her tense tone of voice made all the hair on Sam's arms stand on end.

"Whoa, slow down. Are you okay?" Sam asked.

"What did he say the last time you saw him? I need specifics," Gaia said.

Sam's brow creased as he leaned back against the

low wall surrounding the subway entrance. "Uh. . . not much. We mostly talked about me. . . my new place. . . my new job. . . ."

"Just think for a second. Did he say *anything* about where he might be?" Gaia asked impatiently.

"No. Nothing," Sam said, pushing himself up straight again. "Did you try calling him?"

"His cell phone was disconnected."

"Gaia, what's going on?" Sam asked. "Is Dmitri in danger?"

He heard her draw in a breath and then blow it out right into the speaker—right into his ear. "Listen, this is really important," she said. "If Dmitri contacts you, try to find out where he is and don't, I mean *do not* tell him where *you* are, okay?"

Her voice was full of concern. Concern for him. But why? Dmitri was their friend. He'd done nothing but help them since the day they'd met him—the day they'd found him held captive in the same compound Sam had called home for months. What did they have to fear from Dmitri?

"Gaia," Sam said, lowering his voice as a couple strolled slowly by. "You have to tell me what's going on. What did Dmitri do?"

"I can't get into it right now, but you have to trust me. The man is dangerous," Gaia said. "I can't believe I let him get so close to us."

Sam swallowed hard. Gaia sounded upset—more

upset than he'd heard her sound since her father went missing. He felt his protective nature kick in.

"Is there anything I can do?" he asked, gripping the phone. "Do you want me to come over?"

"No, it's okay," Gaia replied. "I have to go. Just. . . call me if you hear from him."

"Okay," Sam said.

But Gaia never heard it. The line was already dead. Sam swore under his breath and turned off the phone, feeling suddenly helpless and trapped. How could she just call him and say all those things to him with no explanation? He'd been *living* with Dmitri for weeks, for God's sake. What had he done to put Gaia so far over the edge?

There's nothing you can do, a little voice in his mind told him. *She'll come to you if she needs you.*

But the thought was small comfort. For as long as he'd known Gaia Moore, Sam had never seen her come to anyone for help.

"LET ME MAKE SURE I HAVE THIS

Actual Tears

right—Sam Moon was *living* with Yuri?" Tom blurted, pacing back and forth in front of the coffee table.

Gaia and Jake sat on the couch,

looking like two wide-eyed little kids that were being scolded by their father. They watched him warily, like they were afraid that at any moment he might spontaneously combust and take them with him. He didn't blame them. He *felt* like he was about to explode.

"We didn't know he was Yuri," Gaia told him for the fifth time in as many minutes. "He passed himself off as one of Loki's prisoners."

"This is insane. It's just insane," Tom said, his mind reeling. "And you're telling me he helped you capture Natasha?"

Gaia nodded slowly. "He tipped off the CIA. Why would he help the good guys?"

"Well, Natasha tried to kill you," Jake pointed out. "And from what your dad said, it seems like this Yuri guy wouldn't have wanted that to happen."

"Exactly," Tom said, finally pausing in his maniacal pacing. "Once Natasha became a threat to his plans he just gave her up."

"But Dmitri was trying to help me find you," Gaia said, tossing the bag of vegetables she'd been toying with onto the table. "He sent me into this travel agency. . . this front for the Organization to find information on where you were being held."

Tom watched his daughter's mind work as she trailed off, clearly trying to put two and two together. He couldn't have imagined the cocktail of emotions she was experiencing at that moment. He was so proud of her—she was so brave, so intelligent, so resilient. But at the same time, he was frightened for her.

I have to get her out of here, he thought again. *Take her somewhere where Yuri can't find her. This can't go on.*

"But I never found any information," Gaia said finally, pressing her hand into her forehead. "I stole that other file he wanted, but there was nothing on you. Why would he send me on a covert mission to steal from his own organization?"

"A travel agency, you said?" Tom asked, sitting in one of the chairs across the coffee table. "Was it a little place downtown? Between a shoe store and a computer repair shop?"

"Yeah...," Gaia said slowly.

"That's not a front for the Organization, it's a front for the CIA," Tom told her, his stomach curling in on itself. "Yuri sent you in to steal from the CIA."

A thick silence descended over the room and Tom had to swallow back actual tears of frustration. The very thought of the danger that man had put his daughter in—the idea of him manipulating her and Sam into thinking he was some innocent victim—made Tom so ill he wanted to crawl out of his skin.

"Do you remember what it was?" Tom asked.

"Just a file. I never looked at it," Gaia said, slumping back into the couch, dazed. "I can't believe I was so stupid."

"There's no way you could have known," Jake

said before Tom could get out the exact same words. He looked at Jake gratefully. Tom was starting to like this kid.

"Gaia, I think we need to get you out of here," Tom said, leaning forward. He rested his elbows on his thighs and pressed his hands together. "I want you safe. That's all I care about."

"Dad, no," Gaia said firmly, sitting up again. Her blond hair fanned out over her shoulders, framing her beautiful, determined face. "No. I am *not* leaving you."

The tears behind his eyes intensified at her words, but he once again fought them back.

"Gaia—"

"Dad, no," Gaia repeated. She stood up and took a few steps toward the end of the couch, pushing her hands into her hair. "I am not going to run," she said, turning to him. "I've never run before and I'm not going to start now."

"Gaia, you know I'm all for fighting this guy, but maybe your dad's right," Jake said, turning in his seat so he could face her. "This Yuri guy sounds like he doesn't mess around. They almost killed both of us tonight."

"I know," Gaia said. "That's why we have to end this—now. Just think about it, Dad. We bring Yuri to justice and it's over. He's the last link. Loki is gone. . . . If we take Yuri down it'll actually be over."

Tom let her words sink in and felt a flutter of

something new within him. Hope, maybe. Determination, definitely. Gaia was right. With Yuri out of the way and Loki squelched, the Organization would crumble. The last threats to his daughter's life would be obliterated.

But he didn't like the fact that she kept using the word "we."

"I know what you're saying, Gaia," he said, rising out of his chair. "But if Yuri is going to be taken out, you are going to be far, far away when it happens."

"How can you say that?" Gaia asked, whirling around to face him fully. Her eyes flashed, reminding him of the way Katia reacted whenever he picked an argument with her. "Dad, this is our fight. This man is my *grandfather*. He's Mom's father and he betrayed me. He betrayed us all. How can you even think about calling in some team to take care of him? We *have* to do this ourselves."

"Not without some backup," Tom argued. "I don't think you appreciate exactly how dangerous this man is."

"I do," Gaia said, drawing herself up straight. "But we have an edge. We know where he was staying and he left in a hurry. He must have tripped up—left something behind that could help us."

Tom sighed and shook his head. "We can't go in alone," he told her. "You already got jumped there once. He may have sent more operatives."

"But this time we'll be prepared for that," Gaia said.

"I'll come with you," Jake said suddenly, standing as well. Tom saw his jaw working beneath his skin as he crossed his sizable arms over his chest. "I want to help."

Gaia's mouth twitched into a smile that she quickly banished. "We should get Oliver, too," she said, looking Tom in the eye. "Now that we know he had nothing to do with this, he could be good to have around."

Tom's shoulder muscles coiled and he looked away. The very idea of talking to Oliver was almost too much for him to handle. He was going to have to apologize. He saw that now. But even though he'd been cleared in this matter, Tom still didn't trust his brother. He wasn't sure if he'd ever trust the man completely.

When he glanced back at Gaia again, her gaze was unwavering—steadfast. Whether or not Tom trusted his twin, Gaia clearly did. And she was right. Checkered past or no, Oliver's skills would be helpful in this particular operation. It was time for Tom to swallow his pride and call his brother.

"Fine," Tom said finally, trying to ignore the sick feeling that permeated his heart. He crossed to the table next to the couch and reached for the phone. "Let's get this over with."

OLIVER STRAIGHTENED HIS COLLAR

The First Step

and smiled contentedly as he lifted his fist to rap on Tom and Gaia's door. He'd been most surprised when the phone had trilled in the middle of the night and even more surprised to hear his twin's voice on the other end, asking him to come in to the city ASAP. It was an odd time of day for a reconciliation, but beggars can't be choosers.

The door flew open and Oliver blinked, startled. Gaia stood there in a T-shirt and a Kevlar vest, her face flushed and her eyes filled with a sort of grim excitement.

"What's going on?" Oliver asked automatically.

"We have a lot to tell you," Gaia said, stepping aside to let him pass.

Oliver walked slowly into the living room, his mind working double time. At the same moment, Tom stalked in from the hallway, pressing a gun into a hip holster. His button-down shirt was open to reveal his Kevlar vest. Jake stood in the corner by the window, talking into a cell phone. There was an almost palpable energy in the air.

"Ollie," Tom said, lifting his chin. "We need to talk."

Oliver felt his pulse quicken in a way he relished. He followed his brother into a bedroom down the hallway and waited as Tom closed the door. He almost didn't dare to hope.

"Is everything all right, Tom?" Oliver asked.

"No. No, everything is not all right," Tom said, looking him in the eye. There was still caution there, but something had changed. His brother was no longer afraid. "Oliver, I know it wasn't you who kidnapped me. I know you had nothing to do with the hit on Gaia. And I want you to know. . . "

This was difficult for his brother, Oliver could tell. He ached to hear the words, but he didn't prompt them. He had waited a long time for this moment. He could wait until Tom was ready.

"I want you to know that I'm sorry," Tom said finally, his voice husky. "I think you understand why I couldn't fully trust you in Russia, but I'm sorry for how I treated you."

"It's all right," Oliver said, somehow containing the maelstrom of emotions within him. "You had a lot to process."

"Yes," Tom said, tucking his hands under his arms. "To be honest, I still do."

"Of course," Oliver told him, refusing to let his brother's continued wariness get to him. This was a start. A first step. It was all he could ask for.

"But I'm glad to have you back, brother," Tom said, unexpectedly. His voice actually cracked. "It's good to have you back."

Shocked by this sudden effusion of emotion, Oliver was hardly prepared when his brother enveloped him in an awkward, stiff—but still heartfelt—hug. Oliver slapped his brother's back and quelled a wave of tears that threatened to take over. This was it. The moment he'd hoped for. The moment he'd lived for.

The Moore brothers were back.

Oliver pulled away from Tom and clasped his shoulder. Neither was comfortable with outpourings of emotions. They'd done what they needed to do and there was clearly some other serious business at hand.

"Why don't you tell me what's going on? Why is your daughter out there in a bulletproof vest?" Oliver asked.

Tom took a deep breath and blew it out noisily. "Well, Ollie... You up for a mission?"

"Absolutely," Oliver said, following Tom back out to the living room/dining room area. Gaia was laying equipment out on the table while Jake was still over by the window, his back to the room as he spoke into the phone. "Who wants to tell me what's going on?" Oliver asked, pushing his hands into his pockets.

Gaia shot a look at her father. "You might want to sit down for this," she told Oliver, twisting her hair back into a messy bun. But Oliver stood stock-still. He was feeling fairly euphoric after his talk with Tom. Nothing could bring him down.

"Okay," she said with a shrug. "Remember Yuri? He's alive. We have to get him."

Oliver pulled a chair out from the dining room table and fell into it. "That's not possible," he said. "Yuri's dead. Loki shot him. I remember it like it was yesterday."

"Yeah, well, Loki got duped," Tom said, buttoning up his shirt. Any trace of emotion was gone as he was back to business. "And now Yuri's after Gaia."

Oliver's heart skipped a long beat as he gazed up at his niece, his mind reeling. "This doesn't make any sense," he managed to say.

"I know, but we don't have time to figure it out right now," Gaia told him. "I know the last apartment he was staying in. We're going there to see what we can find."

Oliver watched as Tom helped Jake into a bullet-proof vest and showed him how to fasten the shoulder straps. Gaia pulled a sweatshirt on over her own vest. Her hair stuck out in all directions from the static. They looked like they were getting ready for battle.

But with Yuri? It couldn't be. All these years Loki had been running the Organization—feared, revered, respected. And he'd only been able to do it by murdering Yuri—by showing everyone who the new boss was. What had Yuri been doing all that time? If Oliver knew anything about the man, he knew that he couldn't have been just sitting around twiddling his thumbs. Yuri loved the Organization—it was his baby. He must have hated Loki for taking it away. He must have been plotting revenge.

"Will you come with us?" Gaia asked.

Oliver swallowed hard. "Of course I will." His family needed him. He would go wherever they asked. It was just going to take him a little while to process all of this. It was as if the whole world order had shifted in the space of three seconds.

"Oliver? Are you okay?" Gaia asked.

"I'm fine," Oliver said, clearing his throat, trying to banish thoughts of Yuri and what he might want to do to the man who had tried to take his life.

"Where did you get all this equipment?" Oliver asked, picking up a stun gun and inspecting it. He had to put thoughts of his own safety out of his mind. This was about protecting Gaia and Tom. It was time to focus.

"I kept it in a locker in storage," Tom said. He picked up the last vest from the table and handed it to Ollie. "Good thing, too. Who knew I'd need it for something like this?"

"Well, you were always the smart one," Oliver half joked.

He slipped into the vest and zipped up the front, glancing at Gaia, who smiled back at him. Oliver's heart warmed. Suddenly he felt like part of the family again—part of a team. And for once, he was on the right side.

"All set?" Gaia asked, looking at Jake over Oliver's shoulder.

"Yeah. I talked to my dad," Jake said, yanking a sweater on over his head as he approached them. "I'm good to go."

"Gaia?" Tom asked.

"Ready," she replied with a nod.

"Ollie?"

Oliver pulled his jacket on over his vest and nodded, determined. "Let's do it."

To: Y
From: X22
Subject: Genesis

Capture unsuccessful. Please advise: X22

To: X22
From: Y
Subject: Re: Genesis

You stupid, blithering idiot! How could you
fail to catch one small girl? I know she is
powerful, but I told you this. I warned you. How
many men did you send in? Did you not bring
weapons? Are you that idiotic?

I would like you to proceed by sitting on your
hands while I get this done right. Continue
reports on Cain and Abel. Don't screw up again.

Visions of his
body being flung
across the room,
of a giant
fireball **jake**
exploding out **the**
the side of the
building, of **spy**
Gaia's limp, dead
form, flashed across
his mind's eye.

JAKE FLATTENED HIMSELF UP AGAINST

The Roller Coaster

the wall of the hallway outside Yuri's apartment, feeling once again like he was in the middle of a Vin Diesel movie. After what had happened here the last time, he had expected to be peeing in his pants from fear, but he was strangely calm—excited, but calm. Maybe he was getting used to this stuff. Maybe he even had a future in the spy game.

How cool would that be? Jake thought, trying not to smile. This was not an appropriate situation for smiling.

Tom signaled to Jake and Gaia to stay put and stay quiet, then nudged open the broken door with his toe. He took a few steps inside, inspecting the area. Jake glanced at Oliver, who gazed back, his cool blue eyes telling Jake to take it easy—be patient.

Suddenly Tom reappeared in the doorway.

"Let's go," he whispered.

The team tromped through the door and into the apartment. Jake paused before entering, looking both ways down the hall to see if anyone was lurking, but there was no movement.

When Jake walked into the apartment, Gaia, Oliver, and Tom were standing in the living room, taking in the scene. Blood dotted the floor around the smashed coffee table. The men he and Gaia had knocked out, however, were all gone.

"Fan out," Tom said, sweeping his arm toward Jake and Gaia. "I want to get this over with. Bring us anything that looks suspicious."

"I got the bedroom," Jake said, heading for a closed door near the back of the apartment. Oliver followed as he carefully stepped over a few bills and envelopes on the carpet, in case they were important, and grasped the brass doorknob. He opened the door and was about to walk in when he heard a click and a beep.

"Stop!" Oliver shouted, causing Jake's heart to jump.

Jake was about to pull his hand away from the doorknob, but Oliver touched his arm, stopping him.

"Don't move a muscle," he told Jake.

Jake swallowed with difficulty. He wanted to ask what the hell was going on, but he was afraid to open his mouth. Oliver dropped to the ground, turned on his side, and slid through the space between Jake's legs and the door.

"What's going on?" Tom asked, approaching them with Gaia close behind.

"It's C4," Oliver said, shining a tiny flashlight up toward the top of the door. "It's wired from the wall down to the doorknob. He moves, it blows."

Jake's knees wobbled dangerously and he pressed his eyes closed. He'd seen enough spy movies in his lifetime to know that C4 was a seriously nasty explosive. Visions of his body being flung across the room, of a giant fireball exploding out the side of the building, of Gaia's limp, dead form, flashed across his mind's eye.

Oh, no. He really *was* going to pee in his pants.

"How much?" Tom asked.

"Enough to take off the top of this building," Oliver said. "But it's a rudimentary device. Not a problem."

Jake liked the sound of that. He opened his eyes and saw Oliver pull a pair of clippers out of his utility belt. Then he reached up with the flashlight toward Jake.

"What?" Jake asked.

"You'll need to hold this with your other hand so I can see what I'm doing," Oliver said.

The beads of sweat along Jake's hairline organized themselves into one large rivulet and danced right down the center of his nose. He was sweating, he was shaking, and he wasn't sure how much longer he could hold on to the doorknob, let alone the flashlight. He looked down at Oliver helplessly, feeling like the useless wuss he clearly was.

"You can do it, Jake," Gaia said in his ear, her voice firm and full of confidence. It was also completely devoid of fear. Apparently when she knew she was about to be blown to bits she didn't let it bother her.

161

Jake nodded slowly. He grasped the flashlight in his sweaty fingers. Oliver guided Jake's hand until the light was pointing where he needed it to be. Jake's heart hammered in his ears and he found himself silently praying—something he hadn't done once since his mother died. He'd kind of had a problem with God since then.

Oliver cut the casing off the red wire and looked at the circuits inside. Then he did the same to the green wire, and the blue. Jake held his breath. If this was such a rudimentary device, then what the heck was taking so long?

"Got it," Oliver said, once the circuits inside the yellow wire were exposed.

He placed the wire-cutters around the circuits and Jake waited for his life to flash before his eyes, but it didn't. All he saw was his mother's face, then his father's, then his mother's, then his father's. His dad was going to be really pissed at him if he died and left him all alone.

Then Jake heard the clip and the door swung free of his grasp. He sucked in a breath, still alive.

"See? No problem," Oliver said, holding the door open.

Jake stumbled into the room and fell onto the bed, his knees finally giving out. He felt an overwhelming urge to cry, but the second Gaia stepped into view he squelched it. He'd already proven himself to be enough of a wimp right in front of her face. He wasn't going to be a blubbering baby as well.

"You okay?" Gaia asked, standing in front of him.

"Fine," Jake replied, pressing his hands into the bedspread. "Can't say the same for my ego."

Oliver and Tom headed back out into the living room and Gaia sat down next to Jake, a few inches away. "I should've never asked you to come here," she said.

"You didn't. I volunteered," Jake reminded her, pushing both hands into his hair.

"But I didn't try to stop you," Gaia said. She looked down at her clasped hands between her knees. "That's not like me."

"And it's not like me to stay behind no matter what you say," Jake replied. He took in a long, shaky breath and let it out in a loud burst of air. "But I gotta say, I'm not so sure if I'm cut out for this stuff. Five minutes ago I was James Bond and now I feel like I left my spine somewhere in the living room."

He hung his head, ashamed, the rapid beating of his heart pounding in his ears.

"What, you think you're some kind of loser because you got scared?" Gaia asked.

Jake scoffed. "You have a way with words."

He saw Gaia flush out of the corner of his eye and smiled slightly. "Jake, you wouldn't be *human* if you weren't petrified by what just—"

Gaia abruptly stopped talking and looked away. Her jaw clenched and he could see her fighting something off—something she didn't want to think about. So maybe she was affected by the idea of being blown to bits.

"You're gonna be fine," Gaia said, standing—averting her gaze. "Let's get back to work."

There was something she wasn't telling him—Jake could sense it—but now was not the time to ask. He could hear Oliver and Tom crashing around in the living room, searching. The longer they stayed here, the longer Yuri was out there, free to plot whatever he was plotting. Jake made himself stand up and start moving.

While Gaia searched the closet and dresser, Jake rifled through the drawers in the bedside tables, which were empty except for a few pencils, a pair of glasses, and an old watch. He dropped to the floor and looked under the bed. There was a bunch of random stuff shoved underneath the mattress and he started pulling it out. A sleeping bag, a pair of tall rubber boots. . . and then his hand hit something hard.

Jake's pulse seized up as he yanked it free. It was a laptop and it looked like someone had taken a sledgehammer to it. The screen was mangled and half the keyboard had been smashed to bits, but the hard drive was still inside.

"Check it out," Jake said, standing. He set the

computer on the bed as Gaia crossed the room in two long strides.

"Dad!" she shouted, excited.

Tom and Oliver had entered the room in less than a second. Together they all gathered around the laptop, knowing this could be what they were looking for.

"Where did you find this?" Tom asked.

"Under the bed," Jake said. "Look—whoever destroyed this thing wasn't paying much attention— the hard drive is still intact."

"So it is," Oliver said, picking up the computer and inspecting it. "Which means we should be able to extract whatever is on it."

"Good job," Tom said, clapping Jake on the back.

Gaia smiled and Jake felt himself relaxing—grinning even. Suddenly all his fear and shame were washed away, replaced by the pride of accomplishment.

"See?" Gaia said. "You're fine."

"It's a roller-coaster ride, kid," Oliver said with a small smile. "But you'll get used to it."

He thinks I'm good, Jake realized. *He thinks I can do this for real.*

Tom clapped his shoulder again and Jake followed the others out of the room, practically glowing. Oliver was right. Excitement followed by dread, followed by sickening shame, followed by elation and pride. It was a roller coaster. And Jake could definitely get used to the ride.

GAIA AWOKE TO THE SMELL OF frying bacon and was sure she was still dreaming. Breakfast was usually courtesy of Dunkin' Donuts, Krispy Kreme, or, every now and again, McDonald's. She couldn't remember the last time breakfast had actually been made in this apartment. If ever.

Bliss

A city bus squealed to a stop somewhere on the street below and it knocked Gaia out of her groggy state. She sat up, everything suddenly rushing back to her—the storming of Dmitri's. . . no, *Yuri's* apartment in the wee hours of the morning. The argument she'd had with her father over her going to bed (she wanted to stay up, he insisted she get some rest). Gaia whirled around to look at the digital clock. It was 10:07. She flung the covers aside and headed for the kitchen.

"Morning!" Oliver said from the head of the dining room table.

He was sipping a cup of coffee and tapping away at a computer keyboard. Before Gaia had reluctantly hit the hay, he'd linked Yuri's smashed hard drive to Tom's PC to see if he could get something out of it.

"Anything?" Gaia asked, yawning hugely.

"I'm getting there," Oliver replied.

"Gaia! Want eggs?" her father asked, appearing at the window between the living room/dining room and the kitchen. Gaia's stomach grumbled loud enough for him to hear. Oliver and Tom both chuckled.

"I'll take that as a yes," her father said, disappearing again.

Gaia walked over to the doorway to the kitchen, her bare feet slapping against the hardwood floor. She was about to lambaste her father for letting her sleep so long, but when she opened her mouth, nothing came out. Seeing her father, standing there at the stove, pushing eggs around with a spatula, she was suddenly overwhelmed.

This was it. This was the moment she'd been waiting for for over a year. It was a regular Sunday morning. She was still in her pajamas, her father was making breakfast in a pair of jeans and a worn-in sweater. This was normalcy.

"I made them dry, just how you like 'em," her father said, turning around with the frying pan in his hand. He took one look at Gaia and paused. "You okay?"

"I . . ."

She had no idea what to say. Part of her wanted to grab her father and hold on to him, partially to make sure this was really happening and partially to make sure he wouldn't get away again. But that was far too melodramatic. So instead she just stood there, wringing the hem of her oversized T-shirt between her hands.

Gaia's father's face softened. He walked over to her, leaned down, and planted a kiss in the middle of her forehead. Gaia, in that moment, felt bliss.

"I know," he said with a smile. Gaia smiled back. He did know.

"I've got something!" Oliver called from the dining room.

Gaia forgot about breakfast and rushed back to the table. Tom dropped the frying pan back onto the stove and followed. They took position behind Oliver at the computer screen, which was filled with a list of numbers and letters.

"What is it?" Gaia asked.

"It's a list of coordinates, I believe," Oliver said. "Each line seems to have a set of longitude and latitude coordinates embedded into it."

"Cells of the Organization?" Gaia asked, glancing at her father.

"Could be," he replied. "Could be fronts or safe houses. . . "

"Or targets," Oliver said ominously. "We have no way of knowing. And there are hundreds of them. It would be impossible to check all of them out."

Gaia swallowed, a feeling of helplessness settling in over her shoulders. When she'd first heard Oliver's psyched tone, she naively thought he'd figured out exactly where Yuri was, but it could take months to decipher this list—figure out what it meant and whether it was useful.

"So what do we do now?" Gaia asked, looking from her father to Oliver and back again.

Her dad stood up straight and rolled his shoulders back. "I may just have an idea."

TOM STRODE DOWN THE DIMLY LIT

So Close

hallway leading to Natasha's glass-fronted cell, feeling more focused than he had in years. He was close—he could feel it. All he needed was one more piece of the puzzle to fall into place and he would have Yuri. The nightmare would be over, once and for all.

Now he just had to convince Natasha to give him that last piece, to show him how it all came together.

Tom paused in front of the transparent wall and watched Natasha rise from her cot and approach the glass. A line of tiny holes ran across the front, right at mouth level, so conversations could be had through the bulletproof substance. Tom pulled the list of coordinates and other random numbers out of his breast pocket and slapped it up against the glass, the printout facing the prisoner. For a moment, neither of them moved.

"What does it mean?" Tom asked, his glare boring

into Natasha as he pressed the paper into the glass with his palm.

Her eyes moved back and forth quickly over the page in front of her and he could practically see the gears in her brain working. She knew what the gibberish meant, that much was clear. What she was undecided on was what to do with that knowledge.

"What does it mean, Natasha?" Tom repeated. Her eyes flicked to him as if she was surprised by the sudden interruption in her thought process. "Intel is going to figure it out eventually. You may as well tell me now."

We're so close, he thought, trying to keep his expression impassive. *So. . . close.*

Natasha's mouth curled into her trademark smirk. "I will give you no more help," she said. "You have yet to release my daughter."

"That's because the intel you gave us last time didn't get us anywhere. You know how it works, Natasha. You lead us to an arrest and then we make good on the agreement," Tom told her. "You give me this. . . you help me bring in Yuri, and Tatiana goes free."

"How stupid do you think I am, Tom?" Natasha snapped, her eyes flashing. "You can keep us both here for the rest of our lives dangling my daughter's freedom in front of me whenever you want something. No." She turned her back on him and paced away. "I will give you nothing more. You have betrayed my trust."

Tom saw red and it was all he could do to keep from pounding his fists against the glass. *He* had betrayed *her* trust? Who had wheedled her way into his life? Into his *heart*? And then tried to kill his daughter, for God's sake!

"You know what this is, don't you?" Tom said, the paper fluttering slightly in his hand. "You could help me if you wanted to."

Natasha turned her defiant profile to him and he knew he was right. He knew that somewhere in her mind was the information that he needed—the information that would ensure Gaia's safety. And she was denying him.

"I could have helped you," Tom told her through his teeth. He wondered if the human body could actually shake apart from repressed rage. "I could have gotten you both out of here. You've just sealed your own fate. And your daughter's."

Then he turned on his heel and rushed back down the hallway. The MP at the end of the hall unlocked the door for him and Tom strode through. All he could think, over and over, was that he had failed. Natasha was their last hope for tracking down Yuri, but so far he had failed to get her to talk. And time is of the essence.

If anything happened to Gaia now, it was all on him.

SAM WOKE UP LATE SUNDAY MORNING

to the sound of his cell phone singing the theme from *Star Wars*. He pressed his fingertips into his eyes, then fumbled on the floor for the jacket he'd been wearing last night. The number displayed on the screen was unfamiliar and started with an area code he'd never even seen before. Confused and half asleep, he hit the talk button and brought the phone to his ear.

"Yeah?" he said gruffly, falling back into his pillows.

"Sam? It's Dmitri."

Instantly Sam was awake, heart hammering, senses on the alert, sitting up straight in bed. *He's a very dangerous man,* Gaia's voice said in the back of his mind. *Find out where he is.*

"Oh. . . hey," Sam said, because he had to say something. He bunched his sheet up in his lap and clasped it against his chest, praying for the right things to say. He couldn't mess this up. Gaia needed him.

"I had to leave again," Dmitri told him. "Have you been to the apartment?"

"Yeah. . . I was there yesterday," Sam said, his brain working overtime to choose his words carefully. "Is everything okay?"

"Yes, everything is fine, but I need to see you and Gaia," Dmitri told him.

He's a very dangerous man. . . .

But he didn't sound dangerous. He sounded like Dmitri, the kindly old man who had been a victim of Loki's, just like Sam had been.

"Where are you?" Sam blurted. Luckily it was a logical question under the circumstances. If Dmitri wanted to see them he was going to have to tell him where they would meet.

"I can't tell you that right now," Dmitri said. "But I need you to bring Gaia to the art museum in Philadelphia tomorrow afternoon. I will meet you on the steps at exactly two P.M. I'm trusting you to do this, Sam."

"Whoa, whoa, whoa, Dmitri, what the hell is going on?" Sam asked, his courage growing slightly. Anyone would be completely baffled and freaked by this phone call even if he didn't suspect that Dmitri was bad news. "You can't just expect us to go all the way to Philadelphia without giving us a reason."

"It's for your own safety," Dmitri told him calmly. "Sam, we have to trust each other."

Sam took a deep breath against the hammering in his chest. Gaia told him to trust her and now Dmitri was telling him to trust him. There was a point in time recently when Gaia had shown no confidence in him whatsoever—when she'd accused him of trying to kill her and turned her back on him entirely. Meanwhile, Dmitri had never done anything but help him.

173

Sam had a choice to make. Who was it going to be? The girl who had broken his heart and stabbed him in the back, or the man who'd given him a home and money to get back on his feet?

Sam closed his eyes, his stomach clenching. "Okay," he said. "We'll be there."

It is an odd feeling, knowing there is not a soul on Earth you can trust. I thought I knew Tom. I thought that he would make sure that the CIA made good on its promise. They told me that if I talked, they would free my daughter. I talked, yet my daughter is still in prison. Still sequestered from life. Still suffering. I thought I could trust Tom. But then, how can I blame him, after what I have done to him?

I could have told him what those numbers meant. I could have told him exactly where Yuri is. But what is the point? If Tom goes there, he will die. If Gaia goes there, she will be taken. And Yuri will find some way to punish me and possibly Tatiana as well. Yuri is everywhere. He is everything. And betraying him is a grave mistake. I learned that the hard way.

Sooner or later Tom would have deciphered that Yuri was alive. I gave him nothing when I gave him that information. But if Yuri were to find Tom on his doorstep he would know who sent him there and Tatiana and I would pay with our lives.

I have to do what little I can to protect my daughter. My silence is all I have left.

Still, I hope I am wrong. I hope that Tom will find Yuri and bring him to justice. That Tom will prevail. Yuri must pay for what he has done to us. He must pay.

Who knew that donning Kevlar could be so intimate?

nothing to lose

GAIA, JAKE, TOM, AND OLIVER SAT

Choosing Him

around the dining room table on Sunday afternoon, each poring over a separate copy of Yuri's list of coordinates. Maps covered the table. They were marked with red dots in various places, indicating the listed locales. The work was hard and tedious and the longer it went on, the more coiled Gaia became. They were never going to get anywhere this way and they knew it. Just figuring out the locations meant nothing unless someone told them the significance of the list.

The advantage was gone. Yuri was out there somewhere and they were never going to find him.

A sudden rap at the door took them all by surprise. Gaia got up and checked through the peephole. Sam stood on the other side of the door, looking around him like a lamb who'd just been tossed into the lion's den.

"Sam? What's wrong?" Gaia asked, ripping the door open.

"He called me," Sam said, holding out his cell phone like it was an explosive device.

Tom was on his feet in an instant. "Who? Yuri?"

"No. Dmitiri," Sam said, walking into the room and taking in the maps, the endless cups of coffee. . . Jake. And then Oliver. Sam took an instinctive step back and Gaia took an instinctive step closer to him to help him feel safe.

"Dmitri and Yuri are the same guy," Jake said, leaning back in his chair. He rested his muscled arm across the top, nonchalantly showing off his brawn.

"Well, who's Yuri?" Sam asked, ignoring Jake and turning away from Oliver.

"My grandfather. It's a really long story," Gaia began.

"Forget that now. He contacted you?" Tom asked, walking over and taking the cell phone from Sam's trembling fingers.

"Uh. . . yeah. . . it's the last number in there," Sam said, visibly fighting to control his emotions. He stuffed his hands under his arms and pressed his elbows down into his sides. "He wanted me to bring Gaia to meet him. He said two o'clock tomorrow afternoon on the steps at the Philadelphia Museum of Art."

"Philadelphia?" Oliver said, looking over Tom's shoulder as he scrolled to the phone number. Both brothers' faces lit up when they saw the digits displayed there.

"We've got him," Tom said, meeting Oliver's gaze. Gaia's heart took a leap as her uncle looked up at her and smiled. After all this work, after being stonewalled by Natasha, after hours of brainstorming, Sam had just walked in and given them the key.

"How could he be so careless?" Tom asked. "All we

have to do is trace this number through the satellite provider and we have his exact location."

"He wants Gaia and he's getting desperate," Oliver said. "Kidnapping her didn't work so he went to his next best hope."

He looked at Sam as he said this and Sam's face went ashen. Gaia had to get him out of there before he got sick or worse. She opened the door and pulled Sam out into the hallway.

"Are you okay?" she asked him.

"This is all a little weird," Sam admitted with an embarrassed laugh. "Dmitri is your grandfather? What the hell is that about? And why is he so dangerous?"

"Sam, my grandfather is a very bad man," Gaia said, looking into Sam's green eyes and feeling more grateful toward him than she'd ever felt toward anyone. "And you just helped us find him. We're going to get him because of you."

Sam swallowed and looked down at his shoes. "Gaia, I. . . I don't even know what to say. I'm. . . glad I could help?" he added with a shrug.

"I'm going to explain all of this to you, I swear," Gaia said. "But right now I've got to get back in there and help them."

Sam nodded. "Is there anything else I can do?" He sounded almost hopeful that she'd ask for more. But he'd done enough. And now all she wanted was for him to be safe.

"You have no idea how much you've done already," she said. And then, on impulse, she reached up and hugged him, tightening her arms around his neck. Sam held her so close she could feel his heart beating against her chest, matching the quickened pace of her own pulse. When she pulled away and looked into his eyes it was so simple to imagine herself kissing him. Choosing him. Being with him.

But she couldn't. She was moving on. And Sam had to move on, too.

"Thank you," she told him sincerely.

And before he could say anything more, she slipped back into the apartment and closed the door on Sam.

An Actual Girl

GAIA SAT ACROSS FROM JAKE AT THE dining room table early Sunday afternoon, watching him shovel food into his mouth. She couldn't believe how quickly everything had changed. It had taken less than an hour for her father and Oliver to track Yuri's cell phone down to an address in north Philadelphia. Once they'd come up with a game plan, Oliver had run out to the corner deli and bought sandwiches, salads, and fruit to fortify them for the trip. None of them had taken in a normal meal all day and Oliver was of the opinion that they had no chance against Yuri unless they were well fed and focused.

"Enjoying that?" Gaia asked, raising her eyebrows as Jake shoved half a turkey hero into his mouth at once.

"Uh, you're one to talk," he said, eyeing her chest. Gaia looked down to find a big chunk of potato salad stuck to the front of her light blue T-shirt.

Oh, that's attractive, she thought, wiping it up with her finger.

Jake smiled at her, his blue eyes twinkling, and Gaia flushed. Every time she saw Jake, the temperature of whatever room they were in seemed to skyrocket. More and more she found herself blushing around him. And smiling. And wondering what her hair was doing. She found herself acting like `an actual girl`.

"Gaia, you have your battle gear?" Tom asked, walking in from his bedroom.

A girl with battle gear, Gaia reminded herself. Somehow she had a feeling she would never qualify for a femininity award.

"Yeah," she said, wiping her mouth with the back

of her hand. She grabbed her bulletproof vest from the chair next to her and pulled it on and zipped up the sides. She reached over her left shoulder and groped for the nylon strap, but couldn't get it in her grasp.

"I got it," Jake said, rising from his seat. Gaia couldn't help noticing he used an actual napkin to wipe his face. He came up behind Gaia and lifted the strap. Gaia could feel his breath on her neck and tried not to react, but there was nothing she could do to control the omnipresent tingle.

Sam may have made her pulse race earlier that day, but Jake excited something new inside of her—something she felt in every inch of her body, heart and soul. There was no point in denying it anymore. She was falling for him.

"You okay?" Jake asked, as he snapped the strap to her shoulder and tightened it.

Gaia swallowed hard, her throat constricting. Who knew that donning Kevlar could be so intimate?

"Fine," Gaia replied. She went over to the table and picked up the paper plates and bags and soda cans. "You better get ready."

Her arms full, Gaia kicked open the kitchen door and dumped everything into the trash. She paused in front of the sink to catch her breath and get her pounding heart under control. Through the kitchen window she could see Oliver, Jake, and her father talking in low tones, going over the game plan as Jake secured his protective gear.

Aside from the vibe of attraction constantly sizzling between her and Jake, there was also an air of determination in the room that affected everyone, not least of all Gaia. This was it. By the end of the day today, it would all be over. She would be free.

Life as she knew it was about to change. For the better. For good.

Gaia took a deep breath and Jake tore his attention away from the elder men, looking over at her. Their eyes met and Gaia froze. As if in slow motion, Jake's eyes softened and he smiled a slight, private smile. It turned Gaia's insides to goo and she had the sudden, almost overwhelming desire to rush right out there, grab him, and kiss him.

Jake's smile widened as if he knew what she was thinking, and Gaia forced herself to look away, `closing the little shutters over the opening`. She turned around and leaned back against the sink, her hands braced against the counter, her elbows behind her.

Gaia did want to kiss him. More than anything. And she would. Later. After it was over. When they were both safe and sound and victorious.

She would kiss Jake Montone as soon as she had nothing to lose.

"IF ANYTHING GOES WRONG AND

Grandpa

you can't speak into your handheld, just press this button," Gaia's father explained, holding up his tiny walkie-talkie. "You press this button on the side and the rest of us will be able to track you anywhere within a ten-mile radius."

Gaia nodded her understanding. Every order, every instruction her father had given that afternoon had been repeated in layman's terms again and again as if he thought he were speaking to a group of kindergartners. She knew he just wanted them to be prepared, but enough was enough. Gaia was more than ready to go.

She looked out past the bushes that concealed her, Jake, Oliver, and Tom, gazing across the wide lawn at the mansion hulking against the twilit sky. At least a quarter mile of open green grass separated the little team from the target. If Yuri had any guards stationed outside, which was an obvious no-brainer, they would spot Gaia and the others before they made it five feet from the brush.

She considered mentioning this, but she was sure her father, Oliver and Jake were all well aware of the situation. Unfortunately, there was nothing they could do about it. This was the best route onto the grounds unless they wanted to walk en masse up the driveway out front.

"Remember, we want to head for the basement. If he's got a panic room, that's where it'll be," Tom added.

Come on. Enough instruction, Gaia thought, her leg jittering beneath her. *Let's get this over with already.*

"This Yuri guy sure knows how to live," Jake said, scanning the back of the huge house.

"That's all about to change," Tom told him. "Okay, Jake and Oliver take the west side, Gaia and I will go east."

Everyone nodded and a thrill of excitement rushed through Gaia. This was it. If they succeeded here today, life as she knew it was over. How totally cool.

"Move out," Tom said.

Gaia cast Jake what she hoped was an encouraging look before following her father through the woods toward the right side of the house. Every twig and leaf that crunched beneath their feet sounded loud enough to wake the dead. Gaia kept one eye trained on the house, but there was no sign of life. So far, so good.

Her father suddenly paused beside a huge oak and pressed himself back against the trunk. He motioned to Gaia to stay down, but over the top of the brush Gaia could see what had stopped him. A single gun-toting guard moved from around the side of the house to the back, patrolling along the perimeter.

"That's not too obvious," Gaia said sarcastically.

"He has his back turned," her father said flatly. "Stay low."

He rushed out of the bushes, legs bent, back down, moving quickly across the lawn. Gaia followed him, wondering if he was scared, if he was worried that they might not pull this off. It was one rare moment in her life that she was actually grateful she was a freak who couldn't feel fear. Yuri seemed like the type of character who could inspire terror in anyone. It was still so hard to imagine Dmitri as a psychopath.

They made it to the wall with no incident and sat back against it, taking shallow breaths. Gaia trained her ears toward the other side of the house, listening for anything out of the ordinary, but was met with silence. Wherever Jake and Oliver were, they were okay. So far.

"I'll check the window," Gaia's father told her. He stood up and ran a circuitry detector along the bottom of the window above Gaia's head. The green light blinked rapidly and Tom attached it to the glass. He pressed a button, then crouched down again.

"What's that do?" Gaia asked.

There was a sizzle and a pop from above them and her father stood up and opened the window. No alarm.

"It shorts out all the wiring in the vicinity," he explained, motioning for her to climb inside. "Let's go."

Impressed, Gaia swung her leg over the window and lowered herself into a vacant room. No furniture, no artwork, no light fixtures. Everything was still.

"Looks like we picked the right room," Gaia whispered when her father appeared beside her.

He nodded tersely and headed for the door. Gaia pressed her lips together and told herself to remember why they were here. Her father had a reason for being all business. This was a huge mission and if he wanted her to keep her mouth shut—as he seemed to be telling her by his own example—she would do just that.

Her father checked outside the door, then motioned to her to follow. They speed-walked along the wall down a long corridor that appeared to open up onto a large room. The hallway split at one point, but her father stayed the course—heading for the front of the house. Suddenly Gaia heard male voices up ahead and she and her father both froze. He looked around the corner and pulled his head back.

"Two guards, playing poker," he whispered to her. "Stay here."

Gaia resisted the urge to protest. Why was she always staying behind him, staying low, staying back? Didn't he trust her to hold her own—to help more?

Her dad stepped out of the hallway, dart gun drawn, and fired. There was a commotion and a gun went off. Gaia's father ducked back into the hallway and a piece of the wall across from them exploded.

"There are two more," he told Gaia as the shots and shouts intensified. "They walked in from the other room." He reloaded his dart gun and looked her in the eye. "I'm gonna hold them here. You go back to that fork in the hallway and see if you can find a way to the basement."

Gaia's heart thumped as he jumped into the fray again and fired a few more shots from his dart gun.

"Why are you still here?" he hissed when he ducked back again.

"I'm not leaving you here with three guards," she told him, pulling out her own dart gun.

"Yes you are." He grabbed her arm and nudged her back in the direction they'd come from. "Go!"

Gaia hesitated.

"We're here for Yuri, Gaia," he said fiercely. "I know you can take him. I'll be right behind you."

That was all she needed to hear. Gaia drew herself up straight and ran double time back down the hallway, buoyed by her father's confidence. Every door along the new hall led to another unused salon or bedroom, but at the very end of the hall, Gaia found a reinforced steel door—quite unlike the standard wood doors she'd already tried.

This looks promising, she thought.

She turned the knob, but it was locked. Gaia had a

loaded gun in an ankle holster, but she had been instructed not to use it unless absolutely necessary. Besides, she didn't want to draw attention to herself by blasting the lock to smithereens. Instead she crouched to the floor and pulled out a lock-picking pin and fork from her utility belt. She hadn't practiced this particular skill since she was in grade school and Loki had secretly trained her behind her parents' backs, but even then she was an expert.

Gaia inserted the tools into the lock, trying not to pay attention to the continued gunshots in another area of the house. She had to focus. Her father would be with her any minute.

Suddenly the mechanism inside the doorknob clicked and Gaia's pulse jumped. "Like riding a bike," she whispered.

She tried the knob and held her breath as it turned. Standing, Gaia opened the door ever so slowly, waiting for more gunfire, an order to stand down—something. But the door swung open and Gaia stood there, looking down a darkened set of stairs.

Bingo, she thought, replacing her tools in her belt. She drew out the dart gun again and started down the steps, walking as lightly as humanly possible. The stairs grew narrower toward the bottom and ended at a wall. The only direction Gaia could go was left. She pressed herself back against the wall and checked around the corner.

190

One guard stood before another metal door at the base of another set of stairs coming in from the right. He spoke rapidly into a wrist mike while more voices crackled through the speaker in his ear, so loud Gaia could hear the distortion all the way down the hall.

"I need a guard at the back door!" the man said into his mike. "Someone secure the back basement door."

At that moment, he looked up and saw Gaia emerging from the stairs.

"Too late," she said with a shrug. Before he could even pull his gun out, she had flattened him with a dart to the chest. Then Gaia raced down the hallway, her adrenaline pumping at a fierce rate.

This door was secured with an electric keypad lock. There was a keycard slot down the side. Gaia crouched to the ground and flipped the comatose guard over. She searched his pockets and found a card with a metallic strip attached by a metal wire to his belt. She yanked as hard as she could and the wire snapped.

"Let this work," Gaia said under her breath.

She checked over her shoulder for her father or for the guard her downed-man had ordered, but saw nothing. Pulling her gun out for good measure, Gaia stood and slipped the card through the lock box. The red light on the side turned green and a loud clang emitted from the doorway.

Gaia stepped back, held her gun up with both hands, and kicked the door with all her might. It flew open, slamming back against the wall, and Gaia trained her gun straight ahead.

"Don't move!" a voice shouted.

Yuri stood on the other side of a richly decorated room near yet another, even thicker, door. He had a gun trained on Gaia's head. His eyes widened ever so slightly when he saw her.

"I said, don't move!" he told her again.

"You're not going to shoot me," Gaia said.

She reached back with her foot and slammed the door behind her. Any of the guards would have key-cards as well, but the closed door would buy her a few extra seconds if they did come.

"What makes you think that?" Yuri asked as she sidestepped into the room, her gun pointed right at his face. He followed her with his own weapon, circling around a leather couch to stay across from her.

"Because, I'm your only hope now, right? I'm supposed to be groomed to succeed you, aren't I, *Yuri*?" She paused and ground her teeth together. "Or should I call you Grandpa?" she asked with a sneer.

"Do you think I'm going to let *you* kill *me*?" he asked.

"Not planning on it," Gaia said. "I'd rather see you rot in a federal prison for the rest of your life."

Yuri chuckled. He ran one hand along his freshly

shaven jaw line and smiled at her. "You can't turn me in," he told her. "I have video of you stealing files from a CIA office. If I go down, granddaughter, so do you."

Granddaughter. Somehow, the word lost its warm and fuzzy feel when spoken by a man pointing a deadly weapon at her face.

Gaia felt sick, but she didn't let it show. He may have been her grandfather, but he was clearly still the enemy.

"Are you actually trying to *threaten* me?" she asked, her elbows locked. "I thought you were supposed to be some kind of sociopathic genius, but you're just another idiot if you think that that matters to me."

Yuri continued to smile, his eyes glittering. "Careful, now. My sociopathic idiot blood is running through your veins."

Gaia swallowed back the bile that instantly appeared in her throat. She didn't have an answer for that.

"Just think about it, Gaia," Yuri said, seeing an opening. "If you join me I can help you reach your full potential in a way your father never can. He's holding you back. He doesn't want you to know what you're capable of, but I do. Gaia, I want the world for you. . . ."

He lowered his gun and started to pace at a safe distance, relaxing as he talked. Gaia followed him with her gun by her arms, which were starting to shake, by her vision, beginning to blur with tears. Frustrated that he seemed so calm. He didn't think she would shoot him. He didn't think she had it in her.

"It's what your mother would have wanted, Gaia," he said, pausing and turning to look into her eyes. "I'm your grandfather. Don't you think Katia would have wanted us to be together?"

"She hated you," Gaia spat, one tear brimming over. "She fled her country because of you. If she were here right now, she'd tell me to kill you."

Yuri paled slightly and in that moment Gaia felt truly murderous for the first time in her life. She had never killed anyone in cold blood. She'd never even punched someone who hadn't attacked her first. But right then, she knew she could do it. She could take this evil bastard out right then and probably even feel good about it. No guilt. No remorse.

But he is your grandfather, a little voice in Gaia's mind told her. *He could tell you things about yourself. . . your history. Things you may otherwise never know.*

Gaia was too close to this. She had to get control of herself. Hand trembling, she reached down to her belt and hit the button on the side of her mini-walkie-talkie.

"What are you doing?" Yuri asked, brandishing his weapon again and taking a few steps toward her.

Gaia fired a warning shot over his shoulder, taking out a few books on a shelf behind him. Yuri froze.

"I missed on purpose," she told him. "Move again and you're worm food."

Yuri swallowed hard and eyed her gun. Gaia only hoped someone would come and relieve her before she used it again.

TOM STALKED ALONG THE PERIMETER

Time to Die

of the house, doubling back to the window he and Gaia had come through the first time. During the firefight he'd managed to subdue four guards, but the chaos had taken him outside. He needed to retrace his steps so he could find the hallway he'd sent Gaia through.

How could I have let her go alone? Tom berated himself, struggling to catch his breath, racing more from nerves than exertion. *Yes, she's capable, but she's your daughter, idiot.*

Suddenly the red light on his GPS receiver started to blink and Tom whipped it free from his belt. Gaia had hit her panic button, but the information on the digital tracking screen couldn't have been right. According to the dots on the display that represented his location and Gaia's, she was right on top of him.

Or beneath *me,* Tom realized, his heart seizing up.

He looked down and spotted a long, low window near his feet. Tom dropped to the ground and peered through the glass. There, just below him, was Yuri himself. And he was pointing a gun at Gaia's face.

Tom's paternal instinct didn't even register the fact that Gaia also had a weapon trained on Yuri. All he knew was that he had to get in there and help her. He had to get in there now.

Flipping over onto his back, Tom turned around so that his feet were facing the glass. He said a quick prayer, pulled his legs back, and thrust them forward, shattering the glass. A cacophony of alarms sounded out across the grounds. Tom squirmed through the window, landed hard on his feet, and tumbled right into Yuri, taking him down in a pile of limbs.

Yuri's knee came down on Tom's forearm and he heard the snap before he felt the intense shot of pain. He shouted out, a primal growl, and struggled to free himself, but it was no use. Yuri may have been old, but he was still powerful. Without his right arm, Tom couldn't win.

"Get off him!" Gaia shouted with all of her energy.

"Gaia, don't!" Tom shouted, knowing that if she joined the scrum she would be disarmed.

Suddenly he felt an arm around his neck and was hauled to his feet. Just then the door behind Gaia burst open and Jake and Oliver rushed in, guns at the ready. They flanked Gaia and all three watched in grim surprise as Yuri grasped Tom to him and pressed the barrel of his gun to Tom's temple.

"Dad!" Gaia shouted helplessly, her gun still drawn.

Tom tried to speak, but Yuri's grip choked him.

"I want all of you to see this," Yuri said.

From the corner of his eye, Tom could see that Yuri held something in his right hand—the hand that was free while his forearm pressed into Tom's larynx. It looked like some kind of remote control, but Tom couldn't be sure.

"Tom and I are going to be leaving here together and if any one of you tries to stop us I will shoot him, then blow this entire place."

Gaia's gaze flicked to Tom. He knew his own eyes were filled with fear and he wished for a moment that he had Gaia's power—that he could show his daughter a pair of clear, undisturbed eyes—but he couldn't. He didn't care about himself, but he didn't want her to die. And it seemed like Yuri was more than willing to make that happen.

This is it, Tom thought, looking at his brother with grim resignation. Looking at the three guns pointed at himself and his captor. *It's time for me to die. And either Jake, Oliver, or Gaia is going to have to kill me.*

I realized something about myself today. I realized that I love Gaia Moore. Not just love her like, "Oh, yeah, love you, too." But I love her with every ounce of my soul. I love her more than I've ever loved anyone before. In fact, I don't think I ever *have* loved anyone before, because this feels totally different than what I had with Heather last year or with Anna back in high school. This feels real. This feels more than real. It feels. . . transcendent.

There's nothing I won't do for her. That's what brought this realization home. If I can choose her over a man who has been nothing but a friend to me. If I can put her safety before my own. If I can stand in the very same room with the person who snatched me away from my life, my family, my friends for months and not go insane. If I can do all of that for her, then it must be love.

I told her that I'll meet with

SAM

her uncle and I will. I'll do that and anything else she asks of me. Anything to prove my love to her. Because she loves me, too. I can see it in her eyes. This Jake guy seems like he's in right now. Like he's involved in whatever's going on with Dmitri or Yuri or whoever the hell he is. But that doesn't matter. Jake is too new. Too green. He can't possibly know Gaia as well as I do. Gaia and I have a history—a whole heart-wrenching, mutual lust and longing kind of history. And that doesn't just go away because some mojo-having tool enters the picture.

No. Gaia loves me. It may be buried. It may be confused with something else. It may be a while before she realizes it. But Gaia Moore is mine. We were meant to be together. We're soul mates.

And sooner or later she's going to realize it, too.

She'd done plenty of stupid things in her **peaceful** life, but now **silence** was not the time to add to the idiocy list.

The Idiocy List

"KILL HIM!" TOM GROWLED, HIS throat constricting in pain, his voice sounding like something otherworldly. "Open fire! Kill the bastard!"

Gaia gripped her gun with all her might, feeling as if it was the only thing in the room over which she had any control. The touch of the cool steel against her hand grounded her—helped her focus. She knew what her father was really saying. He wanted them to take them both out—Yuri *and* her father if necessary—just to take Yuri down.

Sorry, Dad. Not gonna happen, Gaia thought, staring into his eyes. She wasn't about to lose her father now. Not when they were so close to being a family again. Not when they were close enough to taste their own freedom.

"I know you won't do anything stupid, granddaughter," Yuri said, his glare boring into her skull as if he could read her thoughts.

Well then, you obviously don't know me that well, Gaia thought. She'd done plenty of stupid things in her life, but now was not the time to add to the idiocy list.

Gaia assessed the situation before her, the seconds dragging away like hours. As far as she could tell, she had one option. It wasn't a clear shot, but if her aim was true, it would work.

She looked at Oliver. *I'm making my move,* she thought, hoping she somehow conveyed that message in her face. Then she gave Jake the same look, lifting her chin ever so slightly to tell him where to go. If Oliver dove right he should be able to take cover behind the leather couch. If Jake dove left, he could duck and roll behind a wooden credenza. It wouldn't give him much protection, but it was something.

Jake narrowed his eyes slightly and Gaia knew he understood her.

She turned her head, closed one eye, and took aim. The last thing she saw before the bullet left the chamber was Yuri's mouth opening in surprise.

Jake and Oliver leapt for cover as the bullet grazed the shoulder of Tom's already maimed arm and embedded directly into Yuri's. Both men tumbled backward and the detonator flew from Yuri's grasp, skittering across the floor and coming to rest right in front of the sofa behind which Oliver now crouched.

Yuri fired into the air as he fell, but his ammo hit nothing but wall, ceiling, and bookcase. Tom gained his balance and dug his knee into Yuri's shattered shoulder. A gut-wrenching cry ripped through the room, but Tom didn't hesitate. He grabbed Yuri's gun with his left hand and stood, his broken right arm held protectively against his chest, blood oozing from the wound on his shoulder.

Gaia stepped up next to her father and pointed her own gun down at Yuri as well. Jake soon joined them. Oliver dismantled the detonator, then trained a fourth weapon on their mark.

Broken and defeated, Yuri lay on his back on the floor, sirens screaming through the night. Gaia saw him glance toward the door where three guards now lay, sleeping soundly.

There's no one left to save you, Gaia thought, gazing at him coldly. He seemed to realize this at the same moment, closed his eyes, and laid his head back on the floor.

"It's over," Gaia's father said.

Gaia looked at him and smiled. "It's over."

GAIA AND JAKE WALKED DOWN THE

Sweet Relief winding driveway behind Oliver and Yuri, who shuffled along, his feet and hands shackled. Small electric lights lined the drive, casting a soft glow over the area. The rumble of an engine split the air and all four of them paused as a pair of headlights swung into view. A moment later, the black van Oliver had procured for their road trip came around a bend in the driveway.

Tom was in the driver's seat, one hand on the wheel, the other taped against him in a makeshift sling.

The brakes squeaked as he brought the van to a stop a few yards ahead of them. Tom got out of the car and went about helping Oliver lift Yuri into the back of the van. The moment all three men disappeared behind the vehicle, Gaia felt a thrill run through her.

This was it. This was her moment.

She looked at Jake. He gazed back at her. About a thousand crickets chirped in the darkness around them, but aside from their song and the quietly idling engine, there was nothing but peace. Peaceful silence outside. Peaceful silence in Gaia's heart.

It was over. And that morning she had made herself a promise. If they came through this alive and well, there was something she was going to do.

Gaia took a step closer to Jake and she saw the question in his eyes just before she wrapped her hand around his neck, pulled him to her, and kissed him like she'd never kissed anybody before. There was no hesitation. No uncertainty. No concern for what he thought, what anyone else would think. Gaia knew what she wanted and for once in her screwed-up life, she felt free to take it.

Jake wrapped his arms around her back and lifted her until she was standing on her toes. He had a confident, strong kiss. Not sloppy or overeager or unsure.

His touch sent chills up and down Gaia's back and through her heart. It cleared her mind of everything except him. His lips on hers, his fingers in her hair, his arms clutching her to him.

It was more than perfect. It was surreal. And when they heard the van doors slam, they pulled their faces away from each other, but never let go completely. Gaia looked up into Jake's clear blue eyes as her mind slowly started to function again. Jake closed his eyes and touched his forehead to hers, letting out a sigh that sounded like sweet relief.

This is where it all begins, Gaia thought, a fluttering of happiness tickling her heart. *Out with the old life, in with the new.*

TOM TOOK HIS SEAT AT THE GLEAMING

Taking Lumps

black table in the debriefing room, as if he were about to face a firing squad. His sore arm throbbed within its cast for the first time all morning as if it sympathized with his plight. There had been no doubt in Tom's mind when he'd taken off to find Yuri on his own that he would meet with dissent upon his return. But he had hoped that the success of his mission—the fact that he'd just turned over one of the world's most wanted criminals—would deflect the ire of his superiors somewhat. From the level of tension in the room, however, it appeared that this was not the case.

Director Vance sat directly across from Tom, flanked by Agent Frenz and Agent Jack Freelander from Internal Affairs. Their expressions were grim except for Agent Frenz, who seemed to be smirking without moving one muscle in his face.

"Well, Agent Moore, what have you got to say for yourself?" Director Vance said, lacing his fingers together on the table, his shoulders hunched forward. Even with bad posture the man was intimidating.

"You're welcome?" Tom asked archly.

Freelander laughed but quickly covered his mouth with his fist and disguised it as a cough. With his good arm, Tom nonchalantly reached for the clear pitcher of water on the table and poured out a glass for the man, then slid it across the table toward him.

"I'd advise you that being flip will get you nowhere," Vance said. "I believe I told you not to go off on your own."

Tom sighed. If Vance had really wanted to prevent Tom from his mission, he could have stopped him. He could have had him detained at the door for disobeying a direct order. But the fact was that Vance had always known Tom was their best shot for bringing down Yuri. He had let the whole Philadelphia mission happen by not doing enough to stop Tom. That meant they had both gone against procedure. Unfortunately, it wouldn't look like that to any IA committee because Vance had covered his ass by ordering Tom to lay off.

Tom had brought down a highly dangerous international terrorist and he was going to get no credit. Instead he was going to be reprimanded. He knew this and had accepted it, but that didn't mean he was going to just sit here and take his lumps quietly.

"Am I suspended or not?" Tom asked, leaning back in his chair. His shoulder twinged and he managed, somehow, not to wince.

Vance took a deep breath and looked at Freelander. The smaller man took a sip of his water and placed the glass down on the table.

"Under normal circumstances a suspension would be in order, but these are not normal circumstances," he said. "The internal affairs committee has reviewed your reports and the statements of several agents and has determined that it would be against this country's interests to deactivate you at this juncture."

Tom held his breath, uncertain if he should allow himself to believe what he'd just heard.

"What?" Frenz blurted, leaning forward to see Freelander past Vance's sizable frame. "How is he not suspended?"

"Agent Frenz," Vance snapped, holding up a hand. Frenz sat back in his seat, petulant. Tom tried not to smile. "Agent Moore, you will be taking the rest of the week off, however, and this time I will not be calling you to come back in. I suggest you take these few days to relax, spend some time with your daughter, and not do anything stupid."

"You can count on it, sir," Tom said, letting the grin break through.

He stood slowly as Frenz and Freelander exited the room. He flinched in surprise when Vance extended his arm across the table. There was a split second of hesitation before Tom lifted his left hand and shook with his superior.

"Good work, Moore," Vance said.

"Thank you, sir," Tom replied.

Vance pulled his hand back and straightened his suit jacket. "I never said that," he warned.

"Of course not, sir."

"We'll see you next week," Vance told him, holding the door open for Tom.

"Yes you will," Tom replied. As he slid by Vance, turning sideways instinctively to protect his broken arm, Tom lifted his chin. In the end, the meeting had gone better than he'd imagined. And now he had a few days off to do with them what he wanted. He didn't even have to think twice to know what that was.

"*Spend some time with your daughter,*" he thought, recalling Vance's words as he headed for the nearest exit. *I like the sound of that.*

WHAT THE HELL AM I DOING HERE?

Repentance

Sam wondered, pressing his back up against the armrest on the wooden bench in Prospect Park as he watched Oliver approach. The moment Sam laid eyes on the man his throat filled with bile and his veins with hatred and fear. He had chosen the park because it was a public place—always crowded on spring days like this one with joggers and stroller-pushing mothers and cops on horseback. But even with the dozens of people milling around within a hundred-yard radius, Sam suddenly felt alone. Utterly alone—just like he had for those months he'd spent in this bastard's excuse for a prison.

"Sam," Oliver said, stopping next to the bench. He wore a new-looking black trench coat over gray pants and a white shirt. His expression was unreadable, his eyes soft.

God, I hope he doesn't try to squeeze out a few tears, Sam thought, fighting against the sickness in his throat. *Why did I ever say I would do this?*

"Gaia and I are both grateful that you agreed to meet me."

Right. Because of Gaia.

"Let's get this over with," Sam told him, gratefully spotting a uniformed police officer at the far end of the winding path their bench fronted. "Say what you've got to say."

Oliver tucked his coat under himself and sat down next to Sam. If there were any way to move farther away from the psycho, Sam would have. But as it was, he was trapped. All he could do was hope that the apology, or whatever this was, would be short and sweet.

Unfortunately, the silence started to drag. Oliver reached into his pocket and pulled out a large coin— one of those old, rare, fifty-cent pieces—and started to roll it over, end over end, on top of his fingers. Sam stared at the movement of the coin, mesmerized by the agility it took to control it. Then the man's leg started to bounce up and down and Sam snapped out of his momentary trance.

"Look, if you've got nothing to say," he said, starting to get up.

"Sit down!" Oliver snapped, his voice harsh.

A cold, blasting chill shot through Sam. Against his better judgment he fell back onto the bench—mostly because his leg muscles ceased to work the moment the man exploded. That was not the voice of a repentant man. It wasn't even the voice of a man who wanted to *fake* repentance.

Sam swallowed hard. He watched the coin spin faster and faster. Watched the leg twitch spasmodically. From the corner of his eye, he kept a close watch on the cop's position.

"Oliver," he said quietly. "I've. . . never seen anyone do that with a coin before."

Instantly, the coin stopped. It fell flat on top of Oliver's fingers. The man looked down at it as if he'd never seen it before. The leg stopped moving. Oliver's brows knit together. He pocketed the coin and looked up at Sam.

"I hadn't even realized I was doing that," he said apologetically. "Nervous habit, I suppose."

Sam nodded, attempting to keep the shivers that were coursing through him like waves at bay. There was something frightening going on here. He hated to admit it, even to himself, but this man did not seem to be the person Gaia thought he was.

"I've asked you here today to tell you that I am deeply sorry for everything I've done," Oliver said, looking Sam in the eye. "To you, to Gaia, to everyone who had the misfortune of coming into contact with—"

Don't say it. Don't say it, Sam told himself. But he had to. He had to find out if he was right.

"With Loki," he finished.

Immediately, the coin came out again. The flipping resumed. The leg began to twitch. Oliver, Loki, whoever the hell he was, stared out across the park toward the nearby woods, his eyes narrowing into slits.

It's him, Sam thought, the fear like knives to his skull and heart. *He's back. He's coming back.*

"I've got to go," Sam said, standing quickly this time.

"Where, Sam?" the man asked, his voice entirely

different than it had been moments before. He sounded amused—venomously amused. "Where do you think you're going?"

But this time, Sam wasn't stupid enough to pause. He took off in the direction of the police officer even though his apartment was on the opposite end of the park. His instinct was to be as close to as much protection as humanly possible, just in case.

Nothing happened, however. Loki didn't chase him. He didn't try to gun him down. He just let Sam go, his pulse racing the whole way. As soon as Sam reached the edge of the park and acknowledged his good fortune in still being alive, he turned his steps toward the subway, checking over his shoulder every few seconds until he could have given himself whiplash.

I have to warn Gaia, he thought, his pace quickening. *I have to warn her that Loki is back.*

"OLIVER KICKS ASS. I MEAN, literally. That man is the Terminator," Jake said, putting his feet up on the just-delivered wooden coffee table at Gaia's apartment. "You should have seen

Possibilities

how quick he took down those two guys at Yuri's. I hope I'm still that good when I'm old."

"Jake?" Gaia said.

"Yeah?" he asked, crooking his arms behind his head as he leaned back.

"You're doing it again. The rambling thing," Gaia told him.

"Sorry. Won't happen again," Jake joked.

As Gaia scooched down into the couch until she was almost at eye level with her feet up next to Jake's, he leaned over and planted a kiss right on her mouth. Gaia's heart did a few million somersaults. Jake slumped back next to her, smiling. If Gaia wasn't so happy she knew the both of them would have been making her sick right now.

"Are we going to watch this movie or what?" Jake asked.

Gaia grabbed the remote and started the DVD player. She'd only agreed to watch Jake's favorite movie, *The Fast and the Furious,* when he'd told her she could crack as many jokes as she wished during the viewing. But even though the choice of film was less than optimal, Gaia couldn't help smiling as the credits started to roll.

This was so normal, vegging on the couch watching a movie on a Tuesday afternoon after school. When, exactly, was she going to wake up from this?

There was a knock on the door and Gaia and Jake exchanged a look.

"Gaia, it's Sam."

Jake rolled his eyes and Gaia jumped up from the couch. She knew that Sam and Oliver were supposed to meet this afternoon and she'd fully expected a rundown phone call from one or both of them later this evening, but a drop-by was a surprise. Gaia glanced through the open kitchen door as she passed it, checking out the microwave clock. It was only 4:45 and they were supposed to be meeting at four. How had Sam gotten here so fast?

"Hey," she said, opening the door. "What's up?"

The two-word question was barely out of her mouth when Sam had passed right by her and into the living room. Gaia let the door slam and followed. Jake pushed himself off the couch and faced Sam as he entered the room.

Great. Just what I needed to puncture the mood, Gaia thought. *A little more macho posturing.*

Jake picked up the remote and paused the already noisy movie. For a moment, Gaia stood behind Sam, uncertain of how to proceed, feeling guilty over inter-rupting a private moment with another guy. But then she reminded herself that however her heart felt at this moment she'd already made a decision to start over. With Jake. And there was no reason to hide that.

It was her life. Her decision.

She walked around the L-shaped extension of the

couch and joined Jake on the other side, standing next to him.

"You guys remember each other, right?" she said, the words coming out in a speedy jumble.

"Sam, right?" Jake said, crossing his arms over his chest.

"And you're Jake," Sam said. His gaze only rested on the other guy for a second before flicking to Gaia. "Can I talk to you alone?"

Gaia could see that Sam was scared. She gave Jake a guilt-filled glance, then led Sam down the hall toward her room. She paused just outside the door and looked Sam in the eye.

"What happened?" she asked in a whisper.

"Loki is reemerging," Sam told her quietly, his eyes darting toward the living room.

Gaia scoffed. "Not possible."

"Gaia, you know I wouldn't lie to you about this," Sam implored, sounding desperate. "We were sitting in Prospect Park and he kept zoning out. And whenever he did he started twitching and. . . and he was playing with this coin, all methodical. . . you know? It was scary."

Gaia felt as if she'd just swallowed something too hot too fast. But she shook it off. This was not possible. Oliver was Oliver now. But Sam's green eyes were pleading with her, begging her to believe him—maybe even to help him. And why not? He was terrified of being imprisoned again. Or worse.

Suddenly Gaia knew that she'd done the wrong

215

thing when she'd sent Sam to meet with Oliver. It was all there again—right on the surface—the hopeless hours, the beatings, the agony of being caged up like a worthless animal. Sam looked tortured again. She felt it within her own heart.

"Sam. . . I. . . I'm so sorry," Gaia said. "I shouldn't have made you go."

"It doesn't matter," Sam told her. He reached for her hands and held them both in hers. Gaia resisted the urge to look toward the living room. What would Jake think if he saw this? "It doesn't matter," Sam repeated. "I just wanted to warn you. Loki's back. You have to do something. You have to protect yourself."

The sincerity behind his concern touched Gaia, but she knew it was unfounded. She was safe now. They all were. Sam had to get used to it as she had.

"Sam, it's going to be okay," Gaia said. "Nothing's going to happen to you."

Sam took a deep breath and looked at the floor. "You don't believe me, do you?"

"I. . . can't," Gaia said.

"Fine," Sam said, nodding. He pressed his lips together and lifted his eyes to meet hers. "Just be careful."

Then he reached out and touched her cheek, his palm cupping her face. Gaia's skin tingled with warmth. Seconds later he was gone, walking off down the hall. She waited until she heard the front door close before rejoining Jake in the living room.

"What was that all about?" Jake asked flatly.

"Nothing," Gaia told him. "He just wanted to make sure I was okay."

"Isn't that my job now?" Jake asked, point-blank. No double-talk. No games.

"It's always kind of been *my* job," Gaia told him.

Jake cracked a smile, reached out, and grabbed her hand. He pulled her down onto the couch and into his side.

"Well, now you have an assistant," he said, laying his arm on top of hers.

Jake's attitude toward Sam was comforting. He wasn't going to walk out on her for having a past that kept rearing its dramatic head. Jake Montone could take it.

"So, are we going to watch this movie or what? I hate late fees." He picked up the remote again. Gaia sighed and allowed her cheek to lean into his chest. As ridiculously tricked-out cars screeched across the screen, she told herself to forget about Sam. He'd readjust. He'd be okay. And so would she. They would all be just fine.

It was time to stop dwelling on other people's feelings. It was time to stop thinking about what might happen tomorrow or next week or next month. For the first time she could remember, life and all its possibilities were open to her.

Gaia Moore was ready to start living.

        Things I have:
A father
An uncle
A maybe boyfriend
A home
A future

        Things I don't have:
Fear
A grandfather (at least not one
I will ever acknowledge)
Psychos tracking my every move
Uncertainty

For once the scales have
tipped in my favor. And life is
good.
Life
Is
Good.

Read an excerpt from the
latest book in the hot
new series

SAMURAI GIRL

BOOK FOUR

THE
BOOK
OF THE
WIND

$$\boxed{1}$$

The flames surrounded us.

I shivered inside my coat and watched as my house—well, the house I'd been living in for the past month or so—spat and hissed in a mountain of fire and smoke. Fire engines rushed to the scene. Eight men tumbled out of the truck and started rolling the hose toward a fire hydrant.

"Everyone get back!" one of them yelled.

Hiro pulled on my arm. "We have to move back, Heaven," he said.

I felt cemented to the ground. Cheryl, my housemate, was trapped inside.

Who set this fire?

Marcus?

I had left him back at the subway station. Cheryl had come home by herself in a cab. The driver had promised to walk her to the door. Hiro and I were only minutes behind her in another cab.

Meaning . . . if I hadn't gone back to the club to get my bag . . . I would've been inside the house, too. The heat started to affect my skin. The smoke began to burn my eyes. I felt light-headed and woozy. My whole body ached.

"Come on," Hiro said again. "We've got to get out of here."

I stared up at my bedroom window and thought, fleetingly, of my sad assortment of personal belongings trapped inside. The jeans and sneakers I bought when I first got to L.A. My crumpled-up photograph of my brother, Ohiko, which I carried with me in my shiro-maku wedding kimono. Various clothes belonging to Hiro. I didn't have much—I hadn't saved enough money yet to really have many material possessions. But still, everything that was mine since I'd come to L.A. was turning to ash and fluttering away.

My eyes filled with tears.

"Heaven, we've got to move," Hiro said, tugging on my arm. "Come on."

A large piece of the roof cracked and fell mere inches from us. Hiro jumped back, but I stood and stared. The flames leapt and danced.

"You're acting foolish!" Hiro said, pulling on my sleeve.

"Wait," I said softly. I saw my little bedroom window, behind the branches of the big cedar tree. Flames danced around the window frame. Was it possible that maybe Cheryl hadn't come home? Perhaps she'd gone somewhere else . . . like to the diner or maybe to the hospital to get her ankle looked at. . . .

Hiro dragged me under a tree. "You're pale," he said, moving his face close to mine. "Come on. We have to get a cab and get out of this neighborhood." He pulled at me. "Heaven . . . you've been so strong so far."

It was true—I *had* been completely strong up until this moment. I had just defended Cheryl from Marcus, who was more terrifying than I'd ever imagined. I'd narrowly avoided death, meeting a subway car head-on. Marcus had dragged Cheryl away from the club knowing I'd follow them. He *knew* that I'd been suspicious of him from the get-go. And he *knew* I'd defend Cheryl. He'd lured me down to that subway station. It had all been a plot to corner me.

And the fire. It was most likely for me as well.

I breathed in and out, trying to get a grip. The firemen worked on, spraying parts of the house to stop the flames. I stepped out from under the tree and moved toward the burning piece of roof again.

"Who wants me dead so badly?" I said aloud. Could it be the Yukemuras?

But it didn't make sense. The Yukemuras, dangerous as they were, didn't want me dead. Yoji, the head of the Yukemura clan, needed me to marry Teddy for the agreed-upon "booty." They had to have me alive. At least for a little while longer.

"Surround and drown!" one of the firemen bellowed. "The inside's collapsing!"

No. It had to be someone else.

I crept up a little closer. My mind circled back to one person. *Mieko.*

Mieko, my stepmother. I'd called her a couple of days ago. I needed to see how my father was doing—he'd been in a coma for almost a month. And when I heard her familiar voice come on the line, she sounded friendly—loving, almost.

And believe me, Mieko isn't the friendly type.

We didn't talk about our family. Instead Mieko grilled me about what I was doing. What was my address? she asked again and again.

"It looks like we've got a class B here," one of the firemen shouted into his radio. "Send us some backup."

Marcus had mentioned Mieko. In the subway station he'd said, "Your mother says hello."

How did Mieko know Marcus?

More voices rang out. "Check the window! Is anyone still in there?"

Bricks crashed to the ground.

But I *hadn't* given her my address. I'd gotten off the phone before I gave away any important information.

But if she knew Marcus . . . who was kind of dating Cheryl . . . who lived with me . . .

My head spun. *Why* did Mieko know *Marcus*?

I stared up at the burning house and my hands curled into fists. The heat made my eyes water. The photo of Ohiko up there was burning up, right now, possibly because of

Mieko or Marcus. Its sides were at that very moment curling and blackening. The fire would eat away Ohiko's face.

All at once, before I knew what I was doing, I ran to the house. The firemen had hosed down the front yard, and the grass squished under my feet. One of the men grabbed my arm with his thick glove as I rushed past.

"What are you *doing*?" he asked.

I shook free of his grip. I heard Hiro's screams from behind me. The smoke was overpowering, but I pushed my way in.

The inside of the house was like nothing I'd ever seen. Orange flames shot from the mantel, the couch, the floor. All of Cheryl's little knickknacks—and she had a lot of random stuff—were charred and blurred into a huge ball of fire.

I heard noises from upstairs.

"Cheryl?" I screamed. I ran to the stairway, but the whole thing was lit up in flames. All of a sudden a rush of air shot toward me, and I saw fingers of fire dance down the banister.

My God. If Cheryl was up there, she was definitely dead.

I looked around me. I'd never realized how *loud* fire was. The sound of the crackling and the growing flames was *deafening*. And it was surrounding me.

Ohiko's photo was up there. That was the only thing I had left of him. What if I forgot what he looked like? I wind-milled my arms right and left, lifting my feet, trying to avoid the flames. A loud crash behind me made me flinch. I wheeled around; the chimney had fallen off the far wall. The flames were devouring it.

Screw it. I had to get out of here. The smoke stung my eyes. I looked down at Cheryl's end table. Her grand-mother's necklace, a gold chain with a large antique amethyst stone, was draped over the edge of a small bowl. Nothing was on fire yet.

Before I knew what I was doing, I grabbed it, and rushed out the door. The smoke blinded me.

I shoved the necklace into my pocket. Firemen rushed around me. "Are you all right?" they screamed. Two men picked me up and carried me away from the house.

"Why the hell did you go in there?" one of the firemen yelled. "Are you out of your *mind*?"

I coughed. Hiro ran up to me. "What were you *doing*?" he asked.

I didn't say anything. I felt deadened. My heart beat fast.

"We've got to get out of here," Hiro said. "Fast. This isn't safe for us." I could tell he was pissed. And worried. "Come on, try to stand up."

I stood up, but my knees buckled. The smoke had made me dizzy.

"All right all right, sit down for a minute," Hiro said. "I don't know why you went back in there—you could have been killed! The inhalation of smoke alone could have knocked you out!"

"I'm okay," I said. I didn't want to tell him about Cheryl's necklace. He'd ask me why I'd taken it. And I didn't know why myself.

I breathed in and out steadily, trying to remember my pranayama breath. I could hear the stream of water hitting the side of Cheryl's house. *Get a grip, Heaven,* I told myself.

I slowly pressed my palms to the ground and lifted myself up. I felt a little better. Hiro chased down a cab. He opened the door for me. "Come on, get in," he said. "We're going to get far away from this."

I fell onto the seat and could smell the smoke on my clothes. Hiro climbed in, too. The cabby idled, waiting for us to tell him where to go.

"Where are we going?" I asked. The fire lit up his face. The orange glow made him look more handsome than ever. His cheekbones seemed prominent; his eyes were deep-set and sensual. I even got turned on looking at the curve of his forearm. On the cab ride over here, I'd gotten butterflies from the way he looked at me. Our knees had gently touched. Hiro had grabbed my hand. Looked carefully and soulfully into my eyes.

Despite my delirium, chills ran up and down my spine just thinking about him.

"I don't know where we'll go," he said, looking over his shoulder at the burning house.

"Where to?" the cabby grumbled.

"Wait just a second, please," Hiro said, then turned to me. "Let's go back to my place."

"No," I said. "Your house is an obvious target. What if it's being watched right now? Maybe we should go to a diner or something to sit and figure this out." I fumbled with the strap of my bag. I also didn't want to go to Hiro's because his girlfriend, Karen, might be there. I hadn't faced her since we'd had a huge fight about Hiro in the park a couple of days ago.

"I don't think we should be anywhere well lit right now. Nothing seems safe," Hiro said, looking out the back window. "What about one of the empty warehouses we've done training sessions in? Like the one down on Winston?"

I thought of the abandoned warehouses in downtown L.A. Creepy. When the Yukemuras had kidnapped Karen (a big reason why Karen and I had been on the rocks lately—that and the fact that she wanted me to "stay away from Hiro"), the "exchange" had taken place at a decrepit parking garage somewhere downtown. It was beyond spooky. I had a feeling the Yukemuras frequented areas like that. Vibe was down there, too. I didn't really feel like going back into that mess.

"Nope," I said. "No way."

Great. We'd pretty much determined that I had nowhere left to go. Instantly I was homeless again. "We should just drive out of the city, far, far away," I said, not very sarcastically. I felt completely drained of energy. Hiro had had to deal with this problem twice before—once when I'd showed up on his doorstep, blood spattered and terrified, and then when I'd had to move out due to a random attack right in front of his apartment building on Lily Place. I mean, he had to be getting sick of shuttling me around so that I would always be safe. No wonder he wasn't into me.

"Really, getting out of the city would be the best thing to do," Hiro murmured.

"You kids going anywhere or what?" the cabdriver bellowed. "This smoke is getting to me."

"One moment, please. I'm really sorry," Hiro said.

"Maybe there *is* somewhere I could go that's not in the city," I said softly. But it was such a long shot. I knew Hiro would say it was too dangerous.

"Where?" he asked.

"To see my friend Katie," I said. I couldn't believe I was even telling him my idea. But I felt nervous sitting there in the cab, not moving. "My tutor, remember? She was my best friend in Japan. She moved to Vegas—that's where she's from—after my wedding. I mean, she wasn't *at* my wedding or anything. She moved back a couple of weeks before I got here." I put my finger to my lips. "I wonder if she even knows what happened."

"So you're saying . . . Las Vegas," Hiro said slowly.

"I think that may be best," I said.

"Do you know where Katie lives?"

"Well, no," I said. I'd called information once before to track her down, but there was no listing for her. And I'd left her mother's number in the hotel room on the day of my wedding. "But . . ."

Hiro didn't say anything. I would have loved to see Katie

again. But I didn't know where she *lived* in Vegas, or where she worked, or if she was even still there or not.

I pressed on. "I do remember that she said she was moving to Vegas after my wedding to get a job in one of the casinos."

Hiro looked at me incredulously. "Isn't that a strange transition to make? From being an English tutor to working at a casino?"

I shrugged. "I don't know," I said. "Katie . . . she's a risk taker. She came over from the States to tutor me, didn't she? Why not go to Vegas after that?"

"Huh," Hiro said. I frowned.

"Besides," I said. "It's not like I have much going for me here in L.A." This was true: I had no friends. Cheryl was dead. Hiro and I could never be together. And he had a beautiful girlfriend who hated me and wasn't afraid to say it.

Hiro didn't say anything. *Maybe he agrees,* I thought.

"I could take a bus there and look for her," I continued. "The bus would be much safer than a plane—more anonymous. And I have some money on me from working, so I could stay in a hotel while I looked for Katie."

Hiro cleared his throat after a few moments. "I think that might be the best idea," he said slowly.

I nodded. "I think so, too," I said. But inside, my stomach started to gurgle with anxiety.

"Take us to the Greyhound bus station," he told the cabdriver. We zoomed off.

I looked at him. He shrugged. "You're right," he said.

"The case you made for going to Las Vegas is a better idea than anything we can come up with in L.A."

"Of course," I said, hiding my shock. "Let's go, then."

I stared out the window as the cab zoomed toward the freeway. Hiro looked out the other window. I longed for the togetherness we'd been feeling on the cab ride to my house (*Hiro touching my hand, Hiro telling me how strong and incredible I was, Hiro denying he was moving in with Karen, Hiro's gorgeous face, his hot body, his delicious skin, his soft hands . . .*)

But he thought I should go to Vegas.

We pulled up to a large lot in front of a squat, dimly lit building. A few buses were idling in the lot. The red, white, and blue Greyhound logo flickered on the top of the building.

"Swanky," I whispered.

Hiro leaned in to the cabdriver. "We're dropping her off," he said. "If you could wait here for a moment for me . . . I'm going back to Echo Park." The cabby nodded.

"You're having the cab *wait*?" I said, my voice breaking a little. All of this was catching up to me. One minute, we were standing in front of my burning house. Suddenly the next, Hiro was shuttling me off to Las Vegas with barely a good-bye! He was having the cab *wait* for him! Meaning . . . he only wanted to see me off for a minute or two! When did he think a bus was going to show up?

"I don't have any clothes," I blurted, uncertain. "They've all burned up in the fire."

"You can get new ones in Las Vegas," Hiro said. He wiped his palms on his pants. I glared at him, suddenly angry. It was pitch-dark out. There was no one at the bus station. It was *creepy*. What was his problem? Why was he just leaving me like this, on the curb? What had made his mood change? How could he just drive home and snuggle into his warm bed with Karen at his side while I staggered onto some smelly bus to a city I'd never even seen?

My throat went dry. I didn't want to show Hiro how nervous I was. Instead I let my emotions turn to controlled rage. *Fine. So he thinks I should get out of town. Well, then, I'll go. Sayonara.*

I walked up to the counter as chill as possible and checked the timetable. A bus for Las Vegas would be leaving in an hour. I glanced behind the ticket window, but it was dark and empty. I turned to Hiro, but he was standing with his back to me, facing the car. I breathed out, frustrated, and walked as calmly as I could over to the Greyhound To-Go machine console. I shoved money in, and out popped a ticket. I examined it, trying to figure out what it said under the dim lights.

"The bus is in an hour," I said, walking back to him. Hiro turned. The cab lights lit up his face, and my heart flipped over.

"So," I said in an authoritarian voice. I wanted to be fully in Independent Heaven mode when I said good-bye to Hiro. "What about training? If I find Katie and everything— I mean, *when* I find Katie—I'm going to want to keep up my training. Should I check in with you every once in a while?

Are you going to want to give me drills or something?"

Hiro shook his head slightly and stepped closer to me. He put his hands softly on my shoulders. Tingles instantly rushed through me. "Listen," he said. "This is very important. You have to listen to me carefully. When I get back into this cab and leave you, I want you to forget all about me."

I breathed in sharply.

"I want you to forge your way ahead, Heaven. Make your own life. Become your own rock. Train according to your own needs. Find your training within yourself." He spoke slowly and evenly, not quite looking into my eyes but instead at a faraway place, past the bus station.

I stared at him, completely dumbstruck. "Say *what*?" I sputtered finally.

He stood there, arms crossed, a look of total serenity on his face. I mean, Hiro always had a pretty deadpan expression on his face *anyway*, but I expected him to crack up soon.

He shook his head. "I'm not joking. It's your mission. This is very serious."

I felt a movement behind me and flinched. But it was only the stationmaster, unlocking his booth. He nodded at me. "You're here a little early, aren't you?" he asked. I looked back at Hiro. I had an hour to kill. They could find me here. The people looking for me. The people who set fire to that house. The Yukemuras. So many people.

He didn't meet my gaze. "I have to go," he said.

"But . . . ," I squeaked. "The bus . . . is in . . . an hour!" *Don't lose it,* I told myself. *Keep it together.* Instead I blurted, "Does this mean you don't want . . . me . . . around?"

Hiro looked out at the cab. He purposefully wasn't looking in my direction. What was his *deal*?

"It's not that, Heaven. My feelings for you are . . . very strong. . . . You don't understand . . . but . . ." He put his head down. He bit his lip, turned away. "This is what we have to do." His voice sounded muffled, strange.

"What are you *talking* about?" I said. I knew I sounded desperate. "What do you mean your feelings are strong? Why is this what you have to do? I don't get it!"

"I . . . I can't explain it now," Hiro said. "Forget me. Please. You have to. Now go wait for your bus." He pointed at a bench. I tried to speak, but no words came out.

The cabdriver peered out disintrestedly at Hiro. "You getting in or what?" he growled.

"Good-bye," Hiro said to me, still avoiding my eyes. And then, without even a touch—much less a kiss—he turned and got inside the waiting cab.

"Good-bye," I said softly. I watched him get in the cab and instruct the driver to take him back to Echo Park. I chewed the edge of my lip, then turned away as the cab pulled out of the lot. I didn't want to look at him.